MORTAL
MISSION

A hard sci-fi mystery

PIP SKINNER

PJ Skinner

Prologue

Spontaneous applause echoed through the NASA control centre as a shrill tone announced the arrival of a message from the Mars lander. The mission coordinator dried her brow on her sleeve and leaned forward to speak into the microphone.

'The landing capsule has detached from the spacecraft. The thrusters have engaged and will now adjust the angle of the craft for entry to the Martian atmosphere.'

High fives rippled up and down the rows of seated technicians glued to their screens. One comedian among them yelled 'Get in the hole', greeted by the desired emission of laughter and groans. An animated sequence showing the surface of Mars, and the planned trajectory of the capsule through the atmosphere, played on the main screen at one end of the launch room.

The faces of the assembled press corps loomed up against the glass of the viewing gallery, jostling for an unobstructed view of the operations room for their cameras, looking for the money shot.

'The landing capsule is on its way to the surface.'

'It's already there by now. There's an eleven-minute delay,' said Chuck Gomez, crime reporter, and sometime

1

roving correspondent for Space Monthly. 'We'll know shortly.'

A joint intake of breath stilled both rooms, and all present froze in position as if any movement might cause the mission to abort. The tension in the NASA launch room reached suffocation level as the capsule neared the point at which the parachutes would first deploy. One man dropped a pen on the floor, making everyone jump. Red-faced, he scrabbled on the floor, trying to pick up the errant object which rolled under a desk.

'Leave it, for God's sake,' hissed Edgar Fredericks, the chief engineer.

Fredericks returned his attention to his screen, willing it to show the telemetry indicating a safe landing. The minutes passed as the capsule passed through the atmosphere, its heat shield glowing as it plummeted towards the surface. Many relatively unknown companies had made the components of the spacecraft. Out of the corner of his eye, he spotted the representative of Heathcoate fabrics, peeking out from behind her hands, awaiting the deployment of the parachute. He smiled reassuringly at her, and she grimaced.

In the skies above Mars, NASA's twin Orbiters, MRO (Mars Reconnaissance) and MAVEN (Atmospheric and Volatile Evolution) scanned the airwaves for vital signs from the lander. They would relay any signal they received to NASA from the parabolic radio antennas in Spain and Australia. But no relay arrived. The press corps muttered and shuffled above the launch room, and several of the technicians refreshed their screens in a vain attempt to get a reading. A prickle of anxiety rose up Fredericks' spine and penetrated his scalp. Please. Not again. But the silence held.

Behind the long glass window separating the press gallery from the launch room, arms holding cameras aloft started to droop. Feet shifted in embarrassed

2

impatience. The promised seven minutes of terror stretched to ten.

'Is this normal?' said Bill Hogan.

'NASA were five for five on landings before the last failed mission, but look what happened to that one.' said Gomez.

'Not that we know what happened,' said Hogan. 'But this is freaky. What are the odds of a second failure?'

'I blame China,' said Marge Henning. 'They're not happy the USA will send the first manned mission to Mars. They want to sabotage our space programme.'

'Don't be ridiculous,' said Gomez. 'How on Earth could they do that from here? Anyway, one astronaut on the manned mission in a couple of years' time will be a Chinese national.'

'And we invited him out of courtesy,' said Hogan. 'Why would they kill their own man?'

'I'm just saying what we're all thinking,' said Henning, pursing her lips.

'Speak for yourself,' said Gomez, who moved away from her, rolling his eyes and twisting his finger at his temple.

As the minutes dragged by, the dawning realisation that the mission had failed again deflated the technical team. Many of them slumped into their chairs, still gazing at their blank screens. Edgar Fredericks lowered his head into his hands and let out a deep sigh. He ran his hand through the tight curls bordering his bald crown. *How is this possible? The press will have a field day.*

He stood up.

'Okay everybody, I want data. Monitor the signals from the satellite relay and get me some information. We don't know what the problem is yet. It may be a relay blockage. Meanwhile, I'll need to speak to the press. Get them assembled in the press hall.'

Chapter 1

H attie Fredericks stared into the microscope, blinking with effort as she tried to confirm the presence of a stromatolite in the thin section of rock under the lens. Billions of years of evolution separated her from the primitive algal mat, but that didn't diminish her fascination with these tiny pioneers of life on Earth. *A bit like me. The first of their kind, subjected to a harsh environment unsympathetic to the improvements they could bring to it.*

Hattie pushed her afro out of her face and held it in place with a bamboo headband. Her frown wrinkled her nose, displacing the freckles that meandered across the bridge separating her plump cheeks. She leaned back and rubbed her eyes. Her stomach growled in protest, and she glanced up at the clock. *Twelve o'clock? Damn. If I don't get a move on, a swarm of hungry workers will have stripped the canteen again, leaving behind some scraps of salad and a burnt corner of the lasagne.*

She logged out of her computer and placed the cover over the microscope. She stood up and rubbed the small of her back, groaning. The white floor tiles emphasised the scarlet canvas of her shoes and she wiggled her toes in pleasure at their bright colour. Despite her restrained demeanour, Hattie did not go in for dull clothing. Her white coat hid clandestine rainbow cuffs, which only showed if she rolled the sleeves up. She shook out the creases and hung it on the back of the stool.

After the tomb-like silence of the laboratory, the cacophony in the canteen assaulted her ears. She winced and screwed up her eyes as someone scraped a tin tray clean into the organic waste bin. Opening them, she found herself looking into the grey eyes of Jim Rutherford, who grinned and patted the bench beside him. She made a series of gestures to the food queue and he nodded, mouthing 'I'll save your place'. Colour rose to her cheeks, and she hurried to the queue, hoping he didn't notice. Hattie nursed a soft spot for Jim. As the mission flight engineer, he responded to the almost compulsory nickname of Scotty, even though he originated from Alaska rather than Scotland. His upbringing in a harsh environment with no neighbours and freezing temperatures made him the ideal candidate for space travel.

When she joined the astronauts training for the Mars mission, Hattie put up with suspicion about her qualifications. Being the daughter of the head of NASA did not endear her to the other candidates, despite her obvious abilities. She needed to prove herself before they accepted her. Jim had no such qualms. Both pragmatic and phlegmatic, he took Hattie at face value, and ignored the mutterings about favouritism. She impressed him with her mechanical skills and ability to think outside the box, and he dedicated free time to developing her flying and docking skills.

'Repetition is the key,' he said. 'Make muscle memory.'

Hattie stood in the lunch queue, her stomach rumbling, and looked longingly at the dish of fries. Her latest diet definitely did not include them. Instead, she pointed to the salad and the steamed fish. The caterer raised an eyebrow but did not comment. Hattie swiped her card on the automatic cashier point and collected her cutlery. She took her tray and sat opposite Jim. He frowned at the contents of her lunch.

'You don't eat enough to keep a mouse alive,' he said.
'Lucky I'm not a mouse then,' she said, crunching on a piece of raw carrot, and keeping her diet to herself.

He rolled his eyes and cleaned his plate with a piece of French bread. 'I'm making the most of my food now, before I have to eat space rations,' he said.

'I don't have that problem,' said Hattie, trying to keep the reproach out of her voice.

'You don't know that. Weirder things have happened. Look at NASA's attempts to collect the Perseverance samples over the last couple of years. Who would have predicted two successive failures?'

'Bad luck comes in threes,' said Hattie. 'I'm not sure being chosen for this trip was so lucky.'

Jim looked up to see her eyes crinkling and wiped his mouth with his hand.

'Hilarious. I don't think.'

'Sorry, I didn't mean...'

'It'll be fine. They've been planning this mission for years. The sample collection has just been tacked onto it.' Jim rubbed his chin. 'I guess after five successful landings in a row, we were due a failure or two. I'm glad it's people in charge of landing this time and not a computer.'

Hattie surveyed the frown lines on his forehead, gauging his willingness to discuss the taboo topic of module failures.

'Um, what do you think went wrong?' she said.

'With the landings? Who knows? Perhaps we used up all our luck by going five for five on the unmanned rover missions.'

He paused and rubbed his chin again.

'Anyway, this time our space craft has a different configuration. They tested the type of Starship we'll be using on a six-month sojourn around the moon and on its surface with no problems. We've also sent five separate Starships ahead of us to carry the life support systems to Mars with no errors so far.'

'But isn't one missing?'

'It's probably just a communications error. Anyway, I'm able to fly ours, in case of gremlins, which makes it safer. There's less room for error with humans on board to correct for the unexpected.'

'I guess so,' said Hattie. 'I presume that's why we learned to fly too. It's going to be exciting for you all.'

'We'll be asleep for most of the trip. I'm not sure how exciting that's going to be.'

'More exciting than staying here, I'll bet.'

'At least you passed all the training modules with no problems. There's a big chance you'll be the one to go, if there's a last-minute problem.'

Except for the time I suffered an attack of claustrophobia in my space suit in the dive tank and had to be fished out.

'Maybe. Thanks, Scotty.'

Jim stood up.

'See you around, short stuff.'

'Less of the short,' said Hattie, but he had already gone.

She stood up to get a coffee and added a couple of chocolate biscuits to her saucer. That's the problem. I've got no will power. How can I be an astronaut with my lack of gumption?

'Do you really need those biscuits?' said a voice.

Hattie didn't need to turn around to know who it belonged to. Serena Hampton. Tall, willowy, silver spoon wedged in her mouth. They selected her as second officer for the Mars mission because of her leadership qualities. She also had a master's degree in geology and doubled as the mission's science officer. Hattie watched her breeze through training, jealous at the consummate ease with which she overcame the hardest of tasks.

While Hattie hid her phobia of running out of air, and the thought of diving in a spacesuit made her feel sick,

Serena showed no sign of being fazed by the rigours of training. Her leadership qualities were never in doubt, and the men all followed Serena with their eyes too. Hattie tried not to mind that they only laughed at her, and not with her, but the knowledge they would leave her behind rankled with her as she struggled to keep up with the ice queen.

Underneath all her privilege, Serena possessed an iron will, forged in the shadow of her elder brother, the pampered heir to the Hampton fortune. She kept herself whip thin and looked down her nose at anyone she considered being overweight. Self-absorbed and bitchy, she did not qualify as a team player. *How did she fool the recruiters? There might be no 'I' in team, but Serena didn't go out of her way to make me feel good. Maybe money talked.*

'They're not for me,' said Hattie. 'They're for Scotty.'

'Hasn't he left?'

'Oh, I didn't realise. I'll put them back.'

Serena smirked as Hattie replaced the biscuits.

'Are you coming to the launch dinner?' she said.

Hattie turned around. Serena's face did not betray any emotion. A neutral question? Perhaps.

'Um, I don't think so. It's not in the protocol to have the substitute on the pitch once the game starts.'

Serena raised a perfectly plucked eyebrow.

'You might enjoy it,' she said. 'We don't bite.'

Hattie swallowed her answer.

'Perhaps,' she said, and Serena stalked off.

Despite the invitation, Hattie couldn't escape the feeling Serena looked down her nose at her. It wasn't as if Hattie lacked qualifications to be an astronaut. Hattie started out in mechanical engineering only to be seduced by a supplementary course in geology. She swapped majors and graduated first in her year in natural sciences, majoring in geology and winning a prize for her thesis on the origin and classification of fossil stromatolites or marine algal mats. She only chose the thesis in the first place because she got to spend three months at Shark Bay in Western Australia, but the persistence and tenacity of these organisms impressed her.

The scuba diving course she did counted as a necessity for astronaut training. While she passed the course, she almost drowned in an incident on the reef which left her traumatised. She told no one about it, but sometimes she woke in the small hours, gasping for breath, her heart almost exploding with anxiety. She had planned to get therapy for it, but once they put her on the short list for Mars, she couldn't risk anyone finding out and stopping her from going. Meditation helped, but the fear lurked in the recesses of her brain, raising panic in her breast whenever she suited up.

She followed up her master's degree with a PhD comparing the living stromatolites to those in the fossil record. Her interesting and meticulous studies caught the eye, and soon she counted amongst the few global experts on the topic.

'Honestly flower, why didn't you choose a more interesting animal, like dinosaurs or something?' said her mother, Juana Fredericks, rolling her eyes. 'None of the ladies in the country club have ever heard of strawmatites.'

Hattie shook her head.

'It's hardly surprising, considering they're called stromatolites,' she said, but her mother was no longer listening, sipping her gin and tonic, and looking over the rim of her glass at her daughter, as if Hattie had been swapped for an alien.

Despite all her efforts, she felt suspicion and hostility from diverse members of the scientific unit who resented her hanging around. *Is that why they didn't select me for the mission to Mars? If only they knew how I fought for my place as reserve, despite being the highest qualified of all the aspirants.*

Her father shrugged his shoulders at her frustration.

'It's not my fault,' he said. 'We have to follow strict protocols against nepotism if we want to be true to our mission statement. Be thankful you're the backup. You get all the training and none of the peril.'

But it rankled, and Hattie found it hard to keep up her cheerful exterior, while her interior bubbled with resentment. She had given everything the last three years of astronaut training, and fought her way to the brink of success while others fell by the wayside. She excelled during the six months' survival instruction in Utah, handling isolation and confinement as well as anyone. Her practical side came to the fore as they learned how to repurpose materials to create shelters, and change rovers into motorcycles. Her childhood first-aid classes gave her a head start in their triage classes and her calm nature in the face of trouble impressed the instructors.

But AI read her resentments with other members of the crew and she had to suffer the indignity of anger management courses and deep analysis to make her release her frustrations. Was it any wonder she got annoyed? Chad, Bret and Serena, with their perfect white teeth and flawless skin, looked as if they were manufactured by Mattel. They almost had astronaut stamped on their skins. Ellie worked her way into the crew without a ripple. Industrious and sweet natured, she didn't rub anyone up the wrong way. Jim picked himself with his efficient, multifaceted qualifications for setting up and fixing all the hardware coming on the trip.

The international members of the crew had also been obvious choices. Mo Shariff, computer wizard and scion of a wealthy Pakistani family, Wayne Odoyu, from Kenya, graduated suma cum laude from Harvard with a dual botany-biology doctorate, and Chen Yu, trauma surgeon with a side-line in tropical diseases and acupuncture. Hattie didn't fault the eventual choices, and in reality, she couldn't compete with Serena's cool exterior and calculated charge to the top. The more obvious it became that Serena would beat her to the earth science slot, the more frustrated Hattie became. In the end, AI picked Serena because of Hattie's flaws and despite Serena's. I have only myself to blame. So close and yet so far.

Chapter 2

Noah van Horn, the head of ethics at the Centre for Christian Nationalism, entered his office on the eighth floor and shut the door. He ran his finger over his magnificent mahogany desk and squinted at his digit, checking it for dust. Satisfied, he heaved his three-hundred-pound bulk into a swivel chair covered in battered, black leather, and spun it around to face the window. He admired the view from his office. Below him, the traffic moved silently through the streets. He had been brought up in the noise and bustle of the fossil fuel age and he found the lack of noise peculiar and disorienting. Only yesterday, he had almost been run over when he crossed the street without looking. The silent electric cab had stopped automatically when it sensed him, but the passenger had been less than impressed by the sudden jolt which woke him from a nap.

Behind Van Horn, his computer flickered into life and wished him good morning. He swivelled back to it and surveyed his office with pride. It had been decorated in the old-fashioned style with dark wood and thick carpets. In front of him, the walls were covered with religious imagery; Russian Icons, a Renaissance painting of the Madonna and Child, a framed portion of a stained-glass window containing a representation of Saint Francis of Assisi, and in pride of place, at the centre, an ancient wooden cross. He shut his eyes and muttered a prayer, but his attention flagged as the worries of the day crowded in on him and a large bluebottle appeared out of nowhere and started bouncing off the glass outer walls of his office.

Van Horn panted with exertion as he leaned forward for the scanner to verify his pupil, sweat speckling his brow. He turned away again, as the automatic assistant's caramel voice listed his appointments and highlighted the number of unanswered emails in his inbox. Irritated at being called to account, he spun around and told her to shut up, something he found very satisfying. He selected a channel streaming the news, but his annoyance increased as yet another image of the gleaming Starship with its belly of black tiles appeared on his screen. The newsreader extolled the courage of the astronauts and the pioneering spirit of the average American until Van Horn felt quite nauseous. He drummed his fingers on the desk, mystified.

Why is the mission to Mars going ahead at all? We paid a fortune to have the best bot farms spreading misinformation and lies about it. People are up in arms about the waste of money and the danger to the astronauts. *Why is the administration willing to risk their astronauts' lives after what happened to the last two Mars missions? Why do US governments do anything these days?* It must be money related. They've always been prepared to sacrifice people for profit.

Despite all his lobbying, the Christian National Party (known as the CNP) had been unable to prevent the launch of five Starships loaded with cargo during the last window for flights to Mars. Four of the Starships had landed safely on the southern border of the Utopia Planitia and disgorged their contents via autonomic lift systems. The fifth Starship had disappeared from NASA's screen and had been presumed lost after the CNP had interfered with the communications system on board using their asset in NASA.

However, the CNP had not managed to force a postponement of the upcoming crewed mission to Mars. The four Starships that had landed contained sufficient supplies for five years for the eight astronauts who would only be staying five hundred days. Now countless agile robots were working to set up the mission camp; deploying nuclear fission reactors and solar arrays for power to melt ice and manufacture fuel and oxygen.

Van Horn's computer screen flickered to life. The craggy face of Richard Taylor-Brooks loomed large. His bushy eyebrows sat over his hooded eyes like fat caterpillars, a contrast to his thin lips. Van Horn felt the familiar knot in his guts as he tried to remain calm in the presence of the Chief Executive of the CNP. He affected bonhomie.

'Good morning, Richard,' he said. 'I trust you are well.'

'You trust wrong. I'm not happy with your piss-poor performance, not happy at all.'

Taylor-Brooks frowned into the camera and his eyebrows almost met. Van Horn cleared his throat.

'Yes, well, it's been difficult. I—'

'You are an incompetent fool. Somehow, we have to stop the crewed mission arriving on Mars, but if it doesn't leave Earth, so much the better. We need another delay to increase the opposition to the mission and get it cancelled until the next Hohmann transfer window.'

'I don't think you're being fair. I've increased opposition to the mission by 20%. The public are against—'

'Stop waffling, man. We need to increase the pressure on NASA and I have just the man for the job; a vile scumbag with not a Christian value in his bloodline; perfect when extreme measures are called for.'

'Extreme? I don't understand.'

'His name is Harlan Grimes. He'll do anything for money. I want you to act as the go between for us in our dealings with him. I'm sending you through his contact details. He's expecting your call.'

'But what do you want him to do?'

'You'll think of something. Just stop the mission. Now.' The screen shut off.

Noah Van Horn struggled to contain his anger at being reprimanded after all the effort he had put in. The Mars mission represented all that was evil as far as he understood it. Even the faint possibility of the discovery of ancient, or God forbid, extant, life on Mars, would sweep away any pretence that the Earth was unique, and chosen by God, as the only place in the Universe to contain life. Man was created in his own image. *What if sentient beings were found on Mars? How did that fit with God's teachings?* He felt as if they were intent on desecrating all he held holy, all he had believed in. As a child, he had admired and followed several famous conservative preachers, and had bullied his mother into subscribing to their channels. That was before she died in a car crash, taking his little brother with her.

His father never mentioned her again, nor did he reveal her intention to abandon her religion, and he and his son continued like nothing had happened. After a few years, Noah van Horn got used to the idea that he would never see his mother or his brother again. He had washed cars and cut lawns in the days before robots took over, to save money to go to Christian rallies. He grew up as the apple of his father's eye, the perfect son. *What did kids do to earn their pocket money these days? Design NFTs? Code video games?* He felt like a fossil in this fast-changing world. His religious fervour had not dimmed, but his vision of a return to the old values did not mesh with modern technology and the proliferation of genders.

Van Horn had enrolled in religious studies in university, but had quit in fury after a few lectures, when he realised that he would have to learn about religions other than Christianity. One lecturer even asked them to consider whether evolution was part of God's great plan, continuously expanding and changing and challenging men to do the same. Van Horn had stood up and walked out. He never returned. He looked for something more solid, more constant, less blasphemous, and found it in the Christian Nationalist Party. They understood his longing for the old values and took him in and moulded him into a fervent disciple. He threw himself into the defence of Christianity as written in the Bible and soon found a new enemy, the Cult of the Green Dragon, as environmentalism became known. The denial of science as an explanation for the workings of the planet, and the determination to eradicate the teaching of Darwinism from schools, filled his days. Creationism became his mantra, even though his brain told him that the Earth was more than six thousand years old.

His fervour did not go unnoticed, and he soon rose in the ranks of the Christian Nationalist party, which stemmed from the split up of the Republican party after the nomination of Donald Trump to fight the 2024 election, despite being found guilty of insurrection in 2022. Van Horn had recently resigned from the political branch of the party after a misunderstanding about the use of funds for decorating his villa in Florida, but, despite this, and his relative youth, he had kept his position as the head of ethics in the Centre for Christian Nationalism. The forced resignation still smarted, and he plotted a return to party ranks in the near future.

The door of his office opened and Grace Dos Reis, his personal assistant, came in with a tray. She wore a bright pink linen shift dress with cap sleeves and vertiginous beige heels. Her pretty face and curvy figure brightened up even his darkest moments, and her choice of delicate perfume made his head spin. She wore something called Arcana Perfume Oil, and when he bought her some for Christmas, he found it contained frankincense, rosemary, lavender, neroli and verbena.

Alchemy like her. The cute way she wore different coloured Alice bands to push her neat afro off her face made his heart sing. He couldn't imagine how a girl from high society had ended up in his office, but he thanked God for her every day.

'Is that my coffee?' he said.

'White with two sugars,' she said. 'Just how you like it.'

She placed the cup on his desk and walked out, leaving a faint smell of her perfume, which Van Horn breathed in like life itself. He sometimes wondered if he could bear his job without the ray of light she brought into his life. He sipped his coffee and ate the delicate, sugared cookies she had placed on a side plate. He sighed in pleasure at the treat, trying not to wolf them down in an instant. When he had finished, he clicked on the contact sent to him by Taylor-Brooks.

'Call Mr Grimes,' he said, wiping his head with a pristine linen handkerchief and leaning back into his chair, which groaned in protest. Moments later, Harlan Grimes's rodent-like features filled the screen, pock-marked and greasy under his ludicrous comb-over. *Why didn't he get plugs or something?* Van Horn grimaced and then forced out a smile.

'Mr Grimes? I believe our mutual acquaintance put us in contact.'

'Morning, Noah. What can I do for you today?' said Grimes.

'I'd prefer it if you didn't call me that. My name is Van Horn.'

Grimes sighed.

'Did you have anything on your mind?' he said. 'I'm kind of busy this morning.'

'Yes, I did. And less of the cheek, please. I need you to carry out a mission of the utmost importance.'

'That sounds important.'

'Don't be facetious. The future of the Religious Right depends on it. I can give it to someone more suitable if you can't take it seriously.'

'Apologies, I'm suffering from a sugar rush. You have my full attention now.'

'We need to disrupt the launch by removing a key member of the crew.'

'And how do I do that? They are already on base, in quarantine. I can't get inside.'

'I'm sure you'll think of something.'

'I doubt it will stop them for long. NASA has stand ins.'

'I don't need long. The window for flights to Mars will soon be closed, and they'll have to postpone the voyage for over two years if we do this right.'

'Okay. I'll see what I can do.'

'Don't screw this up,' said Van Horn.

'I don't ever miss my target.' said Grimes.

The screen went blank. Van Horn sat staring at it for several minutes before taking out an electronic pad to doodle on. The muscles in his cheeks worked as he pressed the stylus into the interface, which emitted a warning beep in protest. He sat back and chewed the end of the stylus in revenge.

Chapter 3

A s the day of lift off loomed, the misery of being left behind permeated Hattie's whole being. Her instinct to hide away in the laboratory made it hard to avoid the excited talk about the upcoming Mars mission. Sullen and withdrawn at home, she shut herself in her room to avoid her mother's well-meaning, but grating, platitudes. Her interest in space began at an early age. Since her days staring through the telescope of their neighbour, Morty Reisner, she nurtured the ambition of proving that Mars had harboured primitive life, and possibly still did. It became an obsession, especially when the missions to retrieve the Perseverance samples from the surface of Mars had failed. She longed to be the one to analyse the samples, a hope crushed by her exclusion from the final selection.

A burning resentment of the unfairness of life soured her sunny outlook. Not even her beloved stromatolites could cheer her up. Unable to bear the building anticipation surrounding her, she drove out to spy on the SpaceX installations where operations continued around the clock to check and recheck the Starship before launch day. The first stage booster rocket had already been transferred to the launch pad on a repurposed oil rig offshore, but the second stage Starship coated with heat and radiation resistant black tiles stood in the wide bay surrounded by lifts and cranes. Hattie gazed up at the nose cone which contained the seats used during take-off. She pictured herself in one of them, pinned down by G-forces. *Some hope.*

The last of three fuel tankers stood on the low loader ready for transport to the launch pad nearby, reflecting the yellow arc lights which illuminated the surrounding infrastructure. It carried the methane necessary to refuel the mission in orbit. Human silhouettes scurried back and forth on unknown errands beneath the massive Starship bays, disappearing into massive silos and sheds storing spare nose cones and Raptor engines for the Starship assembly line. She had toured the buildings when she first got accepted on the Mars Mission astronaut intake. Elon Musk himself had showed them around, dazzling her with his encyclopaedic knowledge of all the SpaceX programmes and every detail of the Starship. She sighed as she remembered her conviction that it would be her to go on the Mission. Broken dreams. *What is the point of torturing myself from afar? If I want to suffer, I know where to go.*

She got back into the car and turned up the volume on the retro rock and roll that she streamed when she drove anywhere. The surround sound cocooned her as she headed south on auto-drive, her eyes shut to keep out the world. The palm trees lined her route like large cannabis plants. How strange it used to be illegal when it offered so many medical applications. *Thank goodness I wasn't born thirty years ago.* The lights were on in her sister Grace's house, but Hattie drove on past it for almost two blocks before pulling in to the sidewalk. She sat there for twenty minutes before she gathered the courage to get out of her car.

The streets were well lit as she made her way to her sister's house, but no one else ventured out and she reached Grace's house unseen. She strode up the path to the front door, trying to generate confidence. The doorbell chimed, and Hattie could hear the muttering of her sister's voice in the hallway.

Grace opened the door.

'Are you mad? Coming to my house? Did anyone see you?'

'No, they didn't, and hello to you too.'

'What are you doing here?' said Grace.

'As if you didn't know,' said Hattie, crestfallen.

Grace smirked at her distress.

'I forgot you didn't make the grade, miss wannabe astronaut. Are you looking for sympathy?'

Hattie shrugged.

'Can't you ever say anything nice? I thought you were supposed to be a Christian or something.'

Grace raised an eyebrow.

'Or something? God will strike you down one of these days. What do you want anyway?'

'I wanted to see you. Is that a sin now?'

Grace rolled her eyes and opened the door wider.

'Come in then.'

Hattie sniffed the air. The aroma of fresh baked brownies overcame her instinct to turn around and leave again. How did her sister stay so slim? She walked into the sitting room feeling self-conscious about her tight trousers, stretched over a stomach which had swelled since she started comfort eating in her misery at getting left behind.

She sat in a corner of the sofa, shedding her shoes and drawing her legs under her. Grace's face softened as she observed her little sister trying to shrink into the sofa.

'Do you want a brownie? It's a bit late for coffee, but I have some decaf.'

Hattie smiled. Brownie love; the closest her sister ever got to affection these days. They used to be so close before the Christian Right got its claws into Grace. Her conversion from the carefree teenager, who loved to spend long nights drinking and dancing with her sister, to the severe twenty-nine-year-old with a fanatical puritanism took mere months. When Hattie departed for Australia to do her thesis, her sister had been the life and soul of the party. On Hattie's return, she discovered a different Grace, who had been recruited by the Christian Right and emitted the fervour of the newly converted.

The shock devastated Hattie. In one fell swoop, she lost her wingman and confidant, replaced by someone who resembled an inhabitant of Gilead. Now the shock had dissipated, replaced by sadness.

'How's work?' said Hattie, savouring a bit of fresh brownie.

'The same as ever. Smiting the sinful, and punishing the non-believer,' said Grace, in an uncharacteristic jibe at her position of PA to Noah van Horn in Christian Nationalism's ethics office. 'And you?'

'Still staring down the microscope at micro-organisms,' said Hattie. 'And trying not to be jealous of the others.'

'You're lucky you're not going,' said Grace. 'I've heard many rumours about the mission.'

Hattie stopped eating and examined her sister's expression. Grace's brown eyes avoided hers.

'What do you mean? What have you heard?'

'Oh, nothing. Just people mouthing off.'

'What about?'

'Oh, you know. The cost of the missions when poor people are starving.'

'The Christian Right has one of the newest, most expensive buildings in New York. How come they don't help them?'

'God punishes sinners. They must have done something wrong to be in that state.'

'You don't believe that, do you?'

'Let's not fight. I'm glad you came over. It's been too long since I saw you.'

Grace sat beside Hattie on the sofa and put her arm around Hattie's slumped shoulders.

'You're so brainy. Why don't you put your talents to work for God instead? We could do with some less robotic recruits.'

'I already work for God. He gave me a brain and I'm using it to improve the future for mankind. What's wrong with that?'

Grace frowned.

'There is no life on Mars,' she said. 'God created the Earth to be the exclusive manifestation of his works. He made man in his own image. The Bible doesn't mention life anywhere else. It's just not possible.'

'But isn't that why we're going? To prove for once and for all that alien life has not begun on another planet in our star system? Your friends should have the courage of their convictions. Anyway, life on another planet doesn't disprove God. It just proves our lack of understanding of his works. Perhaps we are too stupid to understand his grand plan?'

Grace shrugged.

'There is no flexibility in the fundamental doctrine. It is written.'

Hattie sighed.

'Can I stay tonight?' she said. 'I don't think I can bear to be alone.'

Grace pursed her lips.

'Okay but don't tell anyone you stayed here. My work colleagues think I'm an orphan. They've no idea I have an apostate for a sister.'

'Seriously? Is that why you're using Mum's maiden name?'

'It's easier to avoid awkward questions about you and Dad. Stay here. I'm just going to put sheets on the guest bed.'

'Can I help?'

But Grace had gone, shutting the door behind her. Hattie felt a flutter of sympathy for her sister and her absurd double life. *If she believed all the fundamentalist stuff, why didn't she disown her family forever?* Maybe

23

blood was thicker than water after all. Her instincts told her Grace was becoming less enamoured of the strictures and doctrines of the Christian Right, but she would wait her out. No need to poke the bear. Grace will let me know when she is ready to leave that behind. The door opened and Grace put her head into the room.

'The room is ready for you,' she said.

'Thank you, sis. Sorry to be a wimp, but I'm off to bed now. Pretending to be happy for my fellow astronauts is exhausting.'

'Ask God for strength and humility. I find it helps.'

'I will, thank you,' said Hattie. 'See you in the morning.'

She climbed the stairs and let herself into the spare room. Tears filled her eyes as she spotted her childhood lamp projecting the starry night sky onto the ceiling. She slid beneath the Star Trek themed sheets, also from her childhood, and lay on her back watching the constellations change and the planets fade in and out. *Why did Grace keep all this stuff?* Their mother, Juana, told Hattie that she threw it all out while Hattie did her Master's degree in Australia. Hattie had been heartbroken, but Juana did not have a sentimental bone in her body.

'When I was a child, I talked like a child, I understood as a child, but when I became a woman, I put away childish things,' her mother said when Hattie complained.

'Where does it say my mother threw away my things?' said Hattie.

'I threw away Grace's toys too, but she didn't fuss. She took everything to the dump.'

But she didn't, did she? Hattie smiled and hummed the tune to Star Trek in her head. To boldly go where no man has gone before. She shut her eyes and pretended to be in a sleeping pod on the Starship. A sleepy prayer issued from between her lips, but she didn't ask for humility; she asked for a place on the mission. Scotty told her stranger things happened, but had they really?

Chapter 4

C huck Gomez rang up the stairs to the conference room in the astronauts' building. His shirt stuck to his back under his faux leather jacket. He snuck a look at his watch. Bang on time. No need to panic. He stopped outside the hall and ran his hands through his mop of brown hair. He grinned at the prospect of the press conference. *Would there be any surprises? Unlikely with NASA in charge. How would the crew appear? Nervous? Excited? This should be good.*

The heavy double door groaned under his push and swung open to reveal a packed hall. His eyes darted back and forth across the lines of seats, but a self-satisfied back occupied them all. A few stragglers stood at the back of the hall, fiddling with their all-in-ones. He patted his pockets and the reassuring shape of his rite in the rain notebook took his pulse down a couple of beats. Other journalists made fun of his old-fashioned paper notebook, but he took it on the chin.

'I'll keep it, thanks. A notebook doesn't run out of charge, day or night, and it won't stop working if I drop it, or dunk it in a puddle.'

He wasn't a Luddite. Like everyone else on the planet, he owned an all-in-one, not the latest model, but perfectly serviceable. He had also purchased a bale of notebooks in an online auction, and he reckoned they would see him out; that and the box of HB pencils salvaged from a warehouse where he had covered the story of a murdered girl. He shifted from one foot to another to take the weight off, and then he spotted a space on one of the sidewalls, much nearer the front. Maybe he could get a question in after all. He edged towards the space with his fingers crossed that it would still be there when he got there.

Too late, he realised they had left a gap beside a swinging door, which opened onto a passageway to the building's kitchen. The door swung open towards him as he arrived, almost knocking him out and causing a ripple of laughter from the nearby journalists. He leaned against the wall and put a foot out to stop the door swinging past ninety degrees. The odour of fresh baked pastry curled around the door, tantalising him. As usual, he had failed to fuel up before the meeting, and his stomach rumbled in protest. A pretty journalist heard the growl and sniggered at him.

'Hungry?' she said.

'Always,' he said, winking one of his big brown eyes at her, making her blush.

A hush fell on the audience as the astronauts filtered onto the stage in their light blue overalls with the NASA crest on their right breast. Gomez recognised Chen Yu, the crew's medic, from an interview they had done with him. His small, neat body looked out of place against the meaty linebacker shapes of the blond, blued eyed officers, Bret Grayling, the captain, and Chad Farrant, the first officer. Behind them, Ellie Barrett, the geochemist and remote sensing expert, got pushed aside by Serena Hampton, the science officer and homecoming queen. Wayne Odoyu, the biology and botany expert, slipped in with Mo Shariff, the robotics wizard. Both men kept their eyes fixed on the table top, uncomfortable with the limelight. Ellie putting her hand on Wayne's arm. He frowned and shook it off. She pretended not to notice. *A crush? Or something else?* He scribbled a comment in his notebook.

Serena Hamilton sat between Chad and Bret, her glossy hair and radiant smile a focal point for the press photographers. *How can anyone look that smug when they're about to climb aboard a giant bomb to hurtle through space? Perhaps I should rephrase the question before I ask it.* But he didn't get a chance. Most of the questions came from the front row, and to his trained ear, sounded as if someone had them planted beforehand. Pat answers from the trio in the centre confirmed his suspicions. Chad looked as if he had had his teeth whitened for the occasion, smiling his way through the press conference as if the voyage had already been completed and the astronauts had returned triumphant.

Ellie, Wayne, Mo and Yu wore the fixed grins of people who wondered if NASA had wheeled them in for decorative purposes only. Gomez reviewed the line up again. Hang on. Where was Jim Rutherford? He counted as the most important member of the crew. His skills would be essential for the smooth running of the machinery, and the assembly of the Moxy and Methane plants on the surface for the safe return to Earth. Gomez scribbled hieroglyphics into his note book, and put his hand up, frantically trying to get picked.

'Well, folks,' said Edgar Fredericks. 'That's about it for now. We'll see you back at the launchpad in a few days.'

The astronauts stood up, waved at the press corps, and headed for the wings. Gomez took a deep breath.

'Where's Rutherford?' he shouted.

Only Mo Sharrif turned around. He mouthed something. It might have been fever, but the reply got lost in the tumult of chair legs scraping across the floor and excited exchange of notes. Frustrated, Gomez shoved his notebook back into his pocket and zipped it up. Another waft of fresh baking filled his nostrils. Without considering the consequences, he slipped through the door, following his nose to the kitchen. He peered through the open door where a small army of sous-chefs dressed in face masks and surgical gloves were putting the finishing touches to a stunning array of dishes.

Beside him, on a table near the door, sat an open box from the Far East Sushi restaurant with a purple dragon logo prominent on its lid. Inside it was a tray of sushi arranged in the shape of a flower and decorated with pieces of ginger and small bowls of soy sauce. He edged closer to the table, intending to filch a couple of petals from the flower and rearrange them so the loss would not be obvious. As his fingers hovered over the plate, a slim man grabbed his wrist and squeezed it hard, making Gomez drop to his knees in pain. He stood up, rubbing his wrist. Aikido? My brother used to do this to me before he disappeared.

'Miss Hampton ordered the sushi,' said the man, glaring at him through ice-blue eyes. 'She counts the pieces. She would not appreciate your grubby fingers all over it.'

The head chef stormed down the aisle between the food preparation benches, his eyes bulging out of his head. He poked a finger in Chuck's chest.

'What the hell are you doing in here? Don't you know you could contaminate the food? The astronauts must be healthy for the trip.'

He paused for breath and noticed the box on the table.

'Oh, is that the sushi? Thank God. I wouldn't like to experience the wrath of Princess Hampton.'

For a moment, his face relaxed, and he smiled. Then he refocused on Chuck.

'Why are you still here?' he said. 'Out, out!'

Gomez sighed as his hope of a feed evaporated.

'Sorry,' he said. 'I'm from the press. It smelled so wonderful, and I haven't eaten all day.'

The chef rolled his eyes.

'Wait here,' he said.

He strode to a bench and stuffed a buttered roll full of smoked salmon, coming back to Gomez and thrusting it in his hand.

'Here you go,' he said. 'Now, get lost or I'll have you thrown out.'

Chuck sat in his car and ate the roll, transferring notes into his all-in-one and re-running the press conference in his head. He couldn't get over his impression of Bret Grayling, blemish-free in both character and body. Bret looked implausibly like Captain America. No sign of stubble marred his square jaw, and a thick thatch of blond hair emphasised the blue of his eyes. His answers had been solid, and uncontroversial, delivered with a cool detachment. His deputy, Chad Farrant, had almost identical physical attributes, but he fidgeted and grimaced his way through the whole conference, working his jaw muscles whenever Bret took a question that Chad might have answered.

How would the crew get on after months of confinement? Chuck had heard rumours that NASA had shoehorned certain members into the crew to suit the requirements of the United Nations and others for the massive corporations who funded the mission. It seemed like an enormous risk to send a young and untried crew on the most important space mission of the last hundred years, but conventional wisdom favoured the resilience of youth and the ability to regenerate compared to older crew members. Only Bret and Scotty had spent time on the surface of the moon. The others had been to Mars simulation camps in the desert and in the tundra. *Too late now. I wonder if I can get another roll from the kitchen?*

Chapter 5

N oah van Horn stared in horror at his screen. He couldn't believe what he read. Another scandal involving an evangelist preacher and an underage boy. A viral video appeared on his screen and he turned away from the explicit contents. The hypocrite preached fire and brimstone with the best of them, but he couldn't keep his hands off the teenage sons of his flock. Only six months ago Van Horn arranged a large payoff to the livid parents of a young blond parishioner. They kept the incident out of the media, but the youth did not repent, and had to be sent away for aversion therapy. Not a pretty business.

This latest disaster summed up his dilemma. *How could the true religion compete in a world with twenty genders and sex on tap?* At least the cancel culture of the early 21st century had ebbed a little after people retaliated for being told not to wear corn rows in their hair, and saris to parties, by reporting their neighbours to the police for activities such as dyeing their hair blonde or eating Chinese food. The tit for tat nature of the complaints swamped the courts before they reinstated equilibrium and some modicum of free speech and behaviour.

But the religious right experienced pressure from all sides, especially after President Harris stacked the Supreme Court with Democratic leaning judges who legalised all drugs, liberalised abortion and mandated a third sex. The influx of different religions didn't help, he mused. Muslim refugees from strict Sharia-run countries and Catholics from Latin America formed large proportions of the population. They formed impenetrable multicultural ghettos with their own vibrant cultures and beliefs. The doctrine of the Christian Right did not appeal to people who had escaped from similar regimes.

As their influence shrank, the threats from the outside multiplied. The new moon base has put paid to their long campaign to label the moon landings as a lie. Conspiracy theories lost their charm once Elon Musk conceived the brilliant idea of taking some of the prime culprits to the moon and around the Earth, smashing their conviction and converting them to the wonders of space. The resulting press conference had been one highlight of the 2020s.

Van Horn countered this revelation by releasing videos accusing the ex-conspiracists of accepting large bribes, but momentum had been lost. The public became obsessed with space, enabling the government to proceed with its plan to claim the metals on Mars for the United States of America. The public were dreaming of aliens, but their leaders were wide awake to the potential of the red planet.

He pressed his intercom.

'Miss dos Reis? Can you come in for a moment, please?'

Did he detect a sigh? Miss Dos Reis appeared intolerant of his determination to see her face to face despite all the modern technology available to him. She had no idea how much he longed to have her sit on his knee so he could stroke her slim figure and sniff her delicately perfumed hair. *What soap does she use?* The authorities banned strong perfumes in public because of allergies and they went the way of peanuts and other triggers, although a contact told Van Horn to say the word if he required any contraband. Van Horn would have loved a carton of cigarettes so he could smoke by the sea when no one was watching, but being beholden to that slippery scumbag did not figure in his plans. He owned an electronic cigarette, but nothing rivalled the hit he got from a lungful of smoke and the nostalgia that came with it.

Grace entered the room, her corn-rows plaited with pink and purple beads. Her loose linen dress hid her curves, as was correct for work, but he spotted her in the street one weekend, in antique blue jeans and a flowery shirt, which hugged her figure in all the right places.

'Yes, Mr Van Horn?'

She enunciated his name with care and stood looking at the floor, as far from him as possible, her fingers interlaced and a pulse throbbing in her temple. He stared at her for a moment. *Why have I called her?*

'Are you interested in space travel?' he said on a whim.

She didn't look up. Colour rose in her cheeks and she swallowed.

'Space travel, sir? No, of course not. It's not part of God's plan. He never intended for us to leave this planet, which he made for us.'

She bit her lip, waiting. He took pity on her.

'Quite right,' he said. 'I'm just concerned about this Mars Mission. It's doomed to failure. There is no life on other planets, or the Lord would have told us about it.'

Grace raised her eyes to examine him and her gaze seemed to x-ray his mind. Van Horn flinched. Have I given myself away?

'Did you want anything else, sir?' she said.

'No, thank you. You can go.'

She left as silently as she had entered. Van Horn wiped his brow. *Talk about stupid. What is wrong with you?* She didn't guess, but she could have. He turned to the window and gazed out at the sky. *Have we misunderstood God's plan all this time? God created man in his own image.* That meant he gave him an inquiring mind on purpose. *Was it a sin to wonder about the other planets?*

Doubts had assailed him ever since the day he watched a vintage Star Trek film which had been supposed to shock him with its blasphemy. Instead, it charmed him with its message of tolerance, and defence of the weak. He attempted to dredge up some righteous indignation, but it had been half-hearted. Afterwards, he obtained copies of other movies in the series, on the pretext of studying the enemy, but he soon became hooked on the simple messages of tolerance and bravery. It wasn't as harmful as fiddling with small boys, but it counted as sin, and he couldn't stop. Somehow, imaginary aliens who were homosexual seemed so much more acceptable than human ones.

His screen flickered into life. Grimes. *What did he want?* Van Horn considered ignoring the call, but his curiosity won out. The ferret-like face of Harlan Grimes appeared, flakes of pastry visible on his sweatshirt, and one clinging to the corner of his mouth. A glint of triumph flashed in Grimes's eyes.

'Good morning, Mr Van Horn. Would you like an update on my progress?'

'I'd like you to clean the evidence of your gluttony from your shirt and mouth for a start,' said Van Horn.

Grimes raised an eyebrow, and then flicked at his shirt and ran a napkin over his thin lips. His icy blue eyes seemed to pierce right through Van Horn who sat up straighter in his chair, trying to hold in his vast bulk.

'You have something interesting for me?' said Van Horn.

'Turn on the news. I'll wait.'

Van Horn selected the option for live feed and soon a sombre Edgar Fredericks appeared, holding tight to a lectern, whey-faced.

'Yes,' he said. 'That's correct. We found Serena Hampton dead in her room this morning. The coroner has attended, but there is no sign of foul play.'

Van Horn's eyes opened wide and his jaw dropped open.

'How did you? What did you...?' he stuttered. 'You weren't supposed to kill anyone.'

Grimes laughed.

'An unfortunate accident,' he said. 'I hoped she would share her food with everyone and give them all serious food poisoning, but it appears she kept it all for herself. I expect them to attribute her demise to sudden death syndrome.'

The door opened again, and Grace came in carrying a tray.

'Good morning, sir,' she said.

'Is that the delicious Grace?' said Grimes, licking his lips. 'Let me see if you're as pretty as your voice, honey.'

Grace froze and shook her head. Van Horn grimaced at her, and waved her away with his hand, annoyed at Grimes's interruption of their morning ritual.

'She's busy,' he said. 'As you should be. We'll settle up later.'

'Don't forget me,' said Grimes, smirking.

Reptile. How did I become involved with such a foul creature? He seems oblivious to the fact that he has just murdered someone. And how does Richard know him anyway?

Van Horn took a couple of deep breaths before he contacted Richard Taylor-Brooks. Feeling of resentment swamped him as he waited to report in. He understood plausible deniability well enough to realise Taylor-brooks had nominated him as the fall guy.

'Noah? What's up?'

'Grimes has overstepped the mark.'

'What has he done?'

'He murdered an astronaut.'

'Murdered? How the hell did that happen?'

'He took matters into his own hands. I only asked him to delay the mission.'

'It seems he interpreted your instructions in his own way. You should have been clearer, but it's a little late now. Is there anything on the news yet?'

'That's where I saw the news of her death.'

Taylor-Brooks cut off the call. Van Horn wiped his brow and called up the news channel on his screen. He didn't have to search long before he found a live feed from the space centre. A crowd of hastily assembled journalists brayed questions at a frazzled looking Edgar Fredericks who stood behind a lectern gripping it tight with white knuckles.

'No, we don't know what happened yet,' he said. 'There will be an autopsy of course, but so far it appears to be a tragic event unrelated to the mission. Serena Hampton died in her sleep.'

'What happens to the mission now?' said one woman. 'Will you postpone it?'

'No, it will go ahead. We have planned for all eventualities and there is a pool of replacement astronauts with the same training. Now, if there are no more questions...'

He loosened his grip on the lectern and his eyes darted to the exit. A clamour broke out amongst the press corps who surged forward with their microphones. They all had the same question for him.

'Will your daughter Hattie be going instead?'

Chapter 6

T he insistent buzzing of her all-in-one finally penetrated Hattie's dreamworld. She rubbed her eyes, reaching for the unit and tapping the screen. Her sister's face, taut with worry made her sit up in bed.

'What's up, sis? Should you be calling me from work?'

'I'm in the Ladies. It's an emergency.'

'Do you need a Tampax or something? I don't see how I can help.'

'Serena Hampton is dead.'

'Dead? How? Did her head get too big for her body and explode?'

'For heaven's sake, stop messing around, and listen to me.'

'You're serious? Oh my God. What happened to her?'

'They don't know. She died in her sleep. You know what this means, don't you?'

'Sleeping is dangerous?'

'You're going to Mars, you idiot. I've got to go, and you do too. They'll be looking for you and they shouldn't find you in my house. Van Horn would be the one exploding then.'

'Sorry, I'll leave right now. Thanks for the heads up... And for rescuing my Star Trek stuff from the dump. I knew you were in there somewhere.'

'It's me I'm protecting. Get out of my house. Now.'

'Aren't you going to wish me luck?'

But Grace had gone and the screen went blank. Hattie took in a couple of deep breaths, releasing them as slowly as she could. Holy moly. *I'm going to Mars*. Hattie jumped out of bed, her heart racing. She went to the bathroom and splashed cold water on her face. *Am I dreaming? This feels pretty real.* She got dressed without showering and let herself out of Grace's house, glancing around cautiously to make sure nobody saw her. She got into her vehicle and told it to go home. The traffic had lessened after the morning rush hour but Hattie felt exposed and pressed the button to make the windows black out. Her all-in-one pinged and her mother's tear-stained face hovered on her screen.

'Darling, where are you? Dad and I are frantic with worry.'

'Don't panic. I heard the news and I'm on my way home right now.'

'They took your underwear.'

'Who did?'

'Some people from NASA turned up and asked me for it.'

'Ah, they need to sterilise it.'

'It's already clean. Yasmina will be most insulted.'

'For the spaceship, Mum. We can't take anything to Mars that could contaminate our results.'

'Why can't they give you new underwear?'

'The female astronauts have refused to wear boxer shorts and they don't make astronaut bras. Mind you, with a fifth of Earth's gravity, I won't need a bra.'

'Don't be silly, darling. You have to wear a bra.'

'I'll be there soon.'

'I should warn you. A swarm of reporters have arrived outside the house.'

'My windows are blacked out. Open the gate for me and I will park the car in the basement so they won't see me get out.'

Her mother nodded and signed off. Hattie's seat belt tightened around her chest as her heart rate elevated with the adrenaline rush. It's real.

'Loosen my belt,' she said.

Sometimes the automatic functions were a pain. Like when your heart rate went up with anticipation of a kiss and the vehicle trapped you in your seat instead. At least vehicles never crashed anymore. Her father told her roads used to be death traps. Drunk drivers, stoned drivers, boy racers, people with bad eyesight or distracted by cell phones. How did they survive? Automatic cars were boring but at least you got home safe.

As her vehicle approached the entrance of her parents' beach villa, the throng of waiting reporters turned towards her as one – like a murmuration of starlings – and thrust an army of all-in-ones towards the blacked-out windows. Some of them bounced off the glass as she went by them through the gate of the villa making her shrink back into her seat.

'Obstacle in the road,' said the mechanical voice of her car.

'Proceed,' said Hattie.

'Obstacle in the road.'

'Proceed, damn you. Sound the horn. Loud.'

The sharp blast had the required affect, scattering the crowd and opening a path to the villa. Soon the gates were closing behind her and as the vehicle glided into the bay under the house, she let out the breath she had been holding. Her mother burst through the door from the utility room of the villa as it came to a stop, her hand on her heart, a sure sign she had palpitations, or some such motherly ailment. Hattie couldn't stop a grin creeping onto her face.

Poor Juana. Born into a prominent Cuban family in Miami, she married below her, but her husband had surprised her with his ambition. He rose to become head of NASA, and now everyone including her parents lionised him. But Juana suffered the bitter blow of having two children who not only had the temerity to be female, but also showed zero interest in coming out into high society. Grace had joined a cult, or a something resembling one, and Hattie had followed Edgar into NASA. Hattie sympathised, but not enough to compromise.

The door of the car slid open and she jumped out.

'Hi mom. Here I am at last.'

'Where were you? How could you worry me like that? You weren't with that Larry boy again, were you?'

Hattie sighed.

'Honestly, mom, do keep up, I broke up with him about eighteen months ago. I slept at Grace's house, actually.'

The casual phrase made her mother clutch Hattie's arms and peer into her face.

'You saw her? You saw my baby? How is she?'

'Grace is fine, and still almost thirty.'

'She'll always be my chiquita gordita. Neither of you has permission to grow up.'

Hattie followed her mother into the kitchen where her father waited, his face neutral, as if it were just another day.

'Hello,' said Hattie. 'I hear they need a spare astronaut.'

'Seems that way,' said Edgar. 'You have to agree to go first, though.'

Hattie shook her head.

'I don't think I will. I have a concert next week I don't want to miss.'

Juana sobbed theatrically. Edgar put his arm around Hattie's shoulders and looked into her eyes.

'You don't have to go, you know. No one would think any the less of you if you backed out. They do have candidates from other nations who are also ready and willing to go.'

'I know, but I've been waiting all my life for this opportunity and I want it more than anything. If I turn it down, they won't ask me again.'

'How could you be so cruel?' said Juana. 'After all I've done for you, throwing away your life on account of Star Trek.'

'Please try and understand, Mum. It's because of all you've done for me that I'm ready for this. I never fitted in down here. Perhaps I'll find my destiny in the stars.'

'Do something, Edgar. Stop her.'

'Now, sweetheart, don't fret. It's no different to her being in Australia. You can record video chats for her and she'll come back all excited but without the dirty laundry for once.'

But it wasn't the quite the same. No one mentioned the fact that space tried to kill anyone who ventured there. The bombardment with dangerous radiation, altered gravity fields playing havoc with body fluids and structures, the absence of hospital treatment in case of emergency are all potentially fatal. The tiniest leak or crack which goes unnoticed could develop into a life-threatening situation. Space debris could write off the Starship while it refueled in upper orbit. The Moxy plant on the surface of Mars could malfunction along with its two back-ups. A rover could break down far from the habitats or fall down a crevice, taking the crew with it. The Starship could fail to take off from Mars or get damaged in a meteor shower in space.

'When do we leave?' said Hattie. 'Has the change in crew affected the schedule?'

'We need to launch during the next ten days if we want to follow the Hohmann Transfer Orbit to Mars, but you'll have to go to the astronauts' building tomorrow anyway. They need to carry out medical and dental checks on you. You'll need to re-integrate with the crew and be tolerant of their reactions to you joining them. They've had one nasty shock already.'

Edgar smiled to show he was joking, but Hattie heard the message loud and clear. She had always aspired to be part of a close-knit team but somehow her choices resulted in her being alone a lot of the time.

'Are you going to let him insult me like that?' she said to her mother, who held out her arms in answer.

'My funny little one,' she said, kissing Hattie's forehead. 'All grown up and off to explore the universe.'

Chapter 7

C huck Gomez stared at the screen in disbelief, his piece of toast hovering half way to his mouth. He put it down again and watched intently as the newscaster recounted the shocking events. A young woman struck in her prime, just before the biggest adventure of her life. They suspected sudden adult cardiac arrest syndrome. *Weren't astronauts screened for that? If not, they should be.* A picture of a pretty young woman in a bright flowery shirt flashed up on the screen. *Isn't that Edgar Fredericks's daughter, Hattie?* What an extraordinary thing to happen; the daughter of the head of Nasa heading to Mars on the first ever mission.

He abandoned his breakfast, grabbing his notebook and his all-in-one and stuffing them in the pockets of his jacket as he left his apartment. The freeway was jammed going into town but Gomez had no trouble travelling out to the beach where the Fredericks had their villa. Maybe he could get an exclusive story and rack up enough credits to buy a newer vehicle. The battery on this one didn't hold enough juice to charge his all-in-one. Any day now he would get stranded and have the indignity of being rescued by a robot. He couldn't afford the recycling costs of a new battery, never mind a new vehicle, but if he got an exclusive on Hattie, well, that could be lucrative.

He rubbed his hands together, and then smoothed down his thatch of unruly brown hair. He pulled his shirt down over his trousers, to cover the coffee stain he had made at breakfast. *Will I manage to speak to Hattie, or just her parents?* Juana had a reputation as a bit of a snob, but she came from immigrant Latino roots, just like him. Maybe they would find common ground. His cosy imaginings were rudely interrupted when he spotted the large cluster of journos at the gates of the Fredericks villa. So much for an exclusive. He'd be lucky to get a shared quote. He told the vehicle to stop about half a block away, outside an old-fashioned house with pink walls and a green metal gate with rusty hinges. In the garden, an old woman struggled to move a heavy plant pot.

'Can I help?' said Chuck, jumping out onto the pavement.

She peered at him through rheumy eyes.

'Do I know you?' she said.

'No, but I promise I won't harm you.'

'Hm, we'll see about that. Come in then.'

Chuck let himself through the gate and walked down the crunchy gravel path.

'Where shall I move it to? My name's Chuck. By the way.'

'Chuck? What sort of name is that?'

'It's short for Carlos, mam.'

'Ah, a Latino boy. I'm Sybil Reisner. Just pick it up and follow me. My gardener didn't turn up today and I'm desperate to repot the shrub before it dies.'

Chuck picked up the pot and followed her into an ancient greenhouse, built as a lean-to against the southern side of the main building. As they entered, the smell of tomato plants hit Chuck with a strong memory of his grandmother in Colombia. He stood sniffing the air for a moment and the old woman smiled.

43

'You can have some if you would like. I can't eat them all. What are you doing here anyway? I haven't seen you around before.'

'Oh, I had hoped to see the Fredericks, but it appears to be a common idea today.'

The old lady frowned.

'Nice family. It's a pity about their daughter though.'

'Hattie? But isn't she going to Mars? I expect she's ecstatic.'

'Oh, bless you, no, not that daughter. Hattie belongs in space. She's always been an adventurer. I used to find her climbing the trees in out garden. My husband Morty used to let her gaze at the stars through his telescope. They were great buddies, those two. Morty passed away a few years ago though.'

She sighed and pinned a wisp of grey hair back into her bun.

'I'm sorry for your loss.'

'Don't bother with the sympathy. It won't bring him back.'

Chuck took a deep breath.

'Did you say the Fredericks had another daughter,' he said, trying not to sound too eager.

Sybil Reisner appeared not to hear. She trowelled some foul mulch into a larger pot on the floor of the greenhouse, covering a spider who didn't have time to flee.

'Lift the shrub out of the pot. Careful, don't damage it. And rest it on the bottom here.'

Chuck did as he was told and soon the shrub stood in its new pot ready to be moved back to its spot in the sun. He picked it up with a grunt, and staggered back outside.

'There now. Isn't that better?' said the woman.

'It looks great,' said Chuck.

'I wasn't asking you,' said the woman, caressing the leaves of the shrub.

'Um, the other daughter,' said Chuck. 'Can you tell me anything about her?'

'She went all religious on us. A crying shame. Grace used to be such fun. Much like her sister in many ways. They both had green fingers. A lot of the flowers in my garden were planted by them.'

'Grace, is that her name?'

'Yes, I think I have a photograph of them. Would you like to see it?'

Chuck nodded, and the woman fished a battered all-in-one from her apron pocket. She scrolled through the photographs, muttering to herself while he tried not to seem impatient.

'Ah, here they are with my husband. Aren't they a picture?'

Chuck took the phone and gazed at the photograph. Grace and Hattie were very much alike, but Grace had finer features and a slimmer body. They were laughing and Morty Reisner had a gigantic beam on his face.

'What a lovely picture. Do you mind if I take a copy?' said Chuck, taking out his all-in-one and syncing it for a second, just long enough to copy the image.

The woman narrowed her eyes and grabbed the telephone back from him.

'That picture is private. You don't have the right to copy it or use it. Are you one of those horrible journalists?'

'Yes, but I would never do that without your permission. I'm just interested in the Fredericks family.'

'Vermin. I should have known,' she said, shoving him. 'Get out of my garden. Go on. Shoo.'

Chuck backed away.

'I'm sorry for disturbing you,' he said. 'I hope your shrub thrives.'

She hissed at him and he trotted away, ashamed of his theft of the photo, but not enough to delete it. He let himself out of the creaking gate and got back into his vehicle. *Could this be the scoop he had hoped for? He'd never heard of a sister.* He took out his all-in-one, entering Grace Fredericks into the search function. She

45

popped up as the daughter of Edgar Fredericks and Juana Dos Reis. Two years older than Hattie, she had studied history in college and then dropped off the radar. *Where had she disappeared to? Maybe she took drugs or something? It wouldn't be the first time a rich kid from this barrio went off the rails. Had she married young and moved away? Why was there no record of her? One thing was for sure. There must be a trace somewhere.* And he knew just the person to track her down. Before he could look up the number, his all-in-one vibrated in his hand.

'There's another presser about the randy evangelist in an hour's time,' said his editor. 'Get down there and find out what excuse they've dredged up this time. We need to get this our asap. Did you find out anything new at the Fredericks?'

'There's a swarm of journos down there but the gates are firmly closed. I think the presser might be more interesting.'

'Okay get over there and send me your report toot sweet.'

'Will do.'

Chapter 8

H attie stood outside the astronaut quarters at NASA clutching a small bag of personal items and feeling like a child about to go to boarding school for the first time. The sun shone, as it did most days on the Florida coast, and loud birdsong trilled from the nearest palm tree. Just an ordinary day. Edgar Fredericks stood beside her. She resisted the temptation to hold his hand. He shuffled and coughed.

'Your mother wanted to come,' he said. 'She couldn't face saying goodbye.'

'I know,' said Hattie. 'I understand. Tell her I love her too.'

'You be careful out there,' said Fredericks, his voice catching in his throat. 'You've no idea how much I envy you, but it's hard to pretend it's not dangerous to be a pioneer.'

'The danger's part of the fun, and at least I won't be sulking around the house anymore.'

Fredericks squeezed out a smile.

'There's that. I just don't like to feel rushed. This has all happened far too quickly for us.'

'Dad, trust me. It will be fine. I'm more than ready. I'll see you in a couple of years. It will fly by before you know it.'

Fredericks enveloped his daughter in his long arms and hugged her close.

'Give them hell, sweetheart.'

Hattie rang the plain doorbell on the grey metal door set in the high wall around the property. NASA were taking no chances with intruders breaking their quarantine. Large flat feet made their way to the door and it swung open on oiled hinges revealing a uniformed security guard with an expressionless face.

'I'm Hattie—'

'I know who you are. Come in.'

Hattie stepped over the threshold and turned to wave at her father who managed another smile. The guard slammed the door shut and strode into the cool atrium.

'The changing room's over there. You'll need to put your clothing into a plastic bag and step into the sterilizer with any belongings you intend to take with you on the voyage. The door will open after ten minutes and you should change into your uniform and shoes on the other side. We'll keep your clothes for your return.'

'Thank you,' said Hattie.

At least they presume we are coming back.

The door to the atrium slid open and she stepped out of the changing room into a new world. Nothing will ever be the same again.

'Well, if it isn't little Miss Stromatolite.'

'Scotty? Am I glad to see you. I'm feeling a little lost.'

'Now didn't I tell you stranger things have happened. No disrespect to the dead, and all, but you're a sight for sore eyes. Maybe we can start to have some fun around here.'

Hattie grinned.

'May she rest in peace,' she said.

'Amen. Shall I show you to your room?'

'I'd be so grateful. I haven't been upstairs before.'

Scotty glanced at the bag she carried.

'You'll have to leave most of that at home,' he said. 'They don't allow contraband on board.'

'I know. I didn't have enough time to choose, so I brought everything I could think of to whittle down before we take off.'

'How'd the medical go?'

Hattie blushed.

'To be honest, they entered orifices less explored than Mars.'

Scotty roared with laughter.

'It happened to us all,' he said. 'Only some of us are pretending it didn't.'

He pressed the button on the lift and they shot up two floors to the sleeping area.

'Your room is at the end on the right,' he said, as they stepped onto the landing.

Hattie swallowed and looked at the floor. Scotty patted her shoulder.

'She didn't die in there,' he said. 'Her room has been sealed for forensics.'

'You must think I'm an idiot,' said Hattie. 'I didn't dare ask, but I'm replacing her and I thought...'

Chad Farrant emerged from his room and folded his arms, looking Hattie up and down with a sneer on his face.

'Don't kid yourself,' he said. 'You aren't fit to shine her shoes. You're just a stand-in.'

'There's no need for that,' said Scotty 'It's not Hattie's fault Serena died. We need to get on together if this mission is to be a success.'

Chad shrugged.

'We're stuck with you now, I guess,' he said.

'I guess you are,' said Hattie. 'I pull my own weight. You should know that from training. You don't need to worry about me.'

'Oh, I won't,' he said, and went back into his room.

Scotty rolled his eyes.

'Don't take it personally. Serena had him wrapped around her little finger. He's just upset. Perhaps he had a crush on her. He can be good fun when he wants to, and he's a real boffin, despite the football jock exterior.'

'Serena's death must have been shocking for all of you. I'm sorry.'

'We'll get over it. Here's your room. Get settled in. Dinner is at seven. We eat in the first-floor common room.'

Hattie entered the bright room and sat down on the bed. She emptied her bag onto the cover and sorted through it to calm herself down. Shampoo, toothpaste, toothbrush, a statue of Buzz Lightyear with a secret compartment in the base, given to her by Grace, before religion parted them. It would probably be a statue of some obscure saint these days. Her all-in-one contained hundreds of books and as much music as would fit in the memory bank. Chocolate to celebrate their Mars landing, a map of the stars given to her by Morty, her beloved neighbour, who had encouraged her to follow her father into NASA when she baulked at the thought.

She searched the drawers of the small chest beside her bed and found her stash of underwear, now sterilized, and a clean uniform. She took out her stylus and wrote a message to her sister, a note of love and hope for the future. She sent it as a picture like they always used to. Text was not the same and never as personal as a written note. She waited until seven o'clock but Grace did not reply. So, she took the lift to the first floor and entered the dining room. Seven heads turned to observe her as she entered. Had they been discussing her?

'Hi,' she said. 'What's for dinner?'

Chapter 9

A s the day of the launch approached, the yawning chasm Grace had created in her family widened and deepened. She longed to contact her parents and share their emotions, but such a move would jeopardise the new life she had invented for herself. Any slip up could have exposed her and keeping her real identity a secret for so long had been a strain. When Van Horn had called her in to ask her if she had any interest in space travel, she had almost suffered a heart attack. She waited for him to mention it again, or to probe her further, but it seemed as if it had been an innocent enquiry, and not linked in any way to her origins.

And then she heard Harlan Grimes gloating about Serena Hampton's death, almost as if he were involved. She didn't believe it, but she found it hard to understand why a great man, a devout Christian, like Van Horn would associate himself with a low-life like Grimes. Perhaps they were boyhood friends? Grace admired loyalty, but this appeared to go further. However, since the death of Hampton, Van Horn avoided calls from Grimes and made Grace give him thinly veiled excuses. Grimes kept trying, and he loved to make Grace squirm with his filthy insinuations. She wished Van Horn would tell him to get lost.

Her all-in-one pinged and she glanced at the screen. A new message from the Mad Hatter. She stood up and headed for the toilet where she opened the message from her sister. Full of love and happy memories, it was handwritten and brought tears to her eyes. How lucky they were to see each other before Hattie had had to enter quarantine with the other astronauts. If it wasn't for Grace's loyalty to Van Horn, she would go to the launch. Not that she condoned it, but she wanted to pray for Hattie as she set off on her great adventure. *But what excuse could she use in order to be absent for the day? And wasn't it a sin to lie? Was she being tested by the devil?*

Ever since the first days of her association with the fundamentalist church, Grace had harboured doubts about some of the precepts. She loved the purity of its doctrine, but worried about the arbitrary nature of its inclusions. *She had bought Van Horn a shrimp salad on many occasions, but weren't shellfish forbidden? If the bible was the literal word of God, why did he make a man lie down with his daughters?* The organisation had spent huge amount of time and energy trying to disprove laws of science which Grace thought showed His greatness rather than going against His wishes. Even the trip to Mars struck her as the beautiful proof of man's innate curiosity to explore the universe God created. But Van Horn told her it was blasphemy to travel into space and the elders agreed with him.

As the years had passed, Grace felt more and more torn between her love of the church and her reverence for science. Hattie's open disappointment with her choice to join it had been wounding, but their bond had not been completely severed. They had recently began communicating again in a tentative manner, but now Hattie would be gone for years, and unless Grace went back to her parents' house, she might never hear from her again. Some days she considered resigning, but most days she dedicated to the service of the church without complaint.

52

To her great relief, her quandary about going to the launch solved itself when Van Horn announced that the office would be closed for a deep clean on that day. Grace did not suspect any ulterior motives on his part, although the coincidence did surprise her. She could easily melt into the crowd if she wore a disguise and stayed away from her family. Her heart filled with joy as she sent Hattie a message – *I'll be there. Don't forget to wave.*

On the day of the launch, Grace woke to crystal blue skies with only the odd cloud chasing across the sky on soft breezes. She put on a linen dress and took her lightest hooded coat out of the cupboard. She pulled up the hood, put on a pair of large sunglasses, and looked in the mirror. Her reflection made her giggle. She looked like a spy from an old movie, or a celebrity trying to go shopping without being recognised. *Was Hattie a celebrity now? Would she ever see her again?* A sob caught in her throat and she shook her head vigorously to dislodge the thought. Everything would be fine and Hattie would come home safe.

She parked as close to the launch pad as she could and pushed her way through the crowds staring at the beautiful silver Starship which gleamed in the sunlight on the rig platform out at sea. The astronauts should be strapped in by now, going through their final checklists. *I'd pay a million dollars to hug Hattie and wish her luck.* Grace wiped her brow as the sun beat down and she got jostled by the excited crowd. Her disguise did not feel like such a good idea now. She longed to throw off the coat and get some relief from the heat. *Surely no one will see me, or recognise me? It's years since I disappeared from my own life.*

She glanced around, gauging her chances of being discovered and, out of the corner of her eye, she spotted Van Horn. She spun around, pulling the hood further over her head, her heart thundering in her chest. *What was he doing here? Could it be a mission from headquarters? It didn't seem likely. They had issued a prohibition banning followers from the launch. Maybe he had been sent to monitor the launch to prevent members attending?* Grace tried to move away but a murmur of dissent came from the tight packed crowd.

'Come on, lady. It's about to take off. You'll be in the way.'

She recoiled from their criticism and keeping her head turned away from Van Horn, refocused on the launch. The minutes passed, and an expectant silence fell on those assembled. Panic seized Grace's heart in a vice-like grip. She struggled to breathe. *Countdown so soon? Please don't go Hattie, I'll come home I promise.* A tear escaped from her eye and rolled down her cheek.

'Ten, nine, eight,' chorused the crowd.

The Starship started to shake and roar, and bright orange exhaust fumes billowed from the Raptor engines.

'Seven, six, five, four,' said Van Horn, oblivious to Grace, so near to him in the crowd.

'Three, two, one,' mouthed Grace, as the ground shook under her feet, rattling her to the core.

The Starship tore itself from the launch pad, as if reluctant to take off, accelerating away into the blue. Grace found herself waving frantically, as if Hattie would see her down in the mass of cheering people and know that she was loved. *Godspeed, Hattie. Come home safe to me.* She watched with her heart in her mouth as the Starship gathered speed and became smaller and smaller until it resembled a lost star.

She sat down as the crowd thinned out, and soon she found herself almost alone on the grassy bank. She sneaked a glance behind her but Van Horn had gone too, so she took off her coat and let the sea breeze cool her. She removed her sunglasses and hung one plastic arm over the neck of her dress. Tipping back her head, she strained to see the tiny dot in the wide sky but it had disappeared. A shadow passed over her face. She lowered her head to see a man standing in front of her, looking at her and back to his all-in-one with studied concentration, his checked-shirt wet at the armpits and grey-flecked stubble on his chin.

'You're Grace Fredericks, aren't you?' he said.

The shock of being recognised left Grace dumb for a second. She stared at the man, trying to remember him. *How does he know who I am?* He smiled at her bewilderment.

'I'm Chuck Gomez,' he said. 'Correspondent for Space Monthly. I've been hoping to speak to you about *Hattie.*'

'You've made a mistake,' she said. 'My name is Dos Reis, not Fredericks. I don't know Hattie, I just came to watch the launch.'

Gomez raised an eyebrow.

'You sure look like her. I've got a photo right here.'

He shoved his all-in-one in her face, and she recognised the photograph of herself with Hattie and their old neighbour. *Monty? No Morty. That was it.*

'She does look a little like me, I guess. But you've got it wrong.'

Grace stood up, grabbing her coat, and brushing the grass of her dress. Her denial sounded hollow, even to her ears. *I'd love a copy of that photo.* Gomez shook his head and peered at her again.

'The resemblance is uncanny,' he said, taking a card out of his pocket. 'I know you don't want to talk now but keep my details just in case. Hattie will be away a long time and I get inside information from my pals in NASA about the goings-on on board the Starship. You might want to call me sometime.'

'I doubt it,' said Grace. 'I'm not Hattie's sister. You have me confused with someone else.'

But she shoved his card deep into her coat pocket. Gomez grinned.

'Sure, well, have a nice life.'

Chapter 10

The world held its collective breath as the silver Starship with its belly of black heat resistant tiles hurtled into the heavens spewing smoke and thunder behind it. Watched by the NASA and SpaceX technicians who had nurtured the project for years, it rose higher, gleaming in the sunlight, its Raptor engines thundering and causing massive ripples to spread out over the ocean. Journalists and camera crews from around the world broadcast live pictures to all forms of media watched by an audience of several billion.

At NASA headquarters, the staff contained their elation until the Starship cleared Earth and headed for its rendezvous with the refuelling tanker ship in Earth's orbit. Despite their scientific backgrounds, the seemingly random success or failure of the Mars missions had made them superstitious. Most muttered prayers or crossed their fingers despite knowing the die had already been cast. Serena Hampton's untimely demise also tempered their natural urge to celebrate. Edgar Fredericks, who had more at stake in the successful take-off than any of them, pressed his fingers into the desk in front of him and released a sigh of relief.

'No rest for the wicked, guys,' he said. 'Can you check the telemetry for the refuelling please? And can someone bring me a cup of coffee. I've been awake for about seventy-two hours.'

'Congratulations, boss,' said someone. 'You must be so proud.'

A spontaneous round of applause burst rang around the room. Some people stood up and cheered. Fredericks blinked and struggled to contain his emotions.

'Thank you,' he managed. 'Hattie is depending on you, as am I.'

Inside the Starship, emotions were also high. Chad, Mo and Bret exchanged fist bumps and chanted 'USA'. The others lay supine, quiet, overwhelmed by the enormity of it all. The shuddering force of the take-off had not been replicated in their training despite all attempts at simulation. The real thing had pinned them to their seats and driven their breath out of their lungs with a frightening power. The 3-G acceleration lasted for over eight minutes as the Starship reached its orbital velocity of seventeen thousand, five hundred miles per hour. When it reached orbit, the main engines cut off and the gravity inside dropped to zero.

Hattie gazed out into the universe as the Starship exited the Earth's atmosphere into space. She shut her eyes as the pressure on her ribcage increased. *I wish Morty Reisner had lived to see this day. He would have been as excited as me.* When the Starship entered orbit and the astronauts were released from the effects of gravity, Hattie loosened her straps and, as if by magic, floated off her seat. She removed her helmet and took a cautious lungful of air; thankful her ribs had not cracked under the g-force of the launch. The intense blackness of space made her throat tighten despite expecting the transition. The Earth drifted past the viewing window and made her catch her breath.

'It's so beautiful,' said Ellie. 'I mean, I knew it would be, but it's like a precious jewel in space.'

Hattie nodded, dumb with the intensity of her feelings. How often had she replayed the recording of the childish delight of William Shatner, when he got to fly in Blue Origin in 2021? Captain Kirk, her childhood hero, had said; 'To see the blue colour whip by and now you're staring into blackness. This covering of blue is this sheet, this blanket, this comforter of blue that we have around us.' And now the comforter had been ripped off and the Earth looked abandoned, resembling a blue-green ball floating in an infinite sea of black ink.

'I'm engaging the epsilon drive,' said Chad. 'Please don't get up yet.'

This drive rotated the inner sleeve of the spacecraft and created a gravity field equivalent to Earth. The presence of normal gravity in the ship prevented many of the health problems associated with space especially those associated with the eyes and heart. The Starship's design also shielded the crew from almost all of the radiation which bombarded the craft from space. They only had to use a radiation shelter if a solar flare enveloped them. The epsilon system switched off automatically when they were all in hibernation on their way to Mars because their pods were pressurised to 1-G. The epsilon technology made everything simpler, including eating, drinking, and going to the toilet. It meant that clothes could be washed and things left in place without floating away. The Nobel Prize for Physics appeared nailed on for the designer of the Starship's washing machine, a slightly sheepish entrepreneur who had been trying to use a centrifuge to make ice cream, or so he said.

Once gravity had been restored, Bret, Mo and Scotty prepared the Starship systems for automatic refuelling in orbit. They sat at the console on the command deck monitoring the screens which had a continuous stream of readings from all over the Starship. The consoles were embedded in the all-white surrounds of the deck, almost blinding in its brilliance. The whole Starship had an inner sleeve which prevented radiation from entering the living quarters. A tubular staircase ran down the centre of the Starship with several exits at each level, making it as easy to use in zero gravity as induced gravity.

Hattie and Ellie stood at the picture window gazing out into space. Ellie put her arm around Hattie's waist.

'We're outnumbered,' she said. 'We need to stick together. To tell you the truth, I didn't like Serena much. It's very sad that she's dead, but I never had anything in common with her.'

'I would like that,' said Hattie. 'I feel like a bit of a fraud, to be honest, an outsider.'

Ellie's blue eyes opened wide.

'A fraud? But you're a famous scientist. And you're not an outsider. Scotty likes you a lot too.'

Hattie tried to hide her face as she flushed bright red. 'Scotty said that?'

'Well, not exactly, but I know he thinks it. We've been good friends since the beginning of training. I know it's hard for you to slot in, after spending most of your time in the other team, but everyone's really nice and they are all amazing scientists. Give them time to get used to you. Serena's loss hit them hard, especially Chad. He needs time to adjust.'

Ellie's heart-shaped face moved closer to Hattie's chubby one, as she searched Hattie's brown eyes for confirmation. Hattie grinned.

'Well, they don't have a lot of choice now, do they. We're all trapped together in this tin can for months.'

'It's lucky we get to sleep for most of the first eight months. No tension or discord while we're all comatose.'

But Hattie wondered how they would all get on when they woke up. Her father had told her politics had intruded into astronaut selection, and he had worried about the pressure that might be exerted on different members of the crew by their national governments. The case of the three Russian astronauts who wore spacesuits in the colours of the Ukrainian flag during the war in 2022 had not faded from memory. Their gesture was feted in the world press but on their return to Earth, they disappeared and were not heard from again.

'But isn't it a UN mission,' Hattie had replied. 'Surely politics will be forgotten?'

'Politics and religion influence every decision made on Earth,'; said Fredericks. 'It doesn't do to be such an idealist.'

But she couldn't help it. And now her faith had been vindicated. She would fulfil her life's ambition despite all the obstacles. She could hardly wait. A barked order from the bridge interrupted her musings.

'Okay everyone. Helmets back on and strap in again. We're going to start refuelling.'

Bret and Scotty sat at the control panel monitoring the sequence as the Starship manoeuvred alongside the tanker.

'Prepare for refuelling sequence,' said Scotty.

'Roger that,' said Bret.

They both sat waiting to confirm the transfer.

'What's the delay?' said Bret.

'For some reason the secondary seal on the fuel inlet has not opened,' said Scotty. 'I'll run a diagnostic.'

Hattie felt a drop of sweat wend its way down her cheek.

'I had hoped to travel further than this,' muttered Yu.

'It's just a glitch,' said Wayne. 'Calm down.'

'I am calm.'

'Fredericks's voice echoed in the cockpit.

'We can see no reason for the fault in the quick disconnect system. We'll keep trying on our end. Scotty, can you suit up, please? You may need to go outside to do some old-fashioned mechanical checks on the entry valve.'

'Is that safe?' said Hattie.

'I have a degree in engineering,' said Scotty, causing everyone to laugh.

'I'll come with you,' said Chad. 'There's probably something that is jammed and you might need help.'

'Okay, get suited up and select some tools for the job. Then run through the safety checks and hang fire until I give you instructions,' said Bret.

Scotty and Chad shinned down the central staircase to the elevator level where the suits were stored. They stood in the automatic bays and waited for the machine to apply their suits and seal them tight. They put on their tanks and sat with their helmets on their laps, going through the safety protocols and waiting for instructions.

'We are go for the spacewalk,' said Bret's voice. 'I know you've done this many times before, but don't get careless. If we can't find the cause, we'll be going back to Earth.'

The two men opened the massive protective door to the airlock. Red lights started to flash and warnings echoed around the ship. The door shut and the air evacuated. Chad gave Scotty a thumbs up which he returned and they pressed the inner buttons confirming permission for the door to open. They floated out into space under the eyes of the world as billions were glued to the drama in the sky above them. Fredericks and his team monitored every breath of the two astronauts as they made their way to the quick-disconnect panel. The cover slid back revealing the quick-disconnect ports. Chad and Scotty clipped themselves to hooks inside the cover for safety. They reviewed the panel, comparing it to the diagram on their space pads.

'What is that?' said Chad, pointing at a steel cap over the methane entry point.

'I have no idea,' said Scotty. 'NASA, do you copy?'

'We see it,' said Fredericks. 'Give me a minute here.'

Scotty floated closer and examined the cap. It had been crudely welded to the panel and wouldn't take more than a quick wrench to release it.

'I can easily remove it,' said Scotty. 'Maybe it was put on to protect the system during transport and they forgot to remove it.'

'That's pretty careless,' said Chad. 'It doesn't sound likely, but what other possible explanation can there be?'

'The technicians say it shouldn't be there. Take it off with as much care as you can,' said Fredericks. 'As long as the connection port underneath is in perfect condition, we can't see any problem with the underlying electronic circuits. We'll run some diagnostics to be sure but otherwise we are still green for go. I'll find out who did this.'

'And put a rocket up him,' said Chad.

'Very funny. Get back inside and let's get this show on the road.'

Scotty levered off the cap which floated off into space before Chad could grab it.

'I guess it's Murphy's law,' said Chad. 'All the technology in the world can't stop stupid.'

'I guess so,' said Scotty.

Chapter 11

I f Scotty or Chad had any misgivings about the weird glitch during refilling of the oxygen and methane tanks on board, they kept them to themselves. The rest of the crew applauded them as they returned to the bridge.

'Well done, guys. All ready to go,' Bret said, strapping himself back into his seat. 'Confirm valves open on Starship.'

'Confirmed,' said Chad.

'Transfer authorised.'

The refilling took several hours and the crew nodded off in their seats, hit by the exhaustion of their build-up to the trip. Finally, the Starship separated from the tanker automatically and the engines fired up to start them on their way again.

'And we're off,' said Bret. 'Eight months to history.'

'Good luck,' said Fredericks. 'The future of space travel is in your hands. We'll see you all soon.'

'Roger that,' said Chad.

'Goodbye, Dad,' whispered Hattie, under her breath.

When all systems had been turned to automatic, and the Starship had set out on its nine-month journey, Yu stood up, somewhat unsteadily and waved his arms.

'I'll prepare the hibernation pods on the sleeping deck. Hattie, do you want to give me a hand?'

'Of course,' she said. 'I love putting people to bed.'

'Putting them to sleep more like it,' said Wayne.

'By telling them anecdotes about stromatolites,' said Mo.

He winked at her as he pulled off his helmet. Mo had already shown a keen interest in developing an algorithm for the simple identification of fossilised stromatolites. 'AI can do anything,' he told her. It was a pity he was such a jock, and laughed at Chad's jokes.

Hattie followed Yu down the stairs to the sleeping area one level below the command deck. It had been put there to remove it as far from the noise of the engines as possible. The narrow bunks with integrated desks and personal storage had been placed around the outer wall, and the hibernation pods were arranged around the central console like petals around the centre of a flower. Everything gleamed white which irritated Hattie. *Could they have not used a few other colours?* A plaque on each hibernation pod spelled out their intended occupant and their role on board above a digital display monitoring the life signs of the occupants. There had not been time to replace Serena's nameplate, but it had been removed, and a sticker with 'Science Officer' printed on it in large black lettering had been stuck on instead.

'Home sweet home,' said Yu, patting his pod. 'Let's hope yours isn't haunted.'

Seeing Hattie's face fall, he added, 'don't mind me. My sense of humour is fatal at the best of times.'

'Enough with the death jokes,' said Hattie. 'How do I help?'

Once he set to work, Yu's mood became sombre and Hattie was struck by the Jekyll and Hyde nature of his character; frivolous one minute, deadly serious the next. They worked steadily for the best part of an hour until all the syringes were ready, containing the exact amount of sedative required by the physiology and weight of the recipient. Yu checked the life support systems on each pod, ticking off a check list on his all-in-one.

'Thank goodness for modern medicine, eh?' said Yu. 'Imagine having to put up with Chad and Bret for seven months.'

His hand flew to his mouth as he looked around to make sure nobody had heard him. Hattie made a zipping motion over her mouth.

'How come you wanted to be an astronaut?' she said. 'You should have been a comedian.'

'The name Yu means universe. My parents had ambitions for me.'

'But what did you want?'

'I had other dreams, but I had to shelve them. I'll tell you about Chinese culture another time,' said Yu, avoiding her inquiring glance. 'Okay, we're ready for the first victim.'

The crew came down to the sleeping deck one by one. Mo insisted on exchanging high fives and chanting USA with Bret and Chad before he got into his pod. Yu rolled his eyes at Hattie and mouthed 'bravado'. Before long, Mo and Scotty were locked into their pods, safe and sound in the land of Nod, as Yu put it. Next to go down were Chad and Bret, who also allowed themselves to be put into comas with no dramas. Ellie hugged Hattie before she got into her pod.

'See you soon, girlfriend,' she said.

Hattie smiled but the thought of using Serena's pod had made her nervous. She didn't believe in ghosts, but Serena didn't like her. *What if she objects to me using her pod?* When Ellie had been sealed in, Wayne came forward for his turn and Hattie grabbed his arm.

'Will you swap pods with me?' she said. 'Chad and Bret are always teasing me. I don't want to sleep between them in case I have nightmares about them.'

Wayne's face showed what he thought of this odd request. *Would he have reacted better to her fear of ghosts?* But he grinned.

'I don't care who sleeps either side of me, after all, we'll basically be in a medical coma.'

65

'Thanks. Sleep well.'

Wayne climbed into the Science Officer's pod and lay down while Yu connected him up to the heart monitor and drips. He shut his eyes and took a couple of deep breaths. He fell asleep before Yu had administered the drugs.

'Sleeping like a baby,' said Yu. 'You're next.'

Hattie's stomach gurgled loudly, making them both giggle. They hadn't been allowed to eat for twenty-four hours and had been subjected to pre-flight enemas to clean out their digestive systems. Hattie craved oblivion to rid herself of the hunger pangs that assailed her. There would be no control over her diet in space. NASA nutritionists would monitor and calorie-control their intake for optimum health. Their pods would also be monitored to make sure they survived the hibernation. She hadn't been so heavily supervised since kindergarten.

'Of course,' she said. 'See you on the other side.'

Hattie clambered into Wayne's empty pod. Her heart thundered in her chest as she anticipated the lid being closed. Somehow, she had got through training without anyone spotting her acute claustrophobia but now she would have to control it. She smiled at Yu.

'I can't wait to wake up again. I've got so many experiments to do,' she said. *It's really happening.* She lay back, trying to slow down her breathing. In her hand, she gripped the note from Grace – *To infinity and beyond.* Yu noticed her look of panic.

'There's a button on the inside if you need to get out,' he said.

Hattie smiled.

'Thanks. I'd forgotten.'

She shut her eyes and held out her arm.

'This will hurt a bit,' said Yu.

He slid the needle into her vein and pressed the plunger on the syringe. The cold fluid made Hattie wince but before she could complain, she blacked out.

Yu shut the lid of her pod, and then did a circuit of the other pods, double checking the seals and taking notes of the readings on the central console. When he felt satisfied with his checks, he got into his own capsule and sealed the lid from the inside. He slid the drip into his hand and opened the tap.

'Sweet dreams, everyone,' he slurred.

***

Back on Earth, Chuck Gomez settled in to watch replays of the launch and listen to the commentators out do themselves with superlatives about the first manned mission to Mars. His frustration at his abortive attempt to interview Grace had faded away with each glass of malt whisky on ice. At least she had taken his details. *And who knew how curious she might get as time passed without news of her sister?* Chuck liked leverage. He felt guilty about cloning the image from the old woman's phone, but now he hunted ahead of the pack. *Surely a large pay day featured in his future?*

***

Juana and Edgar Fredericks relaxed on the swinging chair on their porch. From there, they could see Sybil Reisner up on the roof terrace of her house, gazing at the stars through her husband's telescope.

'Do you think she can see Hattie?' said Juana.

A board creaked on the verandah. They were not alone. A slim figure approached and sat between them. Grace took their hands and they all sat looking at the night sky. Nobody dared break the silence.

On the viewing platform of the neighbouring house, Sybil Reisner sighed, and put the cap back on the lens of the telescope. She opened her all-in-one and looked again at her favourite photograph of her dead husband. He looked back at her, debonair, smiling, with the corners of his eyes crinkled up. She stroked the screen and a tear slid down her cheek.

'I hope you're seeing this, Morty,' she said.

Chapter 12

C huck yawned and arched his back, stiff from sitting at his desk for hours. He chewed the end of his pencil for inspiration, but nothing would come. The manned Starship had set out for Mars nearly six months before, and there were only so many articles he could write about the public expectation surrounding the mission. Grace had not contacted him after their unexpected meeting at the launch, but he planned to have another go at interviewing her now that the astronauts were due to wake up. His knowledge of her clandestine double life would no doubt be sufficient to persuade her.

The astronauts had been in a state of stasis for the whole journey, essentially a medical coma which preserved their supplies of food and water for their stay on Mars and even last for the journey home, when they could be awake. The return voyage would be used for experiments and monitoring of the effect of space travel on the astronauts, if any of them survived. Chuck did not discount the possibility of them all suffering unfortunate ends after what had happened to Serena. *Much better press coverage for death and glory. My boss would love that.*

He stood up and stretched again. *What's it like to be asleep for so long? Do you dream?* Chuck suffered from a chronic lack of sleep, and he had fantasised about volunteering for the trials of coma drugs for long space voyages. Needless to say, his reality did not allow him to take a couple of months off asleep, no matter how tempting it sounded. He didn't like the risks associated with new medical procedures either. Chuck liked other people to test things out for him.

His stomach growled, and he opened the door of the fridge, more in hope than expectation. Apart from the essentials, like beer and, well, more beer, it echoed with emptiness. The simplest thing would be to order lunch and wait for it to be delivered, but for once, Chuck decided to eat out. He had long wanted to try a new downtown deli where, rumour had it, the pastrami rolls were to die for.

He grabbed his all-in-one and ordered a taxi. Then he stuffed it in his pocket with his notebook and pencil and waited to be picked up from the lobby of his building. The taxi came within minutes, and dropped him outside the deli a short time later, but the lights of the restaurant were out and the doors locked. A neon notice on the door contained an apology to regular customers about the closure, due to a bereavement. Disappointed, Chuck looked around for an alternative and spotted a sushi restaurant across the street. *Sushi.* He hadn't eaten sushi for ages. *I could really fancy some California Rolls and Shrimp Tempura.*

He dashed across the road with his head down hoping not to be caught jay-walking by one of the myriad CCTV cameras scanning the street. He peered through the steamy windows into the sushi restaurant. The joint oozed class and most of the tables were occupied, which always spoke volumes about the quality of the food served. The prices on their menu made him blanch, but he felt faint from hunger already, so he pushed the door and stepped inside.

The restaurant had more internal space than he had imagined, and soon a blotchy-faced waitress had seated him in a corner table where he could spy on the other diners without being observed. She dropped an electronic menu on his table and rummaged in her pockets for a tissue.

'The crab is off,' she said, blowing her nose, and walked away wiping her eyes.

Chuck watched her go before opening the menu and selecting his favourites from the garish selection. *Where have I seen that purple dragon before?* The waitress reappeared with his pot of jasmine tea.

'Would you like me to pour it for you?' she said.

'No thanks,' said Chuck. 'I couldn't help noticing how upset you are. Can I help?'

She forced out a smile and took a deep breath.

'Gee, thanks, no, there's nothing you can do, unless you're a cop. One of our delivery men, Danilo, has been found murdered. He's been missing for months.'

Chuck's fingers started to itch. He reached into his pocket, fumbling for his notebook.

'Maybe I can help,' he said, taking out his pencil. 'I'm an investigative journalist. When did he go missing?'

The waitress cocked her head.

'A pencil?' she said. 'Are you from the stone age?'

'Very funny. I'm being serious. When did you last see him?'

'The night of the launch. I remember because we were so excited about it.'

'The Mars launch? The mission is pretty amazing, isn't it?'

'Oh, no, I'm not interested in Mars. We were excited because we fed one of the astronauts. I don't know which of them, but NASA ordered our special flower banquet for one. The press came and interviewed our manager.'

The purple dragon. Now he remembered seeing it on the box in the kitchen during the launch press conference. And he also remembered the aikido move which stopped him tasting it.

'What did Danilo look like?'

'Oh, young, handsome, charming, Latino.' A sob caught in her throat. 'We were... you know.'

'I'm so sorry. You must be devastated.'

'I can't believe it. Who would kill him? He wasn't mixed up in anything I knew about.'

Chuck tried to remain calm. The man who had grabbed his hand in the gala kitchen had been white, and skinny looking; definitely not Latino.

'I've changed my mind,' he said. 'Can you make my order to go?'

After paying with his all-in-one, and leaving a substantial tip he couldn't afford, Chuck carried the take-out to his car. He sat there, sipping the jasmine tea, wishing he had eaten his lunch in the restaurant instead of trying to use chopsticks in the car. *Something smelled fishy, and it wasn't the sushi.* He needed more information and he knew where to get it. He took out his all-in-one and called Miami's police headquarters.

'Are you busy, Gina? I've got fresh sushi if you want some lunch.'

'I'd rather die than have lunch with you. Or have you forgotten how you treated me in the past?'

Chuck bit his lip. He had been a bastard as usual, dumping her without ceremony when it looked like getting serious. She hadn't taken it kindly and had refused to talk to him again for months.

'That must have been someone else. I always treated you like a queen. Please, Gina, this is important.'

A loud sigh. Chuck waited.

'You said Sushi? Really?'

'Uh huh.'

'Okay, but I want Nigiri and Norimaki. I'll meet you at the bandstand in half an hour.'

Chuck entered the new order on his all-in-one and paid for it with his diminishing credits. He re-entered the restaurant, and picked up the sushi to the pleasure of the manager.

'Back so soon?' she said. 'I'll give you a discount card.'

Chuck sat at one of the green metal tables in the bandstand, wiping the fresh bird droppings off it with a napkin to make it presentable. He waited for almost an hour before Gina turned up. She took her time to approach him, swinging her hips in her tight polyester trousers and flicking her long red hair behind her like a horse's mane. Her green eyes narrowed as she spotted him, and she gave him a look that froze his balls. *No romance then.* He took his punishment without complaint, and beamed at her as she approached.

'Hello, stranger,' he said. 'Long time no see.'

'And who's fault is that? Hand over the sushi.'

Gina opened her box and ate with pleasure, smacking her lips and wiping them with a napkin which came away stained with her bright red lipstick.

'Wow, this is great.'

'It is good, isn't it? I only found the place because the deli had been closed for the day.'

Gina wiped her mouth and took a sip of Chuck's jasmine tea. She looked over the top of the cup through narrowed eyes.

'Okay, so what do you want?'

'What makes you think I want something?'

Gina snorted and stood up, but Chuck grabbed her arm.

'Okay,' he said. 'I need some information.'

She sat down again and faced him.

'About what?'

'Serena Hampton.'

'The astronaut? I thought she died of sudden adult death syndrome?'

'So did I. Until today.'

'What do you know?'

'Nothing yet. It's only a gut feeling so far, but I need help.'

'A gut feeling, uh?'

She feigned indifference, but he had hooked her. Gina Marco loved a mystery.

'I need to know the results of the autopsy. The real results. Can you get them for me?' he said. 'It's important.'

Gina frowned.

'I know the coroner, but he's old school. It may be difficult to get him to spill the beans.'

'Does he have an assistant?'

Gina laughed.

'He does. A young man with designs on me. Maybe I could persuade him to send me an electronic copy of the report?'

'I'd be so grateful.'

'Would you buy me more sushi?'

'Not that grateful. How about a burger? Ouch.'

Chuck rubbed his arm where Gina had thumped it.

'I'll forward it to you,' she said. 'Keep me in the loop.'

Chuck leaned forward and planted a kiss on her cheek.

'Thanks. I promise. Can you do it today?'

Gina sighed.

'Sure. Watch your inbox.'

Chuck got home to his apartment and reread all his notes about the Mars mission. It occurred to him that he had not made much of an effort to find Grace Fredericks. *Surely, she had left some sort of data trail?* He found plenty of information for the first twenty years of her life, and then the trail went cold. A couple of possibilities suggested themselves to him. Either she had got married and changed her name, or she had fallen into a life on the streets. The smart young woman he had met at the launch did not look as if she had a drug problem, or any problem, despite her nervous demeanour.

He searched the marriage records but she didn't turn up there either. *Could she have changed her name for another reason? Was she hiding from someone? How on Earth can I trace her?* Then he remembered the pseudonym she had given him. Grace Dos Reis. *What if?*

He typed the name of Grace Dos Reis into his all-in-one, along with her age.

Bingo! Her face came up on the screen and he recognised the row of freckles running over the bridge of her nose. The Christian National Party? No wonder she changed her name. They would never let someone from a scientific family work in their headquarters. *Did she really believe all that crap in the Old Testament?* It didn't feel right. He cloned her address onto his all-in-one intending to visit her and get an interview that evening.

Suddenly a message notification flashed up on the flat screen in front of him. *Gina. Had she found out already?* He tapped on the screen and it opened. He skimmed the contents.

Chuck, what the hell have you got yourself mixed up in? There's something unsavoury going on. Serena Hampton was poisoned but they're keeping it quiet so as not to delay the launch. They'll fire me on the spot, or worse, if they realise that I've seen the report. I recommend you forget about the autopsy if you want to keep your job. Gina.

He scratched his chin and read it again. Vindication. His scalp prickled. *This could be the biggest scoop of my career. I can buy more than a new battery for my car if I pull this off.* He replied to Gina.

Thanks, honey. That's all I needed to know, Chuck. P.S. Are we still on for a burger?

Chapter 13

H attie tried to open her eyes, but they felt as if someone had superglued the lids together. She moved her right arm and it flopped against the edge of the pod. A wave of panic swamped her. *Where the hell am I? Have I been buried alive?* She started to hyperventilate. The pod opened with a click and her ears hurt as the pressure normalised. She grabbed her nose and blew gently to make her ears pop. Then she sat up, groggy with sleep and looked around, her stomach churning.

Chen Yu hovered at the end of her pod, his face grave.

'Hi, did you sleep well?' she said.

'Not really,' he said. 'Can I help you out?'

'Sure. Where are the others?'

'Oh, they're still asleep. I only woke you because you helped me to load the pods and I needed a witness.'

He rubbed the back of his neck and wrung his hands together avoiding her inquiring glance. Hattie released the sleeping bag and pulled her legs out of it. Then she swung a leg over the side of the pod and Yu pulled her to an upright position. Nausea threatened to make her vomit, but she clung to his arm and took a couple of deep breaths.

'I feel terrible,' she said. 'Is this normal?'

'I'm surprised you can stay upright,' he said. 'It took me several minutes.'

'So, what's up?' said Hattie. 'You look as if you've seen a ghost.'

Yu tried to smile.

'I may have done. NASA woke me because they got a warning signal about one of the pods. I got to it as fast as I could but the fifteen-minute delay in the transmission had been fatal.'

'What do you mean?' said Hattie, now wide awake.

'It's Wayne. He's dead.'

'Dead? Oh my God.'

Hattie took a couple of deep breaths and then glided around the circle of closed pods, grabbing onto the handles until she came to the one with the science officer sticker. Yu pressed the release button to open it. Wayne lay inside, serene, his short afro pressed into the pillow and a peculiar bluish sheen to his skin.

'But how did he die?' said Hattie.

'Asphyxiation, I imagine. Something happened to his oxygen supply.'

Hattie leaned against the next pod, trying to take in the news.

'What do you mean, something happened?'

'I'm not an engineer, I'm a doctor. I just know that he died from lack of oxygen. Look at the colour of his skin.'

Hattie touched Wayne's cheek, still warm, and sighed.

'Poor Wayne. Have you told NASA?'

'I sent them an encrypted message. I'm waiting for instructions.'

Hattie put her hands over her face. *What on Earth is going on? Why would someone tried to kill me?*

'This can't be a coincidence,' she said.

'What can't?' said Yu.

'I swapped pods with him, remember. They've already killed one science officer. I'm the one who's supposed to be dead.'

'Don't over-react. It's a horrible coincidence, not a murder. Besides, we were the only ones who were still awake when he got into his pod,' said Yu. 'And I put you

77

into yours, so the only person who could have done this to Wayne is me.'

Hattie stared at him open mouthed.

'But you didn't, did you?'

'Of course not. How can you even ask me that? Why would I wake you up instead of the others? I knew it was Wayne in there and not you.'

'Sorry, I'm so shocked. Maybe the pod had a fault?'

'Don't you think they checked it a thousand times before we set out?'

'Yes, but this is new technology. Perhaps Wayne reacted badly to the drugs?'

'I don't know,' said Yu. 'It's a mystery, but not one I can solve on board. We should move Wayne to the freezer room so that his body is preserved until we get home again and they can do an autopsy. Will you help me?'

Hattie nodded. As they struggled to put Wayne into a body bag and seal him in, scenarios for the death flooded her brain but nothing seemed to make sense. *Yu was the only one who knew Hattie and Wayne had swapped pods, but what possible motive did he have for killing Wayne? And if he didn't kill Wayne, she couldn't ignore the fact that Wayne died in the science officer's pod. Alarm bells were going off in her head but could the coincidence just be bad luck? And what would the others think?*

Once Wayne's body had been stored at the back of the freezer, Yu made coffee and they sat strapped to their seats in the canteen on the top deck, sucking it out of their cups.

'How long were we asleep?' said Hattie.

'Six months or so. The others are due to wake up next week so there's no point getting back into the pods again. We might as well use the time to get fit. At least there'll be no queue for the equipment.'

A buzzer sounded in the control panel and Yu opened an encrypted message in his inbox. He read it twice, shaking his head.

'What does it say?' said Hattie.

'They found a fault in the software of Wayne's pod, and they regret the tragedy, blah, blah, blah.' He rolled his eyes. 'They want us to keep Wayne's death a secret for now. The mission can't take any more bad publicity after the Serena episode.'

'Maybe they're suspicious too. They probably need time to check the data feeds.'

'Maybe. My guess is that Wayne will officially perish in an accident on the surface, a true African hero.'

'Wow. You're cynical.'

'What do you expect? This voyage is about cold hard cash, just like everything else the government undertakes,' said Yu.

'And the science? What about the amazing discoveries we'll make on the surface?'

Yu shrugged.

'There's no room for idealists on this trip. Our governments are looking for resources for our electric futures. They don't give a toss about life on Mars. Why do you think Bret is on board?'

'Bret? Isn't he an engineer? I thought he came on the mission to set up the first habitats and the Moxy plant with Scott.'

'He's a senior mining engineer. He's supposed to assess the red planet as a resource for commodities for the United States.'

'But this is an international mission,' said Hattie.

'I don't trust Bret. My government thinks he will try and steal the planet for the USA.'

'But shouldn't we do something to prevent it?'

'From what has happened so far, I think staying alive is our main priority. Don't you?'

Hattie nodded.

'If I were you,' said Yu. 'I'd learn the lie of the land. I'm sure Serena would have had the lab set up perfectly for herself, but you may want to log any changes you need in the task file, so Mo has something to do when he wakes up.'

Hattie chose one of the sleeping cabins and unpacked her sparse possessions. She stuck the Buzz Lightyear figure to a piece of Velcro and placed it in a small alcove over the bed, mouthing 'to infinity and beyond' to herself. She placed all her other possessions in the drawers so they would not float away. Then she made her way downstairs to the lab and workstation level where she found Yu chasing his all-in-one across the ceiling.

'Should we initialise the epsilon gravity system?' said Hattie.

'I don't think so. It does make our work more difficult but we should conserve energy until the others are awake.'

'I guess it's good practice for space walks.'

'Hopefully we don't need to do any more of those.'

Hattie and Yu slept zipped up into their suspended sleeping bags hung outside their pods like a pair of giant chrysalides. The confines of the bag induced feelings of claustrophobia in Hattie and she thrashed around as vivid and life like dreams invaded her sleep.

'Can't you take a pill or something?' said Yu, when they woke up. 'You're worse than my dog.'

'I can't help it. I feel trapped. I can't wait to sleep in my bunk,' said Hattie.

'You're lucky. You and Ellie will get a cabin each now that Wayne is dead.'

'That's not why I killed him though,' said Hattie.

She bit her lip but a laugh burst through. Yu shook his head.

'You shouldn't joke about it,' he said, but he laughed too, and the atmosphere that had been generated by the awful discovery evaporated.

In the week that followed, Yu and Hattie fell into a routine based on a twenty-four-hour day. Her experience in the MRDS project in Utah had done a great job preparing her for the daily routine of living aboard a spacecraft in confined spaces. She had always been a loner, so the isolation did not bother her in the slightest. Hattie longed to try out the innovations like the washing machines, and have a shower once a week. Wet wipes kept away her body odours, but somehow, she didn't feel clean without a proper shower. The machines didn't work without the epsilon gravity field but they also used water, which was a finite resource, despite the intense recycling on board, until they reached Mars. The ice fields there would give them a plentiful supply of water to refill their tanks.

Working weightless proved to be fiddly in the extreme. Hattie struggled to remember to stick down her pens and small items to the work top. She spent hours attaching bits of Velcro to them and to the worktops. The onboard laboratory occupied almost a whole floor of the Starship but at eight metres across it did not offer enough room for all eight astronauts to work at once. Hattie had to remind herself that they were now seven, but that didn't make her feel any better. She spent two hours a day on the exercise equipment in the back half of the command level, singing tunelessly to her all in one. As she ran, she wondered if all the other astronauts would wake up or if there would there be more casualties.

She had learned during two years of training about the dangers of working in space, but all her courses on flight safety and operations did not make any reference to astronauts dying in suspicious circumstances. *Were the deaths suspicious? Perhaps Yu was right. It had been a coincidence. A horrible coincidence but why would someone be targeting scientists on a space mission? It didn't make any sense.*

Anyway, the others would wake up soon and the mission would begin in earnest, and she intended to be ahead of the curve in fitness, and in knowledge of the quirks of the Starship. If she could make herself indispensable, perhaps she could fit in better. Her reputation as Ms Fixit might help. Even Scotty had been impressed by her abilities in refurbishing and repurposing waste materials on the training course. *Will I be able to use a soldering iron on Mars?* A frisson of excitement coursed through her at the thought of all the challenges she faced. She turned up the speed on the treadmill.

Chapter 14

H arlan Grimes turned up in person at Noah van Horn's office, breaking their long-standing agreement for him to stay away. He wore an old-fashioned three-piece suit in a shiny blue material which had not aged well and a battered baseball cap. His hooded eyes shone with malice as he stared at Grace, devouring her from head to food.

'Even better in person,' he said. 'Do you have a boyfriend?'

Grace knew better than to answer. She turned her back on Grimes and pressed the intercom button.

'It's Mr Grimes,' she said. 'He doesn't have an appointment. Can you see him now?'

The sigh told her all she needed to know about Van Horn's enthusiasm.

'Show him in. And bring us some coffee please,' he said.

She stayed behind her desk, reluctant to open the door in case Grimes touched her on his way into Van Horn's office. Instead, Grimes put his scrawny fists down on her desk and leaned right over it, breathing in her face.

'I'm a patient man,' he said. 'I'll get me some one of these days.'

He leered down her blouse, and then straightened up again, pulling his trousers up and tightening the belt. Grace managed not to grimace, turning away again like she hadn't heard. *Neanderthal. As if I'd ever have anything to do with him.* She heard the men exchanging greetings and realised she had left the intercom on. *Had Van Horn heard Grimes's threat?* Her finger hovered over the button but the temptation to listen overcame her better judgement.

The sound of a chair being pulled up was followed by Van Horn clearing his throat.

'What the hell are you doing here?' he said.

Grace wandered over to the coffee machine and pressed the buttons to get the correct strengths and sweetness. The whirring of the machine as it ground the beans prevented her hearing the answer, and she cut it off as soon as she could.

'It had better be important,' said Van Horn. 'My patience with you is wearing thinner all the time.'

'I can leave if you like.'

'No, just get on with it.'

Grace put the cups on a tray with some biscuits and carried them through the door. She steered a wide berth around Grimes's chair and balanced the tray on Van Horn's desk. The two men watched her but did not help, willing her to leave again. Grace placed the coffees beside the men and turned to leave.

'Shut the door,' said Van Horn.

The intercom flashed at Grace as she sat back at her desk but she did not touch the button. Instead, she placed her clutch bag over the light so she could claim not to have seen it and pretended to clean the kitchenette.

'You've got two minutes,' said Van Horn.

'My source tells me another astronaut has met their maker,' said Grimes. 'Suffocated in the science officer's sleep pod.'

Grace gasped and dropped a spoon.

'Shut up. The intercom is open,' said Van Horn. 'Grace, turn it off.'

She stumbled over to her desk.

'Yes, Mr Van Horn, I'm sorry. I was washing the cups and I didn't realise.'

'No harm done, Gracie. Just turn it off.'

Grace reached out and pressed the button. She sank down into her chair, her heart thundering in her chest. *Hattie. It can't be. How does Grimes know anyway?* She scrolled through the news outlets with increasing desperation but found no mention of any tragedies aboard the Starship. *But why would Grimes lie?* Forced to wait until he left, she tried not to hyperventilate with shock.

Finally, just as she felt she could bear it no longer, the door opened and Grimes came out. He narrowed his eyes at her.

'You shouldn't listen to other people's conversations,' he said. 'You're looking a bit peaky. I'd soon put some colour in your cheeks.'

'I didn't listen. I forgot to turn off the intercom.'

'Sure.'

He winked and strode away with a backward wave of his hand. Van Horn appeared at Grace's desk, his brow furrowed, and scrutinised her closely.

'What do you think?' he said.

'About what?' said Grace, keeping her voice light and steady.

Van Horn frowned.

'You must remember to shut off the intercom. You might hear something you shouldn't, and that Grimes character is not to be trifled with.'

'I was washing the cups in the kitchenette and I didn't hear anything. Anyway, I'm not interested in what he has to say. He gives me the creeps.'

Van Horn's face relaxed.

'Me too,' he said. 'He's got a cheek turning up unannounced.'

'Do you need anything else today,' said Grace.

'No, I don't think so. Why don't you scoot off home and I'll see you tomorrow?'

Grace nodded. As soon as Van Horn had re-entered his office, she hailed a cab on her all-in-one. Then she grabbed her coat and handbag and took the elevator downstairs to the lobby. Seconds later the cab stopped outside and she got in, keying in her parents' address. She resisted the temptation to call them and instead, continued to trawl through the news sites for news of the Starship, in mounting distress. She discovered an article by Chuck Gomez about the imminent reawakening of the astronauts. Despite her dislike of the man, she found herself reassured by his chatty style laced with real science. *The astronauts aren't awake yet so how could Grimes know one of them is dead? It doesn't make sense.*

By the time she got to her parents' house, some of the panic had ebbed away. Apart from her visit on the night of the launch, she hadn't been in contact with them for years. Their brief union to watch Hattie set off for Mars had reawakened feelings she had hidden, and her need for reassurance in the bosom of her family became stronger every day. She longed to tell Van Horn the truth about them. *But how could she continue her work at the CNP if they found out who she was?*

She got out of the taxi and walked into the garage, pushing her way into the kitchen through the side door of the house. Yasmina had her back to Grace and her bottom swayed to the mamba playing on the music system. Grace tiptoed across the floor and tapped her on the shoulder. Yasmina spun around in fright, Her surprise turned to joy as she saw Grace. A long squeal of joy erupted from her throat.

'Meeeeeeez Grace, you are home.'

She put down the iron and enveloped Grace in a hug that smelled of laundry and lavender. Her cheeks were damp.

'Where's Mum?' she said.

'Your parents are on the porch, having a cup of mint tea. Shall I tell them you are here?'

'No need,' said Edgar Fredericks, appearing at the door. 'We heard your squeal out there. I thought a favourite character had been murdered on your telenovela.'

Yasmina giggled.

'No, they are all alive, thanks be to God. Shall I bring you a mint tea too?'

'Yes, please,' said Grace.

She hardly dared to look her father in the eye, but he didn't stand on ceremony either. He held out his arms, biting his lip, as his eyes swam in unshed tears.

'Come here, Gracey. Your mother will be so thrilled to see you.'

When Grace walked out onto the porch, Juana stood up with her hand to her mouth to stifle a gasp. She tottered forward on her Cuban heels and embraced her. Grace relaxed in the warmth glow of her mother's love but then she stiffened. *What if Grimes knew something they didn't?*

Juana held her at arm's length.

'What on Earth's wrong, darling? Has something happened to you?'

'Sit down, Mum. I heard some disturbing news today and I'm terrified it might be true. I thought Dad should know.'

Juana and Edgar sat back on the swinging chair and she sat opposite, wringing her hands.

'Spit it out,' said her father.

'I overheard my boss talking to a man today, about the Mars Mission. I didn't mean to; Mr Van Horn left the intercom on.'

'What did he say?' said Juana.

'He told my boss that a second astronaut has died on the Starship. Is it true? Only he said they were in the science officer's pod and Hattie—'

She broke off as a huge sob burst from her throat and she scrabbled in her handbag for a tissue. Her parents glanced at each other, and Edgar reached out to hold her hand and shook his head.

'It's not Hattie,' he said. 'It's Wayne Odoyu. But this is top secret information. NASA decided not to release it because they haven't told his parents yet. How on Earth did this fellow know?'

'There must be a leak,' said Juana.

'Hattie's safe?' said Grace, sniffing. 'Are you sure?'

'Yes, positive. She sent me a message to tell me and she signed it Mad Hatter so I'm pretty sure it's her.'

Grace relaxed. Their writing code had not been a secret from their parents. As children, they had always used two names to sign their notes to each other. For Hattie, Mad Hatter meant the contents were true, and Harriet meant they were false. Grace had used Graceful for true notes and Gracefool for made up stories.

'Thank goodness. For a minute I thought. Well, you know...' said Grace. 'But why are they keeping it a secret? Surely, they should release the news as soon as possible or people will think there is something wrong. What happened anyway?'

'One of the hibernation pods malfunctioned, and Wayne suffocated in his sleep. He won't have known anything about it. We are doing extensive investigations to check what could have happened but, so far, it seems it's just an unexpected accident. The pod just turned itself off.'

'But the other pods are still functioning? So how come Hattie sent you a message? Isn't she still asleep?'

'We woke Chen Yu up to deal with the situation, and he revived Hattie to help him,' said Edgar.

'But when will you tell his parents?' said Juana.

'We were going to wait until they got to Mars, and invent an accident so Wayne could be a hero, but if this man knows about his death, the news could get out before we are ready. What is the man's name, Grace?'

'Grimes, Harlan Grimes.'

Edgar sighed and stood up.

'I've never heard of him. He doesn't work at NASA. Perhaps he has a source. Anyway, I'll worry about him later. I'd better go back to work and tell them about this. We'll have to inform Wayne's parents and write a press release. The pressure on us to cancel the mission will only increase.'

'Shouldn't you consider it?' said Juana. 'Two people have died, and our little girl is on board.'

'There's no proof that either of these deaths could have been avoided. Serena died of a heart attack unrelated to the voyage. The pods were checked over and over, and no one could have anticipated one of them switching itself off. It won't happen again. We'll change the software when they wake up.' He scratched his head. 'And space is dangerous. We knew that. Hattie knew it too. She wanted to go. Unless I have proof of serious issues with the Starship, the mission will continue.'

Juana sighed.

'I wish Hattie had stayed on Earth. I can't help feeling something terrible will happen out there,' she said. 'Can't you recall them?'

'It's too late now. They wouldn't have enough propellant to get home. They have to get to the surface of Mars to refuel.'

'It's in the lap of the Gods then. I'll tell Yasmina to cook only for us two. You are staying aren't you, darling?'

'Of course,' said Grace.

Chapter 15

C huck's all-in-one started to vibrate and hop across the counter, emitting an annoying beeping sound. He sighed and stretched out to grab it, knocking over his coffee, throwing the contents onto the carpet. He muttered an obscenity and rolled his eyes. *Who could it be at this hour?* He peered at the screen. *Saul Taggart? They hadn't spoken in years. Not since a drunk Chuck had kissed Saul's wife, Helena, at a NASA party. What did he want?* Chuck tapped the screen and balanced the unit on the counter while he mopped up the coffee.

'Chuck, is that you? I can't see your face.'

'Yup, just dealing with a spillage. Give me a minute.'

'Thank goodness. I didn't know who else to call.'

'I'm surprised you chose me; I have to admit.'

'Water under the bridge. She left me you know. Ran off with her personal trainer. I should have known her sudden interest in exercise didn't add up.'

'Sorry to hear that. I presume you haven't called to talk about your marital problems.'

Saul sniffed.

'She's back now. It didn't work out.'

'Now there's a surprise. What can I do you for?'

'Can you meet me for a drink? I've had some terrible news, but it's not something I can talk about online. It's confidential.'

Chuck had been about to refuse but now his fingers were itching again. A sure sign of a scoop. *Confidential? Maybe. Newsworthy? Possibly. Saul worked as an engineer on the Mars mission. Could he have inside information on the Starship's progress?*

'Sure. What about The Foxhole on the corner of 14th Ct and Alton? We can sit in a quiet corner undisturbed.'

'I'm on my way.'

Chuck loved The Foxhole. The upstairs section allowed you to spy on the downstairs bar without being observed, and the snug couches gave you privacy if you wanted it. The barman upstairs recognised him and gave him a thumbs up. Chuck bought a low alcohol beer, unusual for him, but a precaution, in case he missed something vital from Saul's story. He took out his pencil and doodled in his notebook. *Could this have something to do with Serena Hampton?* He could hardly contain his impatience.

Saul appeared at his side, sweating with exertion. Chuck stuck out his hand and grasped the damp paw offered to him.

'Do you want a drink?' he said.

'Just some iced water for now please,' said Saul.

The barman gave another thumbs-up, and served Saul, who gulped down half of the glass, slopping water down his chin. He grabbed a napkin from the bar and wiped it dry.

'Do you want a refill?' said the barman.

'No, thanks. What are you having?' he asked Chuck.

'A low alcohol beer,' said Chuck.

'One of those, said Saul. 'And let's sit down over there where no-one can eavesdrop.'

Before they were seated with their beers, Saul made a show of looking back down the stairs and checking the other booths. He sweated profusely, and a large damp patch appeared on his back. Chuck had never seen Saul in such a state. This was no trivial matter. He reached into his jacket and took out his all-in-one which he slid onto the table. He tapped the record button, covering the unit with a napkin.

'You didn't tell anyone you were meeting me?' said Saul, sliding onto the couch.

'No, of course not. I've never seen you so jumpy. What's bugging you?'

Saul wiped his brow and lowered his voice.

'I've worked at NASA my entire career, and I've always strained every sinew to ensure I did my best work. I may not be much of a politician but no one has ever had any complaints on the technical side.'

Chuck nodded.

'Anyway, for the past few years, I've been working on the hibernation pods for the Mars mission. We've tested them until we're blue in the face. They have fallback after fallback. They are, to all intents and purposes, infallible.'

'I heard about them. They're an amazing innovation.'

Saul allowed himself a smile.

'They are astonishing technology. They allow the astronauts to sleep through nearly the whole voyage to Mars without the loss of bone or muscle density expected from microgravity. You also avoid the psychological effects of being shut up in a relatively small space with the same people for seven months.'

'It's amazing. Who'd have thought it? So, what's the problem?'

Saul dropped his head into his hands and sighed.

'Oh God, Chuck. What am I going to do?'

'About what?'

'Someone died. One of the astronauts. In their pod.'

Chuck's eyes opened wide.

'Another astronaut dead? They haven't even got to Mars yet. At this rate, none of them will make it home. How did it happen?'

'That's just it. I have no idea. They tell me the pod deactivated and suffocated the astronaut inside, but that's theoretically impossible.'

'What do you mean by impossible?'

'One of the fail-safes for the pod is that any loss or change of pressure inside the sealed pod will cause it to open. It shouldn't have stayed shut. Someone has tampered with it. Or that's what I tried to tell them at NASA. But they won't listen to me. The section head is trying to blame me for the accident. I'm ruined. When people find out, I'll lose my job, my career, everything.'

Chuck took a sip of his beer and scribbled in his notebook. Saul grabbed his arm.

'You can't use this,' he said. 'It's top secret. Off the record.'

'Who died?' said Chuck, ignoring him.

'I don't know, but they told me the pod number.'

'And?'

'It belonged to the science officer.'

Chuck slapped his forehead.

'Holy shit. I can't believe it.'

'Neither can I. I'm fifty-five. I'll never work again after this debacle.'

Chuck looked at Saul expecting to see a wry smile, but self-pity leaked out of his every pore.

'That's a tough break, buddy,' he said. 'Do you have any proof of this failure?'

Saul avoided his inquiring glance.

'I'm not supposed to have any personal copies of the data. But...'

'But what?'

'I've printed all the logs and taken them home. I'm not sure anyone else understands them, and only I can tell if something odd has happened.'

'And have you found anything?'

'No, but I haven't reviewed them all yet. Please keep this to yourself. I had to tell someone, but I shouldn't have told you. It's off the record, all of it.'

Chuck patted him on the shoulder.

'You can trust me. But I need you to tell me if you discover anything strange. Can you do that?'

'Okay. I'll call you once I've reviewed the data.'

'Good, now I've got to go. Another stop before I sleep tonight.'

'But—'

'Sorry, buddy. I can't let the lady down. I'm already late. Let's have a proper drink next time. And don't worry, I'm here for you.'

Chuck tried not to sprint out of The Foxhole. His heart raced, making him feel sick as he reached his vehicle. Once inside, he took out his all-in-one and send the recording of their conversation to his encrypted cloud service. Then he looked up Grace Dos Reis address and keyed it into the computer. The vehicle lurched out into the traffic and he played back his recording of Saul. He shook his head at some parts. *How can a man be so unaware? People are dying and he's worried about his job?*

The car drew up to the pavement outside Grace's house. He could not see any light through the shutters but he tried the doorbell anyway. He could almost feel Grace's eyes upon him through the camera as he wavered on the steps.

'Grace, it's Chuck Gomez. We met at the launch. I've got to speak to you.'

'I know who you are,' she said. 'Go away. I'm not at home.'

'It's vital I talk to you right away.'

'You can't. I'm at my parents' house. And don't you dare turn up here either.'

'Grace, please, this is a matter of life or death.'

'What's the problem?'

'I have to tell you in person.'

'Oh, do you? What a surprise.'

'I'm serious. I found out something today that directly affects you and your family.'

'And you think I don't know about it?'

Chuck paused.

'You've heard about the pods?'

'Yes, it's terrible but it doesn't affect us.'

'It doesn't?'

'No, and I'd be grateful if you'd stop trying to get a story out of me. You're so transparent. Now, go away, and don't come back.'

'But who told you about—'

'Leave. Or I'll call the police. Right now. One, two, three.'

He walked back to the car. *How did she know about the pods? Presumably Edgar Fredericks had told her. But weren't they estranged?* He shook his head. *What can I prove? Nothing yet. I'll have to wait until Saul gets back to me. Then maybe Grace will listen. Meanwhile, perhaps Gina would like that burger.*

Chapter 16

The time had come to reanimate the rest of the crew. Hattie had enjoyed her time with Yu and dreaded the inevitable fall out from Wayne's death.

'Can't we just leave them asleep for another couple of weeks?' she said.

'We have to follow protocol, and we don't know how long they can survive in a coma. There is no choice,' said Yu.

'Let the carnage commence,' said Hattie. 'But start with Ellie and Scotty. We need allies.'

'I think Mo will be okay too.'

'Can't we just leave Chad and Bret asleep?'

Yu giggled.

'You're terrible. Let's do Mo first. We won't tell them about Wayne until they notice.'

He tapped the screen on Mo's pod and the lid opened with a hissing sound as the pressure released. Then he moved on to Scotty and Ellie's pods. Soon they sat up looking disoriented and groggy.

'Welcome back,' said Hattie.

'What's that horrible taste in my mouth?' said Mo. 'Yuck. I feel appalling.'

'Are we nearly there yet?' said Scotty, with a feeble smile.

'I can't feel my legs,' said Ellie. 'Or is it my arms?'

Yu gave the crew a few minutes to acclimatise, and then he checked their vital signs for any irregularities. Satisfied they had all emerged unscathed from their pods, he opened Chad and Bret's pods next. The two men sat up and looked around, their movements in uncanny harmony. Hattie shook her head in wonder. *They look like perfect robots emerging from moulds.*

'Good morning, Commander Grayling,' said Yu. 'I trust you slept well.'

'Not bad, Doctor Chen. I've got a bit of a hangover now though. How do you feel Chad?'

'I've got a foul taste in my mouth but otherwise not too awful.'

Everyone climbed out of their pods and Scotty floated towards the control panel in the wall.

'Attention all crew members. I'm going to initiate the epsilon gravity drive now,' he said. 'Enough to keep the tea in our cups and to convince us that we've lost weight. Gravity will shortly be resumed. Please don't float upside down or you will land on your head.'

The system whirred into action, and Hattie felt her limbs sinking until she stood on the floor of the cabin. She took a few tentative steps and found she could walk without help. Yu also looked steady on his feet. The others struggled to stay upright. Their knees and ankles wobbled, and they looked like puppets on strings. Hattie smirked. *Thank goodness for my exercise routine.*

'Maybe put it on half power for now,' said Yu. 'Until we have gained back some strength.'

Scotty who had sat down on a stool, pointed at the panel.

'Hattie, can you lower the gravity to fifty percent please? I can't stand yet.'

Hattie went over to the panel and slid the indicator downwards.

'Is that better?' she said.

'How come you can stand up?' said Chad, pointing at her. 'I thought women had less muscle than men.'

He looked around, confusion on his face.

'Where's Wayne? Aren't you going to wake him up too?'

'I'm afraid that won't be possible,' said Yu.

'What do you mean?' said Chad.

'He passed away.'

'What? When? Why didn't you tell me?' said Bret.

'About ten days ago, NASA woke me up to tell me there had been a malfunction in Wayne's pod, but by the time I got there, he had suffocated.'

'This one?' said Chad. 'But why haven't you sealed it or something?'

'Not that one. Wayne slept in the science officer pod, and Hattie slept in Wayne's pod.'

'I don't like the sound of that,' said Bret. 'What on Earth's going on?'

'There's no conspiracy,' said Yu. 'Hattie asked to be moved and Wayne offered to swap. Isn't that right, Hattie?'

'Yes, I...' said Hattie.

I was afraid of ghosts? I can't say that.

'So, you should be dead instead?' said Chad.

'Well, I would be, yes, if I hadn't swapped, but it wasn't my idea. Wayne offered.'

'What does Earth say?' said Bret.

'They say it is an unfortunate and totally unexpected malfunction, and they are looking into it.'

'That's some coincidence,' said Chad.

That's what I thought.

'You were the last man to see him alive then?' said Bret.

'Yes, I was,' said Yu.

'How dreadful,' said Ellie, who had gone pale. 'To lose another crew member so soon.'

'It's tragic,' said Scotty. 'And unexpected. What could have occurred?'

'I'll check the systems,' said Mo. 'I should be able to figure out what happened and make sure the error doesn't reoccur on the way home.'

98

'If it was an error,' said Chad. 'It feels more like sabotage to me. I've never been comfortable with this international crew idea. You don't know who to trust. What if someone interfered with Wayne's pod?'

'And what does that mean?' said Yu. 'We wouldn't be here at all without African or Chinese input. The pods are not an American invention.'

'And look where that got us,' said Chad.

'Six months into the voyage without using any precious supplies?' said Mo.

He stared at Chad who did not flinch. Bret put a hand on Chad's shoulder.

'Steady on there. We only just woke up. Our brains will be scrambled. These deaths have shaken us. It's only natural to be unsettled, but we were chosen for our abilities, not our nationalities. Where we are from is irrelevant. It's where we are that counts.'

He puffed out his chest.

'Everyone needs to calm down and get on with their allotted tasks. I suggest that those of us who just woke up take it easy for a few days and concentrate on gym work to build up their muscles again. Meanwhile, we need to review all the data and make decisions based on the facts. Where is Wayne's body?'

'We stored it in the freezer for autopsy when we get home,' said Hattie.

'If we get home,' said Chad. 'This is like that Agatha Christie movie.'

Scotty laughed.

'Come off it. This is the first voyage of this length and whether you like it or not, huge risks exist. There is no guarantee that anyone will make it home. Why do you think none of us has families? It's damage limitation,' he said.

'We may not be married, but we all have families,' said Ellie.

'Okay, that's enough. Chad, I suggest you have a session with AI to calibrate your reactions to this tragedy. We need to start work right away. We can't be distracted by conspiracy theories,' said Bret.

Chad pouted.

'Okay, Commander,' he said.

'Scotty, can you come to the command deck with me and review the systems, please? Meanwhile, Hattie, I presume you have got a head start with our experiments. Please can you show Ellie where you are with them?'

Hattie nodded and smiled at Ellie who looked as if she might faint. Bret continued.

'Mo, I need you to review the data from the pods. Report exclusively to me please. I don't need any rumours making the rounds.'

Hattie caught his eye and flashed him a look of appreciation. Scotty had been right about Bret. He might be a pain with his overt waving of the flag, but he had a calm head, the right man to be in charge. Bret looked away without acknowledging her. She rolled her eyes. So much for being neutral.

***

Bret and Scotty sat on the command deck, flipping through the screens and reviewing the systems from the cargo decks through the radiation shelter and into the crew decks. Bret signed and snorted as if he had something to say. Scotty spun his chair to face him.

'Okay, spit it out,' he said.

'Look, I know you're fond of her, but I can't help wondering.'

'About Hattie? Seriously?'

'Well, think about it. Who profited from Serena Hampton's death? Who should have been in the Science Officer's pod? There's only one person involved with both incidents.'

'But what possible motive could she have? It makes zero sense to me. Anyway, Yu would have had to be complicit and I can't imagine what they have in common.'

'I agree. So far. Listen, Scotty. I wouldn't be doing my job if I didn't at least check for motive. You like Hattie and I'm pretty sure she trusts you. Can you keep an eye on her for me? Just in case.'

'I guess so. I don't like spying on her though.'

'I didn't ask you to spy on her. Just report anything odd to me. Please?'

'Sure. It can't do any harm. Personally, I think Mo will uncover a glitch in the software and it will all blow over.'

'We all be relieved and move on. But until then...'

Chapter 17

Despite the loss of Wayne, and the lingering suspicions among the crew over his death, life aboard the Starship soon adjusted to the planned twenty-four-hour day. Hattie and Ellie took on most of Wayne's practical experiments, and Mo agreed to deal with the data end of things. Hattie's scientific background mirrored Ellie's in many ways and she found her easy to work with. They liked the same music too, so the laboratory soon hummed with jazz and blues favourites.

'Now that's my kind of music,' said Yu, appearing at Hattie's side. 'I wondered if you girls needed any help. I have a grounding in Chemistry from my early years in university, so I could pitch in and help with testing the geochemical sensors if we get instructions from Earth.'

'That would be amazing,' said Ellie. 'We're snowed under here with the extra work from Wayne's tasks.'

'If you're sure you're not too busy,' said Hattie.

'Oh, now that the Epsilon gravity system is working at full tilt, I don't have that much to do. Most of the health monitoring is automatic, and the AI keeps an eye on everyone's mental health. My hard work will commence once we start using the spacesuits. I'll be up to my eyeballs in your medical data and keeping you all healthy will be a full-time job.'

'Cool,' said Hattie. 'Why don't I show you how to slice a rock sample ready to examine for the presence of stromatolites?'

'Why does he need to learn that? I can do it already,' said Ellie.

'We don't know how the tasks will be redistributed now Wayne is dead. It might prove useful,' said Hattie.

'I suppose so.'

'Great,' said Yu. 'Let's get started.'

Meanwhile on the exercise and recreation deck, Bret and Chad tried to outdo each other in physical prowess. For the first few days, they had been weak as kittens and Hattie had delighted in besting them with as much nonchalance as she could muster.

'That woman is getting on my nerves,' said Bret.

'She's just getting her own back,' said Scotty. 'Soon you'll catch up and overtake her again. Why not let her have some fun? You never stopped riding her on Earth.'

'I guess revenge is sweet,' said Bret. 'It's true I was hard on her, but I tested everyone to make sure they could take the pressure. Wayne's death may not be the only one on this mission. Five hundred days is a long time to survive in such harsh conditions with zero experience. We will need to fight for each other on the surface, and it may get rough down there.

'Do you still think she might be involved in Wayne's death?'

'Not really. Once I got over the shock of losing a crew member, I realised how unlikely it seemed. But the failure of the pod is still a complete mystery. Earth has not provided us with the data we need to analyse the fault. They told me that some sort of blackout had erased it. They may be able to access the back up in time but it's not a priority for them with so much else going on. Have we picked a signal from the Mars base yet? We should soon be able to communicate with the vessels which have already landed on the planet.'

'No, not yet, but Earth tells me they are resetting the communications system after that solar flare we had last week.'

'At least we know the radiation shelter works well.'

'It's a bit cosy for seven of us but at least we didn't have to stay in there too long.'

'It worked well as a drill. We should try and rehearse for a series of scenarios soon, so we're not caught on the hop.'

'I'll let you know as soon as communications are restored. We can get a pinpoint GPS fix on the landing area the robots have constructed for us. We should pick up the signalling beacon soon. I'm hoping we can programme the coordinates into the console in the next day or two.'

'I can hardly believe it's really happening. I've spent so many years dreaming of this,' said Bret. 'To boldly go and all that.'

'Me too. It's a bit surreal. All the systems are set up and ready to go. First, we have to land the module on the surface. Once that's achieved, we can concentrate on getting the Starship to base.'

Scotty scratched the stubble on his chin and glanced at Bret who had a faraway look in his eyes.

'I bet you can't wait to be the first? On Mars, I mean.'

'Someone has to try out the spacesuits,' said Bret, grinning. 'I could also be the first to die on the planet if they don't work.'

'I hadn't thought of that.'

'I have. A lot. Chad will film the event. We're going to plant the Stars and Stripes before anyone else on board gets a chance of beating us to it.'

Scotty's eyes widened.

'Hey, wait just a minute. Aren't you supposed to claim the planet for humanity and use the flag of the United Nations? I thought that was the whole point of the mission.'

'You thought wrong,' said Bret. 'I have instructions to claim the planet for the USA. All those massive mineral deposits will be ours.'

'There'll be an almighty ruckus back on Earth.'

'Are you so naïve? The USA paid for the Starships and all the training and equipment for a reason. As usual, the international community was quite happy to let us pay more than our fair share. They screwed us for years in the United Nations and NATO. Now we get to take what we paid for. Who's going to stop us?'

'The Martians might have something to say about this. Maybe they don't want to be a colony of America.'

Bret laughed.

'Hattie says the only Martians are single celled algae. I think my ex-wife used to drink smoothies made out of them. I don't imagine they'll put up much of a fight.'

Scotty frowned.

'Haven't you seen the Blob? Those slimes can be vicious.'

'I'll take my chances. Anyway, I don't have a choice. Some of the world's richest corporations paid for this mission for a reason, and it wasn't to get their names in the news. They want payback, and for payback they need ownership. The Entente Cordiale is toast the minute I land on Mars.'

'Do the others know?'

'No, and I trust you not to tell them. I'm in command here. It won't be a long discussion if it comes up. As a patriot your duty lies with our country and nothing else. That's why only Chad and I will go to surface. I will blame it on the death of Wayne, and the shrinking crew numbers. I'm going to leave you with the com.'

Despite his faith in Bret as commander of the mission, Scotty had serious misgivings about the plan to claim the planet for the USA. He had no interest in politics but the enormity of this decision went against his principles. The apparent coincidence the two astronaut's deaths had spooked him. While he understood the risks of coming to Mars, he had not expected casualties before they even landed on the planet. His logical mind twisted on itself as he tried to make sense of it all. He returned to the command deck and resumed his calculations for the main Starship landing at the Deuteronilus Mensae on the platform constructed by the robots which had landed with the unmanned Starships.

The platform had a similar structure to the one they had taken off from on Earth, but its height had been reduced for accommodating the two stage Starship without the first stage. It had a simple mechanical hoisting mechanism running up the tower and a pair of arms on a swivel, to lift the living quarters section off the top of the Starship and deposit it on the low loader after it had been detached from the cargo bay and lower fuel tanks. Robots would tow the living quarters to the partially constructed hub and connect it to one of the airlocks on the Mars hub, which should by then consist of a central hub with an airlock to the outside, connected by passageways to the Marsha habitation modules and the laboratories formed by the top sections of the landed Starships, except the one they would travel back in.

Mars had started to loom into view, and in a short time they would enter into orbit around the planet. To save fuel, the Starship would enter a highly elliptical orbit around the planet and slowly lower the apogee by making passes through the upper Mars atmosphere and dropping down to a lower Mars orbit over time. Bret and Chad would take the Mars module down to surface first and plant the flag. They would establish themselves in the Mars hub. If that went well, Scotty, Hattie, Mo, Yu and Ellie would land the main body of the Starship on the surface and join Bret and Chad. A lot of things had to go right to even start this mission. Scotty mentally crossed his fingers for a safe landing.

Finally, he shrugged and returned to his calculations. The Starship landing on the surface of Mars would expend most of the remaining fuel for the Raptor engines, meaning that the Sabatier and electrolyser plants would be key to producing the propellant needed to return to Earth. They would have five hundred days to accumulate the methane and oxygen needed, plenty of time if the plants ran correctly, but any major glitches might narrow the window for take-off. He chewed his pen. This would be a major challenge. He let his mind wander as he considered their options.

Four of the original five Starships had made a safe landing on the planet but one had gone AWOL. Since it carried one of the three Moxie plants, this reduced the margins for error on their mission, but it did not qualify as a fatal blow. The missing Starship might have landed safely but be suffering from a glitch in the communications software. They would only discover the truth on landing. If it had gone astray or crashed, and they could locate the Starship, or its wreckage, it could serve as a source of spare parts and provisions in case of a longer stay. Since all of the equipment had been manufactured with maximum reusability in mind, many of the spare parts were standard sizes and could be swapped between modules

Since Mars had one third the gravity of Earth, many tasks involving weighty equipment would be less onerous, but initial testing on the moon had not proved to be a useful dry run for many items. The rovers and mobile equipment had been stress tested at Earth's gravity after an initial focus on lunar testing to ensure they could put up with the rigours of Mars surface travel. Old style lunar spacesuits had been replaced. The massive suits used on the moon and in past space exploration took several hours to put on and take off. As well as being far too heavy for use on Mars, they were uncomfortable, and caused injuries due to their inflexible nature and bad pressurisation. Also, they could not easily be cleaned inside and became filthy and disgusting after a couple of uses.

Scotty remembered the first time he tried on the new generation space suits. They had morphed from a personal spacecraft into a wearable garment. They resembled diving suits, fitted using laser scanning, and printable using the onboard machine when they needed replacing. The genius in their design came from the pressurisation based on the technology used to measure blood pressure. The first time he put on his suit and it tightened around him, Scotty felt as if a boa constrictor had him in its coils and was attempting to squeeze the life from him, but he soon got used to it. The lack of atmosphere on Mars would make the suits a lot more comfortable, and the liquid oxygen tanks, which were made from Twaron fibre, also lessened the load to be carried.

Once he had satisfied himself that all the fail-safes were in place, Scotty went to find Mo who had suffered more than most with his re-acclimatisation to gravity. He could be found most days lying on a couch in the recreation area, muttering as he reviewed the infinite data streams generated by the mission. As a certified jock, Mo had taken his fragility hard. He kept trying to prove how macho he was to the derision of the others.

Mo may not have been good at acclimatising but he had an IQ that flew off the charts. Maybe he finally had an answer to the riddle of the hibernation pod. Despite everyone's attempts to move on, an atmosphere of doubt and mistrust had permeated the relationships aboard the Starship, and it would be nice to have a solution to put minds at rest.

Chapter 18

C huck waited on the side of the road for the robot recovery service to recharge his car's battery. His foul mood did not improve when he heard his all-in-one chirping inside the car. *What now? I'm not late for the meeting yet, but his boss liked to pile on the pressure. Maybe he'd give me an advance to work on the scoop about the astronauts. The story about the second death has not yet broken, and I'm in prime position to publish it first.* Sighing, he reached inside and removed the phone. *Saul Taggart? Fantastic. Maybe he has a scoop for me.* He swiped the screen and stuck the phone to his ear.

'Hello, Saul?'

A loud sob echoed in his ear. He took the all-in one down from his head and focused on the video screen. *Helena Taggart. Still beautiful despite the Botox and whatever she had done to her lips.*

'Helena, it's me, Chuck. Are you okay?'

'It's Saul. The police found him.'

'What do you mean, found him?'

'In the dock. He's dead, Chuck.'

'That's terrible. Did he drown?'

'Someone shot him. Oh God, what am I going to do?'

'Are you at home?'

'Where else would I be?'

With your personal trainer, perhaps?

'Stay there and don't move. I'll be over as soon as I can.'

Chuck put his all-in-one in his pocket but removed it again as it vibrated immediately. A text message flashed up on the screen. *Another hour to wait for the mechanic? They must be joking.* He tapped on Gina's number. Her sulky face appeared on screen, surrounded by a halo of unbrushed hair.

'Yes?' she said.

'Hello doll, you look fabulous today. Can you do me a favour?'

Twenty minutes later, a grumpy Gina pulled up beside his car.

'Why don't you get rid of that old thing?' she said, patting his car.

'How could I do that? It's got sentimental value. Remember the time you and I—'

'Stop right there. Don't you dare remind me of my misspent youth. What's the hurry anyway. Won't the bots be here soon?'

'I've a feeling they'll tow it away for good, and I need to get somewhere fast. Can you give me a lift?'

'Sure. I'm here now, aren't I?'

Fifteen minutes later, they pulled up in front of Saul and Helena Taggart's house, a colonial style bungalow set at the end of a road lined with similar houses fronted with palm trees and elephant grass. Gina's eye's opened wide when she saw the name on the mailbox leaning drunkenly at the side of the pathway leading to the front door.

'Saul Taggart? But didn't you guys have a fight?'

'He's been found dead, and I think it's got something to do with Serena Hampton. I'm going to speak to his widow. Do you want to come?'

Gina frowned.

'I don't know why you're getting mixed up with this. If the two deaths are linked, you may be in danger.'

'You didn't really expect me to ignore a story like this, did you?'

Gina sighed.

'I guess not. You go in by yourself. I didn't know him and, anyway, don't you two have a past?'

'Not really. I kissed her once when I got drunk.'

Gina rolled her eyes.

'All the more reason. Can you get a cab back? I've got to return to work.'

'Do you want to get together later? I think I'm on to something big.'

'Didn't I tell you to stay away from this story? The reaction I got when I tried to see Serena's autopsy frightened me. I've got a really bad feeling about this.'

Chuck shrugged.

'It's my job. You saw the state of my car. I can't even afford a new battery. A massive story like this one could get me back on track. I can't pretend it's not happening.'

'What if someone comes after you?'

'What if I break the biggest story since the re-election of Donald Trump? Please help me with this.'

Gina pursed her lips.

'I've got to go now. But you can call me later if you want.'

She took off before Chuck could reply. He waited until her car was out of sight and then opened the mailbox. Finding nothing, he followed the path to the front door where he straightened his hair and assumed what he hoped Helena would construe as the expression of a man in mourning for a friend. The doorbell rang out in the hall which echoed with the sound of high heels clattering on a parquet floor. Helena Taggart opened the door, the tracks of her tears marked with mascara which had run down her cheeks. Her eyes lit up when she recognised her visitor.

'You're here,' she said. 'I knew you'd come.'

She leaned into him and gave him a hug, her breasts loose in the short nightdress under her lacey nightgown.

111

She smelled of sweat and a strong perfume which made him sneeze and pull away, fumbling in his jacket for a handkerchief. *I thought those were illegal* He blew his nose loudly.

'I can't believe the news about Saul,' said Chuck, sniffing. 'It's all so sudden.'

Helena held the door open for him and ushered him into the lounge. She sat on an enormous squashy couch and patted the cushion beside her. Chuck ignored her and sat on a beanbag next to the couch, almost falling backwards as it shifted under his weight. If Helena was disappointed, she didn't show it. She wiped her eyes and sighed.

'Thank you for coming,' she said. 'I didn't know who else to call. It's not like Saul had many friends, and I know you two made up recently, despite our naughty dalliance.'

How does a drunken kiss qualify as a dalliance? Chuck raised his eyebrows in answer and searched for something to say. He looked around the room for inspiration, made nervous by her inquiring glance. The door to Saul's study hung open.

'May I?' he said, indicating it with his chin.

'Sure, he won't mind now he's gone.'

Grateful for the distraction, Chuck struggled to his feet, and wandered over to peer inside. The large wooden desk usually had a thick covering of books, papers and documents surrounding a rather old-fashioned laptop perched on a block of wood cut from a massive rail sleeper. The wireless keyboard and mouse still sat on the almost empty desk, but a gap in the thick dust told him something was missing. Saul's workstation had been removed.

Chuck could feel his heartrate increase as he surveyed the scene. He turned around to ask Helena about Saul's missing laptop, and found that she had draped herself along the couch in way that suggested she had been expecting him to comfort her. He suppressed an internal shudder. *Why did I ever kiss her? I must have been blind drunk.*

'Um, Saul had promised me the results of some research he had started on, a thing at work. Do you happen to know where his computer is?'

Chuck's rejection of her open invitation did not faze Helena in the slightest. She pulled her nightgown around her and slipped off the couch.

'His laptop? He told me he had some private work to do. I didn't realise it was with you.'

'It was confidential. I guess he died without finishing it. I would like a copy of whatever he managed to finish, though.'

'Oh, I'm sorry. They took it away.'

A chill ran up Chuck's spine.

'Who's they?' he said.

'NASA, I guess. They sent this skinny guy to collect all his work. I didn't recognise him, but he said he worked for Edgar Fredericks.'

'Edgar Fredericks? Okay, look, I'm really sorry but I've got to go. This research is really important and it shouldn't fall into the wrong hands.'

Chuck fumbled with his all-in-one and called a cab on the app. He stood awkwardly behind the settee as Helena raised an eyebrow at him.

'That's all right, Chuck. I don't think you understand how to comfort a grieving widow anyway.'

Helena winked at him, and he blushed.

Chuck paused at the front door.

'I'm sorry for your loss,' he said. 'Saul was a good guy.'

'He was a selfish shit. At least I've got insurance policies on him. That's the saving grace.'

No wonder they got married. They deserved each other.

The taxi Chuck had ordered arrived almost immediately and it took him to NASA headquarters. On the way, his all-in-one sounded and he glanced at the screen. *Whoops.* He tapped the screen and held it well away from his ear.

'Boss?'

'Where the hell are you?'

'Sorry, Earl, my car broke down again on my way to follow a lead. And now I'm in a cab on my way to another. I—'

'Again? That's the second time this month you've stood me up. Get rid of that pile of junk before I do it myself.'

'If this story comes together, we'll both be buying new cars. I've got to interview someone in about five minutes. Can we take a rain check?'

'This better be good. You'll be the death of me one of these days.'

'It's monumental. I promise to fill you in as soon as I can.'

'Today.'

'That could be tricky.'

'I don't care how tricky it is. I want you in my office this afternoon.'

'Okay, boss.'

The cab pulled up outside the administration department of NASA, a bland, stuccoed building with dark windows, and Chuck made his way to reception. He smiled at the receptionist and received a snarl in return.

'I need to speak to Edgar Fredericks,' he said.

'Do you have an appointment?'

She looked him up and down, and waited.

'Not as such, but he needs to see me.'

'Like a hole in the head, I imagine. He's busy today.'

'Can you please tell him my name is Chuck Gomez, from the press corps, and I know about Wayne Odoyu.'

The receptionist sighed and tapped her screen.

'Yes, Mr Fredericks, so sorry to disturb you. There's a man here from the press corp. He says he knows Wayne Odoyu.'

'I know about him, not I know him,' hissed Chuck.

114

He needn't have worried. The receptionist's eyebrows flew up and she turned to him again.

'Fifth floor. Last office on the right.'

Chuck took the lift up to the fifth floor and found Fredericks's office with no problem. The plain interior and cheap desk of the director took him by surprise. Fredericks looked up and examined Chuck from under his impressive eyebrows.

'I recognise you,' he said. 'Aren't you one of the correspondents for Space magazine?'

'Among other things,' said Chuck. 'I also do some crime reporting.'

'And is that how you found out about Wayne?'

'Not exactly. Saul Taggart was a friend of mine.'

Fredericks sighed.

'Saul. Ah. That explains it. What on Earth happened to him?'

'I have no idea. The police think he might have been mixed up in something.'

'Like what? He couldn't have been more of a goody-two-shoes. His job meant a massive amount to him. He wouldn't have risked losing it. What did Saul tell you about Wayne?' said Fredericks.

'That one of the hibernation pods had failed. Saul thought people would blame him for the tragedy.'

Fredericks scratched his head.

'No one blamed Saul. But we still haven't figured out what happened. Did he say anything to you?'

'No, but he had promised to let me know if he found anything.'

Fredericks narrowed his eyes.

'Why are you so interested? Is someone paying you for an exclusive? We can put a court order out to stop you publishing.'

'Whoa there. Don't jump the gun,' said Chuck. 'I'm on your side. Of course, I'd like the story, and to tell you the truth, I expect you to promise it to me now. However, that's not why Saul's dilemma, and his unexplained death, have brought me to your office. I need your help.'

'What sort of help?'

'I believe Serena Hampton was murdered, and her death may be linked to Saul's in some way.'

Fredericks' eyes opened wider.

'But she died of a heart attack.'

'I'm afraid she didn't. Someone poisoned her. The guy who brought her the sushi at the launch dinner was not the usual delivery man. Incidentally, the delivery guy just turned up dead too.'

'The guy who brought the sushi?'

'No, the real delivery guy. He disappeared on the night of the dinner, and someone took his place, but they only found the real delivery guy's body a few weeks ago.'

'Serena ate poisoned sushi? But what proof do you have?'

'Not proof exactly. I met someone who knew the real delivery guy and described him to me. That made me suspicious because I remembered seeing someone totally different deliver the sushi on the night of the launch dinner. So, I decided to read Serena's autopsy, just in case. A source managed to find out that poison was the real cause of death. But when I tried to get a copy of the autopsy, I got a warning to back off.'

'But why? Who would murder an astronaut? I don't understand.'

'I'm not sure. But now Wayne Odoyu has died too, and the person investigating the cause of his death has turned up floating in the harbour. Something stinks.'

'We have a saboteur? Jesus, what about Hattie and the rest of the crew? What can I do to help?'

'I need the data Saul was working on.'

'The data? He took it home.'

'But his widow said you sent someone to collect it, and he took Saul's laptop too.'

Fredericks turned pale and he dropped his face into his hands.

'But we didn't send anyone yet,' he said.

'Maybe the same person who murdered Saul took the information to stop us examining it?'

'That means at least two people are involved because he couldn't have sabotaged the pod. This is getting worse by the minute. We must warn the crew.'

'But how do we know there isn't a saboteur on board the Starship?' said Chuck. 'How do we warn the other crew members without alerting him too? The saboteur can only be in one of two places; here at NASA or on the Starship.'

'Can you send your daughter a private message?'

'Yes, but they aren't encrypted. We didn't think it would be necessary.'

'Somehow you have to warn her without alerting anyone else.'

Fredericks nodded.

'There may be a way. Leave it with me. And keep digging for this other guy. We need to find him. I promise you a world exclusive once we figure this out. Is there anything else you need?'

'Can someone give me a lift home? My car broke down and got towed.'

Chapter 19

B ret Grayling stood, legs apart and hands clasped behind his back in a classic leader's pose. He examined the assembled crew with his piercing blue eyes. Beside him, less composed, Chad scratched his neck, leaving red weals on the surface. Hattie and the rest of the crew waited for their orders; anticipation having reached a peak, as their orbit around Mars had stabilised. Bret coughed and cleared his throat.

'As you know,' he said. 'The original plan for first contact envisaged a crew of four boarding the Mars module and taking her down to the surface of the planet. However, in view of our reduced numbers, NASA orders have changed. Chad and I will go alone on the first attempt at landing, since we are expendable...'

He paused to allow for laughter, but instead blank stares met his grin. He went on.

'We are proud to have been selected for this incredible challenge—'

Ellie raised his hand.

'Excuse me,' she said. 'Why not three astronauts? We've only lost one crew member, and landing the module is less dangerous than landing the Starship.'

'And why two Americans?' said Yu. 'Only one of you should go. The other astronauts should be representatives from the rest of the globe, like Mo and me.'

'Those are our instructions,' said Bret, his jaw tightening. 'It's nothing to do with our nationalities. This is a global first for all of us.'

'Why don't we draw straws?' said Mo. 'That would be fairer. I can see why the commander should go, but why should Chad go too? Surely he should take command of the Starship in case something happens to the module?'

Hattie found herself nodding vigorously, even though she didn't like Chad.

'He's got a point,' said Yu. 'We've all trained for years to get this chance at being the first. There should be an Asian representative in the module.'

'As far as I can see,' said Scotty. 'Bret will be the first person to step onto the planet, and we all know the name of the first man on the moon. But how many people know the name of the second man?'

'Buzz Aldrin,' said Ellie.

'Let me rephrase that,' said Scotty. 'How many people who are not astronauts?'

Ellie scowled. Chad scuffed his foot along the floor.

'Do I get a say?' he said.

'Of course,' said Bret.

'I think Ellie's right. We need to work as a team to stay alive on Mars. Resentments can fester if they're not aired. I don't mind landing the Starship. It's a massive responsibility, but I've trained for it countless times.'

Bret's eyes opened wide and he turned to glare at Chad who shrugged and dropped his head.

'But NASA—' he said

'NASA is many million miles away. They can't make judgement calls for us. It's not sustainable. We can't wait 40 minutes for an answer in an emergency,' said Mo.

'This isn't an emergency,' said Bret.

'But it could turn into one,' said Scotty. 'We've all put the work in. We all deserve a chance to be in the module. Let's draw straws or something. That's the most democratic thing to do.'

119

'And there should be three people in the module. We've only lost one of the crew, and that gives us the best chance of getting half of us alive onto the surface once the Starship lands too,' said Ellie.

'So, there will be Bret, and two others in the module?' said Hattie.

'At least one should be a woman,' said Ellie.

'What do you think, Bret?' said Scotty.

Bret frowned.

'I don't like it.'

'You're in the minority,' said Yu. 'And, as Mo remarked, NASA are many million miles away.'

The tone of his voice did not allow room for argument, and Hattie noticed a stiffening in the stance of the other crew members. Bret did too. He held up his hands.

'Okay. But we'll draw lots, and the first two will come with me no matter where they are from or who they are, male or female. I'll tell NASA something to placate them.'

'But not until it's too late to change our plan,' said Ellie.

A murmur of assent rippled around the crew.

Bret shrugged. He leaned over the console and grabbed a handful of Velcro hoop strips and a waste bag.

'Write your name on a piece of this Velcro and put it into the bag,' he said. 'One each, please, except for Chad.'

He handed them out and waited while people shared their pens and procrastinated.

'Okay?' he said. 'Hattie, can you please do the draw?'

'Me?' said Hattie, putting her hand to her chest.

'Yes, get on with it.'

Bret handed her the bag which she shook a couple of times. Then she shut her eyes and reached in. The feel of the strips on her fingers distracted her from enormity of her choice, and she pulled out the first strip she grabbed, which she handed to Bret. He read the label and held it up for the others to read.

'Chen Yu,' he said.

A groan arose from the others. Yu tried not to look smug and failed. Hattie reached into the bag and pulled out the second piece of Velcro. Bret took it from her and examined it. His eyes widened and then he smiled.

'Hattie,' he said. 'It's you.'

Hattie felt the room spin. She grabbed onto the console to steady herself. The eyes of the crew bored into her.

'It's a fix,' said Ellie, but she smiled.

'Don't be ridiculous,' said Scotty, who hadn't seen her smile. 'How could it be a fix?'

'I think it's the perfect choice,' said Yu. 'She will be the first woman on Mars, and the first African American. I approve.'

'Me too,' said Bret. 'It adds diversity to the landing. Hattie and Yu, you need to come with me, and get briefed on the landing protocols. We need to do a test run through the complete sequence twice before we even consider getting into the module. Mo, can you please check the telemetry systems for the module's broadcasting system? The landing will be beamed live to Earth, and we don't need any glitches. Chad, will you please check the oxygen units?'

Hattie edged towards Bret and Yu. Mo put his arm out to stop her progress.

'But she's only a stand-in. If you want an ethnic minority to go, it should be me,' he said.

'We didn't choose her because she is black. She won the draw fair and square. You need to let her pass,' said Bret.

'Come on, Mo,' said Scotty. 'We'll all be down there soon. What difference does it make?'

A shadow passed over Mo's face. He opened his mouth to say something and then closed it again.

'She must have cheated. The United Nations will hear about this,' he said.

Yu rolled his eyes and beckoned Hattie to follow them.

Hattie stood rooted to the spot for a moment, speechless with shock and excitement. Mo's intervention had been unexpected but now nothing stood in her way. *It's me. I can't believe it.* Her thoughts swirled inside her head as she forced herself to follow Bret and Yu. She looked back to see Scotty holding up an imaginary all-in-one to his head and mouthing *'I need to speak to you'*. She gave him a thumbs up and followed Bret and Yu down to the level of the Starship which contained the module. Bret used the control panel to open the hatch and clambered inside.

'Okay,' said Hattie. 'Let's do this.'

Three long hours later, Hattie stumbled into the canteen, head bursting with new information, and threw a packet of pasta with sauce into the microwave. She sucked at a juice pack and tried to calm herself. *I must send a message home. They won't believe what just happened.* Scotty came up to her table and sat down close to her. As usual, she found his presence both comforting and disquieting in equal measure. *Am I blushing again?*

'How'd it go, Hats? All set for the big adventure?' he said.

'As ready as I'll ever be. I'm having trouble taking it all in.'

'You'll do fine,' said Scotty. 'I...'

'What?'

'I've been thinking about the deaths of Serena and Wayne and I just can't get over the feeling that something is wrong. At first, I thought, well, em...'

'You thought it was me?' said Hattie. 'Seriously?'

'You had motive.'

'Motive? Are you a detective now? What about your suspicious behaviour?'

'Mine? I don't know—'

'Don't you? Why weren't you at the launch press conference and dinner? How did Serena die?'

Scotty's jaw dropped and he opened his mouth to protest.

'And how do I know you didn't interfere with the sleep pod?' said Hattie. 'You've got the skills. I haven't.'

Scotty frowned.

'I was asleep, but you've got a point. Okay, so if it's not us, who is it? Are they onboard with us or working from Earth?'

'I don't know, but I agree with you. Something is not right. We need to find out what's happening before more people die.'

Scotty rubbed his chin.

'There's something else you should know before you launch. Bret is planning on claiming Mars for the United States of America instead of the United Nations. I just don't want you to be surprised.'

'Surprised? But that's terrible. I must stop him.'

'See. I knew you'd say that. But you can't. It's been planned since the outset.'

'And you knew?'

'Bret told me when we woke up from our hibernation. I don't happen to agree, but there's not much we can do.'

'And I thought Mo and Yu were being paranoid.'

'They don't know about this, and you're not to tell them. Once the flag is planted, it will be too late.'

'But this is wrong. Can't we stop him?'

'Look, the politics will be sorted out on Earth, not up here. Just make sure you plant a UN flag beside the Stars and Stripes. They can't stop you and once you've planted it, the Earth feed will show you doing it.'

'Okay, I'll take one with me and attach it to the rover's antenna.'

'That's my girl,' said Scotty. 'Be careful down there. I couldn't bear this trip without you along.'

'Me either,' said Hattie. 'Get the Starship landed safely and keep an eye out for suspicious behaviour. We'll be waiting for you.'

Chapter 20

H attie shoved her feet into her tight boots and fastened the clips with shaking hands before backing into a suiting bay. She took a deep breath, trying to let it out evenly with her eyes shut tight. *You've trained for this. Visualise a sunny day. Breathe in and out.* She pushed her heels against the wall and pressed her palm onto the scanner.

'Initiating spacesuit fitting for Harriet Fredericks. Please do not move.'

The calm AI voice soothed her nerves. *You can do this.* The console beeped a few times. The rings at the bottom of the inner layer of the spacesuit pushed into the top of her boots and sealed with a clunk. Then the suit pulled up past her hips and she thrust her hands into the armholes. The inner suit zipped up behind her and a neck ring snaked around her throat. She shut her eyes again as it clicked shut. Pinned to the panel, she struggled not to panic.

The outer suit rose up her body with a whirring sound, up to the neck ring where it sealed shut. A pair of flexible gloves emerged from the steriliser to one side of her and she put them on, twisting the carbon connectors shut. They were followed by the outer gloves which attached with a snap to the outer suit.

'Confirm suit ready for fitting.'

Hattie cleared her throat.

'Confirmed,' she croaked.

'Initiating.'

The inner suit started to tighten around her like a python squeezing its prey. Tighter and tighter. She held her breath to keep her ribs out but when she let it go, the suit tightened again and constricted her breathing. She raised her hand to hit the panic button. *I can't do this.* Just then Bret walked in.

'Ah, great, you're almost ready. Can you sit in the back row of the rover please? I'll put the spare oxygen unit on the seat beside you and strap it down.'

Hattie nodded, unwilling to speak. She placed her hand on the scanner for release and almost fell out of the suiting bay with relief.

'God, that's tight,' she said. 'I had a pair of jeans like this once.'

Bret lifted her helmet from the console and put it over her head, pressing the button on the side to open the visor.

'There you go,' he said.

Hattie shuffled towards the module, giving thanks for the low gravity of Mars. The suit weighed twenty kilos in Earth gravity but on Mars it would feel like seven. She approached the oxygen tanks which had been pre-checked by Chad. Since the module would land within four hundred metres of the habitats erected by the robots, the tanks did not need to be full, but they were replete with oxygen in case of any unforeseen contingencies.

Hattie liked to check her own gear, a habit from her diving days. She and Grace played a game when they were younger called What If. They used to quiz each other on an endless number of unlikely scenarios from a meeting with their favourite band to dealing with a monster in their wardrobe. Hattie liked to run What If scenarios in real life too. Running a final check on the tanks would calm her nerves. *I'll soon get into my stride. I'm made for this.*

The oxygen units hung in their slots on the wall under the module. Their gleaming white paint still undamaged by radiation or sandstorms. She ran through the test, checking them off one by one on her all-in-one which linked into the central computer. Finally, she noted the oxygen levels in the tanks and took a photograph of the meters before lifting them off the rack one by one and putting them back again. In epsilon gravity, they weighed thirty kilos and she grunted with effort. The tight suit made her feel light headed and she sat down panting, and geeing herself up for the fourth tank. She forced herself to stand just as Bret appeared.

'Ready?' he said.

'Just giving the tanks a last-minute check,' said Hattie. 'Safety first.'

Bret rubbed his chin.

'There's more to you than meets the eye,' he said. 'You should learn to be assertive with the rest of the crew. You have every right to be here.'

'Thanks,' mumbled Hattie.

Yu appeared, a radiant smile on his face and they all backed into their oxygen units. Hattie noticed a piece of bright red material emerging from an external pocket in the leg of his suit. *Is that a Chinese flag? Maybe he has the same idea I have.*

Bret picked up the spare tank with practiced ease.

'We'll take this one with us for spare.'

'I haven't checked that one yet,' said Hattie.

'The gauge says it's full,' said Bret. 'But now that you mention it...'

He picked up another tank.

'This one is heavier,' he said. 'How did you know?'

'I didn't. I just...'

Hot blood darkened her face as she felt his hard stare. Did he think she had interfered with the tank? She forced a smile.

'It's a good thing you checked,' said Bret. 'I wouldn't have noticed otherwise.'

'The leader's safety is paramount,' said Hattie in a faux AI voice.

Bret grinned. The three astronauts entered the airlock together, Bret carrying the extra tank. Hattie envied Bret his muscles. *Maybe having a jock on board had its compensations.* They closed their visors, and checked the seals on their helmets, and then activated the airlock. As the air disappeared, Hattie felt herself float off the floor and she grabbed on to the bars on the wall to pull herself towards the hatch at the front end of the Starship. The hatch opened with a clunk and they found themselves looking at the heat shield of the module.

Sliding though the gap underneath the module, the astronauts entered the door at the side of the module which would morph into a bullet shaped ATV (all-terrain-vehicle) or rover. The interior of the ATV had been designed to take four astronauts in full gear and three cubic metres of supplies. The ATV could also tow one of the small trailers which formed part of the cargo on their Starship and could be used to carry the drill or other ancillary equipment.

The heat shield would break away from the rover before they landed, leaving them under a steel and toughened plexiglass dome capable of resisting thousands of pounds of force. Four large wheels with independent suspension would emerge as the panels were ejected, shortly before the module hovered down to the surface now transformed into an ATV. The oxygen units on their backs were a precaution, as the rover had a pressurised atmosphere, but all the bases were covered in case of a disaster. Robotic rover units would also track their progress to the landing site and wait there in case of emergency transfer.

Hattie crawled into body of the ATV and plonked herself into her seat at the back of the rover. The automatic straps wrapped themselves around her. The seats had been adjusted for wearing tanks but they made her feel even more squashed and claustrophobic. Bret touched a button on the panel and the side door sealed itself with a clunk.

'Confirm astronauts ready for launch,' said Bret.

Hattie and Yu gave him a thumbs up.

'Chad, we are locked and loaded.'

'I copy you,' said Scotty's voice.

'Hey, Scotty. Where's Chad?'

'Oh, diarrhoea, I think. He's been in the toilet for hours. Don't worry. I've got this.'

Bret laughed.

'Remember we are live to several billion people,' he said. 'Watch the language. The sequence is preloaded. It should be automated once you initiate.'

'Roger that. Initiating sequence for module release. Bon voyage folks and happy landings.'

The nose cone of the Starship opened in slow motion. Hattie willed it to speed up. The spacesuit made her nauseous. The cone stopped opening half way and they sat squashed into the rover as the minutes ticked by.

'Bret, we have a problem,' said Scotty. 'The automated sequence has stopped. Mo is having a look to find out why. Hang in there.'

Hattie's heart rate rose again as she fought the confines of the spacesuit and her growing panic attack. She could only see the back of Bret and Yu 's helmets, not their faces. *Were they also having trouble staying calm?* We have trained for any eventuality but many decisions were life or death in space.

'Roger that,' said Bret. 'I need a pee now though.'

'That's what space nappies are for,' said Scotty.

Despite herself, Hattie had to stifle a guffaw. The minutes passed. She managed to calm herself with some deep breathing, and tolerate her discomfort. She took out her all-in-one to distract herself and found she had received a private message from her father. Probably wishing me luck. But it was an image from Grace with a message which read; *I'm sure everyone is doing their utmost to keep you all safe up there. Remember the astronaut deaths were both accidents. Love you. Gracefool.*

Before she had time to reread the note, or wonder about its contents, Scotty came back on line.

'Okay, there's some sort of glitch that only Mo understands. So, I've got him to kill the programme, and I'm launching you manually. If it's good enough for Michael Collins...'

The nose cone started to move apart again and soon the inky blackness of space contrasted with the red blob below their orbit. The module shuddered and came away from its stanchions, floating out into the darkness. The only sounds Hattie could hear were Bret and Yu breathing into their microphones. She shut her eyes and synchronised her breaths with theirs.

'Landing sequence initiated,' said Scotty. 'You're on your own now. See you guys shortly.'

Shouldn't we be saying historic things for people to quote later? I guess Chad had those lined up but Scotty didn't stand on ceremony.

Bret gave a thumbs up and Yu and Hattie mirrored him. A short blast on their thrusters started them on their trajectory towards the surface. Minutes later, the blackness of space acquired a red glow and the module thundered through the thin atmosphere down towards the planet's surface. Hattie kept her eyes shut tight until the roaring stopped. *Seven minutes is a long, long time.* She tried to cross her fingers but her gloves were too thick. Finally, the parachutes deployed, jolting the module, and slowing it down.

'Aren't we going too fast?' said Yu.

'It's our angle of approach that may be problematic,' said Bret. 'Scotty, do you copy?'

'Hearing you loud and clear,' said Scotty.

'Execute protocol six, please. We'll tell you when to remove.'

'Understood. Protocol six and out.'

'What's protocol six?' said Hattie. *That wasn't part of training.*

'Communications block with Earth. They have half an hour to play with as we are ahead of the official schedule in case of mishaps.'

'Mishaps?' said Yu. 'You mean we might crash land?'

'Not much we can do now,' said Bret. 'Brace yourselves.'

The surface of Mars shot up towards them like a massive red fist. The protective panels flew off the lander module and the wheels emerged, causing a muffled thundering sound as they broke the thin atmosphere. The ATV hit the ground with a heavy thud. One of the wheels did not fully lock into position in time, causing the rover to tip over on its side. The spare oxygen tank came loose and hit the back of Bret's helmet. Hattie felt her body crushed against the strapping and hung from her seat.

The rover lay in a cloud of dust. Hattie could hear her heart beating. *I'm alive then.*

'Whoa, that was some ride,' said Yu. 'Is everyone okay?'

'I think so,' said Hattie.

Bret did not answer. He hung in his strapping, his arms loose. Yu struggled to turn around and inspect him. He gave Hattie a thumbs down.

'Hattie, can you get out? Bret's been knocked out and he's blocking the doorway. We need the robots to right the vehicle. If they are here...'

'I think so. Turn off the pressurisation and give me a second to get free of these straps.'

Yu checked Bret's visor and then his own.

'Is your visor down?'

'Yes, ready,' said Hattie.

Yu tapped on the control screen and the pressure in the cabin started to drop. Hattie pressed the release button on her restraints and fell onto the door which had been blocked by the ground. She pushed her boots against it and straightened up to press the exit button on the door above her helmet. The door opened with a hiss. She climbed up the seats and pulled herself out, lying panting for a second, half in and half out of the vehicle.

'Very elegant,' said Yu's voice in her ear. 'Don't kick Bret on your way out.'

'Is he okay?'

'I don't know. The tank knocked him out but he's coming around.'

Bret grunted and moved his head.

'Okay, I can see the robot rovers coming over the ridge. I'll take one over and get the module upright.'

Hattie slid off the vehicle and landed in the red dust. She shook herself to check for injuries and to get the oxygen tank balanced. The salmon pink sky glowed above the line of pockmarked cliffs in the distance. Layered rocks threw shadows on the ground. Bret's laboured breathing was the only sound on her intercom until she picked up the echoing, metallic clunking of the rover wheels on the surface. The wind gusted, sounding like flapping sails or a tarpaulin rippling. Then she spotted Elysium Mons in the distance, looming twelve kilometres above the surface of the planet, majestic through the red dust.

'Are you all right?' said Yu. 'You've gone very quiet.'

'Yes, just catching my breath and taking in the view. Have you seen Elysium Mons. It's quite literally out of this world.'

'Magnificent, isn't it? Even upside down. I can't take in how enormous it is. Oh, by the way, congratulations.'

'What for? Oh...'

Hattie's breath caught in her throat. It's me. *The first man on Mars is a woman. Oh my God.* Her eyes filled with tears blurring her vision of the rover which approached from the south leaving a trail of dust. The rover had extended its camera arms and Hattie felt the weight of history on her shoulders. *I can't let Bret steal Mars for the USA. It isn't right.* She patted her pockets and found the United Nation's flag which she pulled out, shaking out the folds. She made sure Elysium Mons was in the background and let it hang from her hands as the rover neared her, smiling through the visor of her helmet.

'I claim this planet for the United Nations and the good of all mankind,' she said, laying the flag on the ground and putting stones on the corners. The recording button on the rover blinked at her and then stopped. *That's odd, why did it stop. Maybe NASA didn't want any more footage?* With her back to the lander, she took out her all-in-one and surreptitiously cloned the footage from the rover camera. She put it back into her pocket and turned to the lander.

'What the hell do you think you're doing?' said Bret, leaning out of his door. 'Take that flag off the ground, and get this lander back on four wheels immediately.'

'But won't NASA have seen this?'

'They might have, but the feed for global consumption is delayed by half an hour in case of unforeseen circumstances. I stopped the camera recording. I'm the one who gets to be the first, not you. Get me out of here. Now!'

You may get the fame, but I am the first. There is no second chance to be first. It's me, Hattie Fredericks. Grace and her parents would burst with pride when they realised what had happened. No one else might ever find out but no one could ever take that moment away from her.

'Sorry, Commander. I got over excited. Give me a minute.'

Hattie clambered aboard the smaller rover and switched it over to manual control. The rover rolled across the dusty surface and she manoeuvred it as close to the module as she could. Reaching up from the cabin she attached the clip from the winch onto the corner of the undercarriage and the door of the overturned lander. She edged slowly away from it at right angles

132

paying out the rope to give a safe space from her rover. The lander teetered on two wheels and then thudded down onto four. Yu gave her a thumbs up through the windscreen. Bret opened the door on his side of the ATV.

'Are you okay?' said Hattie.

'No thanks to you,' said Bret. 'What were you playing at? Get that rover's camera arm set up again and then get back into the lander.'

Hattie positioned the rover's arm and returned to the ATV. Bret tapped the screen and reactivated the camera.

'Scotty, do you copy?'

'It's me, Chad.'

'Hey, welcome back. Okay, cancel protocol 6 and let's get this show on the road.'

Chapter 21

C huck Gomez looked around the press gallery in the Mission Control Centre for somewhere to sit and take notes, but the place heaved with people. Anticipation had sent adrenaline surging around his body, making him feel nauseous. He wondered if sitting on the floor would be against safety regulations. Everything else seemed to be. *Funny how you could not sit on the floor in Miami, but sending eight astronauts hurtling into space to land on an unexplored planet broke no rules.*

Despite Chuck's conviction about the likelihood of foul play being involved in the deaths of the astronauts, he had not got any further with his investigations. Fredericks could not find any evidence of sabotage at NASA and the authorities had called off his investigation to avoid bad publicity. Fredericks had cited the lack of evidence and asked him to hold off until they announced the death of Wayne Odoyu, which they planned to do after the historic landing on Mars.

The need to purchase a new vehicle had forced him to work overtime after his old one had finally given up the ghost. Luckily, his boss had asked him to follow up on an emerging story about a possible serial killer, a gig which earned him a fat bonus. Now that he had replaced his car, he intended to find the man with the ferret's face as soon as he had the go ahead from Fredericks.

The excitement in the gallery rose and fell as landing time approached. All over the world, crowds had gathered to watch massive screens and take selfies of themselves. Even the recent moon landings had not caused such a huge surge in interest, although they may have primed people for the big one. His all-in-one beeped in irritation at him as his pulse throbbed with anticipation.

Below them, the launch centre heaved with activity. Engineers focused on their screens with intense concentration and others rushed up and down the narrow space between the row of desks, muttering to themselves. Chuck spotted Edgar Fredericks at the back of the room. Tall, grey, and drawn with worry, he nodded and pointed as his lieutenants scurried to and fro. The families of the other astronauts had elected to watch alone at home, in case of tragedies, but he wanted to be close to the action. The chances of something going wrong were higher than NASA had admitted to the public but expectations were so high that it seemed impossible to quell the wave of euphoria. Chuck had never experienced such a surge of hope and excitement. It felt alien to him. And somehow unreal.

When the nose cone of the Starship failed to open automatically, the sound of hundreds of thumbs sending frenzied updates filled the gallery. For once, Chuck had eschewed his beloved pencil and paper, and joined their texting orgy. His head filled with scenarios of disaster and failure, while his heart longed for success. The relief when Scotty nonchalantly switched the opening sequence to manual swept the room like the tide coming in. People vibrated with awe as the lander floated out into the blackness and engaged thrusters. Behind it the nose cone shut in slow motion like the petals of a tulip. Chuck held his breath.

As the lander entered the thin atmosphere it disappeared from the screens again. Instead, the cameras in the command centre of the Starship focussed on the three astronauts at the controls. Then Chad tottered in to view and sat beside Scotty.

'All systems go,' said Scotty. 'Are you okay?'

'Never better,' said Chad, still green about the gills. 'I'll take it from here.'

Those seven minutes of terror again. Chuck shifted from foot to foot. Around him, nails had found their way to mouths and faces drained of blood were turned to the screen, willing the capsule to survive the journey.

'Landing party. Are you receiving me?' said Scotty.

'Loud and clear,' said Bret.

The NASA control centre erupted with cheers, echoed all over the globe in squares and bars and stadiums and houses. Tears of relief mixed with cheers at the astronauts' houses. They're not down yet thought Chuck. The screens around the centre flickered as the focus changed back to the view from the capsule which transmitted fuzzy pictures of the fast-approaching surface. *Aren't they going too fast?*

Suddenly the feed disappeared completely. Bewildered journalists looked to each other for answers. Chuck felt as if someone had punched him in the gut. Down in the control centre, the engineers and analysts looked at each other in shock and started to tap on their screens as if trying to eliminate a plague of ants. Edgar Fredericks, grey with unshared worries, clapped his hands together to attract attention.

'Okay, folks, nothing to worry about. We've lost the feed for a moment but we'll soon get it back. They are over fifty million miles away, and I lose the signal for my all-in-one if I go to the storage room.'

Nervous laughter followed this remark, and heads which had lifted, bent down over their keyboards again. Chuck tried to sit down on a thin window ledge but slid down to the floor where he sent an update to his boss. Out of habit, he took his pencil out of his pocket with his notebook and started to doodle and pose hypothetical questions to himself. *What if they had crash landed?*

Could they be brought to safety by the robots? And if they were dead? The euphoria of the last few minutes had evaporated to be replaced by worried whispering and hissing of questions. Time stood still as they waited for a sign of life from the lander, or the Starship.

Just when all seemed lost, the screen flickered and showed a massive puff of dust. The feed jumped to show Bret Grayling striding towards the camera from the ATV and planting a flag on the surface of Mars. A spontaneous cheer rang out in the control room and once again the journalists' heads dropped as they tapped furiously on their all-in-ones. Bret started to speak but static blurred and gapped the words.

'What's he saying?' said Chuck.

'Search me,' said a colleague, shrugging.

A murmur of complaint spread around the room. Then a young woman came in and passed among them distributing a file containing the speech proclaiming that Mars had been claimed for the USA. A wall of exclamations surged through the gallery, some joyous and others furious.

'So much for international cooperation,' said the journalist from the British Times. 'Bloody Yanks.'

'There's not much we can do from here,' said the Australian standing next to him.

The Chinese correspondents, who had bunched together for the landing, sat stony-faced at their table, tapping out furious articles about American Imperialism. Their joy at the inclusion of Chen Yu in the first landing had evaporated. Chuck shook his head. This would not be the last they heard about it. You couldn't just claim a planet like a piece of lost luggage. This story would run and run. And what had happened during the landing? The missing piece of the recording made his scalp prickle. The ATV looked whole but why had they cut out segment showing the landing, the most interesting bit for space buffs. Maybe he could coax the story out of Edgar Fredericks.

And thinking of the Fredericks family reminded him he wanted to speak to Grace again. *How had she known about Wayne before speaking to her parents?* The source of that information could be key in his investigation.

The girl who had handed out Bret's speech clapped her hands to get the attention of the assembled press corps.

'Ladies and Gentlemen. We will be sending you a highlights package of the day's events on Mars at midday PST on the days we receive them. Owing to the longer day length and extreme cost of broadcasting from Mars, we will not be following events live. The astronauts will be extremely busy and may not always have time to send us anything. Please do not contact NASA for comments on the videos. We will put out bulletins on any important developments.'

She smiled and left the room despite a sea of raised hands and shouts from journalists desperate for clarification. Chuck shoved his notebook into his pocket and stepped outside into the blinding sunshine. He tapped Grace Fredericks's number and waited without expectation for her to answer. To his amazement, Grace's face appeared on his screen, black bags under her normally sparkling eyes.

'Hello, Mr Gomez,' she said. 'I wanted to call you but... I'm sure by now you've realised why I have tried to stay out of the limelight.'

'You mean your job?'

'They'd fire me, or worse, if they found out who I am.'

'They wouldn't hear it from me, I promise.'

'What happened today? To the landing module? First it couldn't be launched and then it disappeared from the screen.'

'I don't know, but I wondered the same thing.'

'Do you think these incidents are related to the astronaut deaths?'

'It's hard to say. I have my suspicions but there's no proof, and space travel can be difficult and dangerous.'

Grace blinked a couple of times and put her head on one side.

'Why did you go to see my father?'

'I thought he might help me trace a laptop.'

'Why did you want it?'

'It belonged to the engineer who designed the hibernation pods.'

'And who took it?'

'I don't know, but I think he's key to the whole thing.'

'My father made me send Hattie a strange message. Do you believe the astronauts were murdered?'

'I'm pretty sure they were.'

'And you think she might be in danger too?'

'I don't know. But you could help me find out and stop the murders.'

'Me? How?'

'Who told you Wayne Odoyu had died?'

'No one told me. I heard it at my office.'

'The CNP building? How did they find out?'

'A man my boss knows came to our office and told him.'

Why? What did Noah van Horn have to do with all this?

'What was his name?'

'Harlan Grimes.'

'Do you have his contact details?'

'No, he doesn't let me have them. He calls Mr van Horn from random cyber cafes.'

'What does he look like?'

'An evil rodent. He's frightening.'

'You've met him?'

Grace grimaced.

'Unfortunately. He came into the office once.'

And how did he know about Wayne?

'So you'll help me?'

'If I can. Please don't call me during the day. Just send me a message any evening and I'll answer.'

'Can you find out about Grimes for me?'

'You're the journalist. I can't ask Mr van Horn without him getting suspicious. He knows I don't like Grimes.'

'Okay. We'll speak soon.'

'Mr Gomez?'

'Chuck, call me Chuck.'

'Okay, Chuck. Please do everything you can. Hattie may be up there with a murderer.'

'Leave it to me.'

Chapter 22

H attie and Yu watched as Bret strode a few metres from their vehicle carrying the short, carbon-fibre flagpole and the American flag. He threaded the flag onto the pole and placed it on the ground. Then he positioned the camera arm on the other rover to point out at the horizon.

'He's not the first,' said Yu, switching the channel to private. 'You were.'

Hattie grinned.

'Don't tell him that. I'm going to pretend it never happened.'

'But you filmed it.'

'I'm pretty sure that part of the recording will get wiped on Earth before it's broadcast.'

'You're still the first.'

'We're the first,' said Hattie. 'All of us.'

Yu switched the rover channel on and Bret's voice reverberated around the cabin. Hattie and Yu listened to him claim the planet for the United States of America. Yu clenched his jaw and Hattie rolled her eyes at him but they did not comment.

After planting the Stars and Stripes into the red soil, and addressing the people watching on Earth, Bret stumbled back to the rover and leaned panting against the side.

'How'd I do?' he said.

'I think they got the message,' said Hattie. 'Congratulations.'

'How are you feeling?' said Yu.

'I don't feel so good,' said Bret. 'That oxygen tank hit me pretty hard. Hattie, can you drive?'

He got into the back seat with Yu and they passed the spare oxygen tank to the front seat. Hattie set the GPS to the position of the Starship hub but realised that following the other rovers down their well-worn track would be more efficient. A fine red dust settled on the sealed dome of the rover, blurring the view, but not obscuring the magnificent vista. She gazed out of the window at the barren dusty landscape as they jolted over the uneven surface. Bret groaned but Hattie could not prevent the rover's hard tyres from transmitting the vibrations into the rover.

'I'll get Scotty to see if he can adjust the suspension when he gets here,' said Hattie. 'But I'm afraid I can't do anything about the shocks for now.'

Small outcrops of layered rock broke through the uneven terrain like sperm whales' mouths poking out of the sea. Everywhere red dust dominated the landscape and the sky loomed pink instead of blue. No clouds intruded into the opaque pink dome. Hattie realised how bleak the landscape looked without so much as a cactus to break the monotony. Could life really have flourished here once? In Utah, on her trips to the Mars simulation Habitat, there had always been patches of scrub or a wandering reptile to catch the eye. Here, only rocks and dust could be seen for hundreds of metres in every direction

Suddenly the gleaming tip of a Starship appeared on the horizon, the steel petals shut to shield the methane tank contained within, enveloped in high tech insulation to keep it liquid. As they drove over the final ridge, four Starships became visible on the Basin, spaced at intervals of about five hundred metres along the eastern flank of the plain.

'Wow,' said Yu. 'They look like skyscrapers. I can't believe they survived the trip here. Don't they look amazing?'

'Stunning,' said Hattie. 'Like Manhattan on speed.'

'Let's hope the Moxie plants have been doing their thing,' said Bret. 'We've got to get Scotty down here asap to make sure the tanks are filling up with fuel.'

The Marsha hub of basalt fibre habitats loomed into view. The tall egg-shaped buildings were set at the end of short tunnels made from the same dark material, which connected to a central dome. Two of the Marsha units appeared to be complete and another had started to rise from the foundations. The basalt fibre panels for the first Marsha habitats had been 3-D printed in one of the Starships' cargo bays from Martian soil, and polylactic acid (PLA), a recyclable polymer composite transported from Earth in one of the space craft. The material had been designed to shield the interior of the habitat from radiation and external extremes of temperature. The robot rovers had transported these panels on trailers and assembled them on site.

'Well, that's a sight for sore eyes,' said Bret.

'Home, sweet home,' said Hattie.

'Let's hope they are finished inside as well as outside,' said Yu.

Hattie manoeuvred the rover alongside the dome and pulled up tight against the airlocked docking port. She pressed a button on the console and exhaled in relief as a connecting tube glided out from the dock until it fitted into the corresponding area on rover. The rover-side door opened with a clunk.

'Keep your suits on,' said Bret. 'We need to check the atmospheric pressure and oxygen levels in the habitat before we take them off.'

He entered the airlock followed by Yu. The door closed behind them and Hattie waited for the inner door to open so that they could enter the extravehicular activity (EVA) preparation chamber. Minutes passed as she gazed out at the Starships, stunned by their majesty. She took a video of the scenery with her all-in-one. Suddenly Bret's voice came over her headphone.

'Are you going to stay out there all day?'

'Coming.'

Hattie powered down the rover and opened the docking door by pressing the panel on the outside. She entered the airlock and listened for the clunk and hiss as the pressure equalized. The inner door opened and she stepped inside the chamber. Bret and Yu were sitting on a bench beside the shower cubicles. On the far wall, Hattie noticed a second airlock for astronauts on foot. controlled by a wall panel.

'Let's go then,' said Bret.

They headed for the entry door to the tunnel which led to the Marsha pod on the left of the dome. The connecting tunnel had not been built for astronauts still suited up with air tanks on their backs so they had to crouch. Hattie noticed how light her tank felt in Mars gravity. They opened the door to the pod and found themselves in the wet laboratory. Pallets loaded with packages wrapped in plastic and cardboard were stacked on the floor beside the work benches.

'Wow,' said Hattie. 'I can't believe how complete the lab is.'

'Those pallets look like hard work to me,' said Yu.

They travelled one by one in the lift to the second floor which contained the dry lab on one side and the kitchen on the other. A large combi-oven and a tall fridge freezer were built into the walls and a counter ran down the centre of the room partitioned so that half ran either side of the kitchen and the dry lab. The cupboards were empty. The floor was covered in shavings and discarded lumps of fibre.

'I guess they don't teach the robots about garbage,' said Yu.

'Another job for the humans,' said Hattie.

The third floor contained the recreation and exercise room. Exercise bicycles and rowing machines were placed like spokes on a wheel in the small gym, all hooked up to monitors with LED screens. A multigym sat at the centre of the half wheel. A faux grass partition separated the gym from a rec-room with couches and what appeared to be a beverage machine. Probably just vitamin drinks.

'As if we're going to need to exercise after the days we have planned,' said Hattie.

'Cool interiors though,' said Yu.

'It's amazing how well the dual shell construction maintains constant temperature and pressure,' said Bret. 'We'll be safe and comfortable in here.'

'It's weirdly normal,' said Hattie. 'Just lacking windows.'

'Come up here,' said Yu, who had risen to the top floor.

Hattie smiled when she saw the neat sleep pods and the smart showers on the top floor. A large water filled skylight beamed light onto a sitting area with plant pots in it.

'I love it. Can I stay here for ever?'

'Don't tempt fate,' said Bret. 'I don't know about you two but I'm ready to eat my own arm. The pressure and oxygen saturation are good according to the monitoring panel.'

'Before you do that, if you guys can empty the rover, I'll look for the food,' said Hattie. 'I need to find some food packs and liquid for us.'

'You can take off your helmet upstairs while we unload the rover into the EVA prep room,' said Bret. 'We'll ditch our suits there when we've finished unloading, and then you can take yours off too.

'Don't start without us,' said Yu.

After the men had gone back down to the ground floor, Hattie shut off her oxygen and removed her gloves. She reached up to remove her helmet. It opened with a satisfying clunk and she lifted it over her head and placed it on the counter. She bent down to review a pile of boxes and then realised she couldn't breathe. Her training kicked in and she spun around to grab her helmet. She shoved it over her head and fumbled with the catch, trying not to panic. The helmet's catch clicked into place and she reached for her gloves. Only one sat on the counter. She attached it to her suit and frantically searched for the second one. It had fallen behind a box on the floor. She wrenched it out and shoved her hand inside, before releasing the oxygen flow in her suit again. The air reached her lungs in an instant and she took a few deep breaths to fill them.

What the hell? Why did Bret tell me, it would be okay to remove my helmet?

Hattie went over to the central control panel in the kitchen. The lights were all green, indicating pressure and oxygen saturation were safe; but they weren't. She got into the lift and travelled down to the ground floor. The wall panel in the wet lab also glowed green. She pressed the door for the airlock to the passageway but it didn't open. She forced herself to think logically. Computers are not infallible. It's just a glitch. She prized the main panel open and pressed the reset button. After thirty seconds, the lights turned red and she tapped the button to establish Earth atmosphere and pressure within the habitat. She pressed the door control again and the door slid open.

Bret and Yu were still unloading the rover when she got to the EVA prep room.

'Have you found us something to eat?' said Yu. 'I'm starving.'

'There is a glitch with the main control panel,' said Hattie. 'I came down to warn you to check your oxygen monitors on your sleeves before you take off your helmets anywhere. I almost passed out upstairs.'

'Probably from hunger,' said Bret. 'Are you sure the oxygen levels weren't correct. I checked them.'

'I'm sure,' said Hattie. 'I reset the circuits now so the habitat should soon fill with oxygen.'

'Never trust a robot,' said Bret, and went back out to the rover.

Chapter 23

Helena Taggart's all-in-one rang for a full minute before she picked it up, breathless, her face red and sweaty.

'Yes?'

'It's me, Chuck.'

'What you do want? I'm in the middle of my yoga class.'

'Should I call you back later?'

'No. Tell me now.'

'Do you remember the man took away Saul's laptop?'

'I guess so.'

'Did he tell you his name?'

'No, he only said he had come on behalf of NASA. Well, he might have. I just don't recall.'

'And what did he look like?'

'Um, kind of skinny.'

'Anything else.'

'Not really. Oh, wait, yes. He had ice blue eyes, like the underside of an iceberg, and teeth like a rat.'

Chuck swallowed. *Harlan Grimes. Again. He's the key.*

'Thanks, that's really useful.'

Helena rolled her eyes.

'The police don't think so. They say he doesn't exist.'

'And the forensics?'

'Why don't you ask them?'

Helena snorted and hung up. Chuck sighed. Another person he would never see again. Not that he cared. *So, Harlan Grimes. Where are you?* Chuck trawled through the internet using every method he knew. He tried not to be annoyed when Harlan Coben kept coming up but not a trace of Grimes. Surely it should be easy to find someone with such an unusual name? But Harlan Grimes did not materialise. Chuck chewed his pencil. If Harlan Grimes was an assumed name, this could be a whole lot harder.

He wanted to ask Grace Fredericks to help him, but she had been adamant, and he needed to stay on good terms with her. Also, while the CNP seemed to be involved, one way or another, he preferred to use her as a conduit for information in the future. Luckily, he knew someone who could help. Whether she would or not remained to be seen. As usual he had failed to keep his promises to her and she kept score.

'Gina, it's Chuck.'

'Hey, long time no hear. I thought you were going to take me out to dinner?'

'And I am. Soon. I'm just a bit busy right now.'

'Busy, uh? How romantic. What do you want this time?'

'Don't be like that. I will take you out when I make a fortune on this story.'

'And pigs might fly.'

Gina sighed. Chuck waited.

'Well, go on then, tell me.'

'Remember that time you took me to Saul Taggart's house.'

'To see his wife? How could I forget?'

'No don't get snarky with me. She's not my type.'

'And I am?'

'Sure you are,' said Chuck, half meaning it. 'I found out who stole Saul's laptop and I think he's the same guy who killed him.'

'And you want me to...?'

'This guy's like a ghost. I've tried every trick in the book to trace him but there is no-one of that name registered anywhere in Miami. Can you ask your friend on the murder squad if they got any forensics on the guy? Fingerprints or DNA; something that might identify him?'

'But they fished Saul out of the harbour. The DNA will have washed off. Where are they going to get fingerprints?'

Chuck ran his fingers through his hair. Grace had told him that Harlan Grimes had been in her office but that was weeks ago. Any prints would have obliterated by the cleaners. On the other hand, Helena Taggart's house had a layer of dust an inch thick. Maybe Grimes had left his prints on Saul's desk? Helena probably hadn't been in there since.

'What if I could tell them where to go?'

'The Taggarts' house?'

'Exactly.'

'But why don't you tell the police where to look.'

'I may have been one of the last people to see Saul and I don't want them getting funny ideas.'

'What will I tell them?'

'Someone gave an anonymous tip to the coroner's office?'

Gina sighed.

'You are such a massive pain in the ass.'

'But you love me anyway.'

'You owe me dinner. And no burgers this time.'

The screen went blank and Chuck stared at it for a while before loading up a blank spreadsheet. He wrote a list of the astronauts who were still alive in the left-hand column and made some preliminary headings along the top: location, nationality, profession, skillset, and, after a delay, motive. He filled most of the cells without any problem using his experience as a sometime space correspondent. But the column with motive remained empty. Then he added Harland Grimes and A.N. other to his list of suspects.

Despite brainstorming for hours, he couldn't imagine why anyone would want to kill the astronauts. Then he added Serena Hampton and Wayne Odoyu to the left-hand column and made another heading at the top; Murdered By. He filled in the cell at the intersection of Serena Hampton and his new column with the name, Harlan Grimes.

Then he considered the possibility Wayne Odoyu had been killed by him too. *But why? What did they have in common?* Of course. He had forgotten Wayne had been in the science officer's pod when he had been murdered. So, someone had targeted the science officers on the Mission. It didn't make any sense yet. Chuck needed more clues. He took a beer out of the fridge and leaned back in his chair, feeling it bite as the cold liquid invaded his stomach.

The beer relaxed him and his mind came into focus. W*hy was Harlan Grimes reporting to Noah van Horn?* As bizarre as it seemed, no matter how Chuck looked at the information he had so far, the CNP could not be eliminated. They were hardly a criminal organisation. Their high political profile made it difficult to believe they would be murdering astronauts without motive. And Noah van Horn ran the centre for ethics, which was kind of ironic given that he had been caught embezzling party funds a few years back.

Chuck's next move became crystal clear. He needed to speak to Noah van Horn, and Grace would have to play dumb. After all, he was trying to save her sister, Hattie. He picked up his phone and sent her a message warning her of his intention. And then he opened another beer and made a list of questions to ask Noah van Horn.

Noah van Horn greeted Chuck with an enthusiastic handshake, his cheeks wobbling with emotion.

'Mr Gomez? It's a pleasure to meet you. I really enjoy your articles in Space Monthly. You have such a witty way with words.'

'You read Space Monthly?' said Chuck, before he could stop himself. 'Thank you. I try.'

Van Horn coughed.

'Of course,' he said. 'It's part of my job to spy on the enemy.'

Was he joking? Chuck ran a shrewd glance over the smug corpulent young man opposite him. Somewhere in there, is a handsome Star Trek Fan, trapped in layers of propaganda.

'Naturally,' he said, and waited.

As he had guessed, Van Horn couldn't tolerate a silence.

'What can I do for you?' said Van Horn, interlacing his fat fingers and flexing them. 'I'm rather hoping for a flattering profile to get me back into politics.'

'And I'm sure I can oblige,' said Chuck. 'Next time. Actually, I have some questions for you about a man I'm trying to locate. My sources tell me you are in contact?'

'They do?' said Van Horn, his eyes widening. 'Would you like a cup of coffee?'

'Sure. Black, two sugars.'

'Ms Dos Reis, can you bring us in come coffee, please?'

Chuck pretended to have forgotten his unanswered question and looked around the room, taking in the opulent fittings.

'That's an amazing icon,' he said, pointing. 'South American, isn't it?'

'Colombian. Yes, it's magnificent. Are you from there?'

'My parents came to Miami from Ecuador but I'm a native, through and through.'

'One set of my grandparents were Dutch,' said van Horn.

'Makes sense,' said Chuck.

152

The door opened and Grace shuffled in with a tray. Without raising her eyes, she placed a coffee in front of Chuck and offered him sugar.

'Ms Dos Reis is Cuban,' said Van Horn.

'Oh, really?' said Chuck. 'That's nice.'

He could feel Van Horn's eyes boring into him as he stirred his coffee.

'Is that all Mr Van Horn?' said Grace.

Chuck noticed her hand trembling. Hold it together there, Gracie girl.

'Thank you. Now, where were we?'

'I need to find a man called Harlan Grimes,' said Chuck.

Van Horn took a large sip of his coffee which scalded the back of his throat. Tears came to his eyes as he choked.

'Who?' he said, avoiding Chuck's inquiring glance.

'Harlan Grimes. He's murdered at least three people that I know of, and I don't think he's finished yet.'

Van Horn went pale and started to pick at his nails.

'And you think I can help?'

'I think someone is trying to sabotage the Mars Mission. And the CNP are a prime suspect.'

'That's libel,' said Van Horn, reddening. 'You have no proof. And I have never met this Grimes character.'

'Please,' said Chuck. 'More people will die.'

Van Horn staggered to his feet.

'I'd like you to leave,' he said. 'Now.'

Chuck stayed in his chair and sipped his coffee. He sighed and stirred it again as if he could get more sweetness from the long-dissolved sugar. Van Horn, who wasn't used to people ignoring his orders, wavered, and then flopped back into his seat.

'Do you really believe in God??' said Chuck, frowning.

'What sort of question is that?' Van Horn spluttered, and shook his head. 'Of course I do.'

153

'So do I, as it happens,' said Chuck. 'But we tend to follow the Ten Commandments where possible in the Catholic church.'

Van Horn froze, a plump rabbit in the proverbial headlights.

'And I don't?' he said.

'Murder,' said Chuck. 'The deadliest sin. Aren't you afraid to go to hell?'

'Me? I haven't killed anyone.'

'I'm sure that's true. But you know someone who has.'

Van Horn took a deep breath and inflated his chest, pointing his chubby finger at Chuck.

'If this Grimes person has killed anyone, he will be judged for it.'

'And what if he plans to kill more innocent people?'

Van Horn's jaw worked and sweat broke out on his brow.

'It's nothing to do with me,' he said, and pressed the intercom. 'Ms Dos Reis? Mr Gomez is leaving. Can you show him out please?'

Chuck stood up.

'I'll be back,' he said. 'Please, just a contact number. He'll never know it was you.'

'Goodbye Mr Gomez.'

Chuck filed out past Grace. He shook his head at her and her face fell. Another dead end? Van Horn had lacked certainty. He'd give him a while to stew on the knowledge that Chuck was on to him and then he'd try again.

Chapter 24

H attie's first days on Mars were not filled the way she had imagined. She stared out of the narrow windows across the silent plain and past the Krusty farm of ten kilowatt nuclear reactors which provided power for the habitats, laboratories, Moxie, and ice melting plants, and the Starship construction equipment such as the 3-D printer. The reactor farm looked like a field of strange alien flowers with its radiators unfolded like metal blooms.

The Krusty reactors were the brainchild of NASA scientist Dr David Poston. When it became obvious that solar panels would be redundant in Mars due to the lack of sunlight and the vast weight of panels needed to power a settlement, Dr Poston had worked with a team to harness small-scale nuclear power. The reactor cores contained a cylinder of enriched uranium surrounded by a beryllium oxide reflector. They were activated by removing single rods of boron carbide, which acted as thermostats to regulate the function of the generator. The fission reaction produced heat which was delivered by heat pipes to power generators known as Stirling converters which were kept cool by the radiator which opened like a steel bloom at the top of the unit.

Hattie longed to jump in a rover and explore the land beyond the Krusty farm, but the job of preparing the habitat for their stay seemed endless. While Bret communicated with NASA and organised the arrival of the Starship, Yu and Hattie got to work unloading the pallets.

'You'd think they'd have put labels on this stuff,' said Yu, slipping a knife under the lid of a cardboard box. 'How are we supposed to find anything?'

'I guess they had more important things to do,' said Hattie. 'Anyway, it's like Christmas. And I love unwrapping presents.'

'Now you put it like that,' said Yu, grinning and holding a teapot in the air. 'I always wanted one of these.'

It soon became apparent that the first pallet contained the kitchen equipment and workstations for the first floor. But they could not find any food. Since they had brought sufficient for a week with them in the rover, and the Starship would soon be landing, Bret kept them on full rations for the time being.

'There's no point starving,' he said.

Hattie loved having constant and reliable power in the habitat, which had been named Homer, following the tradition of using names from the famous cartoon. It meant that she could shower in hot water and watch movies on her all-in-one without feeling guilty. It would also be the best way of ensuring that the hydroponic greenhouse would protect the plant-life they had brought with them to Mars. Now that Wayne had died, she and Yu would be helping Ellie with the project. The robots had almost completed construction of the greenhouse habitat and she couldn't wait to start planting fresh vegetables. Yu's clinic occupied the ground level of Marge, the other completed habitat. Bret had allowed Yu to unpack some essential medical supplies but the rest sat on a pallet on the floor below, waiting to be unloaded. Hattie had made a start on the other pallet containing household essentials.

On the third day, Chad and Scotty prepared the Starship for entry into Mars's thin atmosphere. The land-based crew became solemn with unspoken worries as Chad and Bret reviewed the protocols for landing. The Starship would land in automatic mode using identical criteria to the other four successful landings. Neither the crew on board, nor those already on Mars could do anything to affect the result.

As the time for the landing drew close, Yu, Bret and Hattie suited up and left Homer in the rover. The odd bullet-shaped vehicle nosed its way through the dunes and stopped on a ridge overlooking the plain where the four other Starships had landed.

'It will look even more like Manhattan now,' said Hattie.

'Or Gardens by the Bay in Singapore. Those Krusty units are like mini-Supertrees,' said Yu.

'I'd like to take my wife on honeymoon there,' said Bret.

'As if anyone would marry you,' said Hattie.

As evening approached, the external microphone picked up a muffled sound like large sails flapping.

'The wind has picked up,' said Bret. 'But it won't affect the landing.'

'Bret, are you receiving me?' said Chad.

'Loud and clear, buddy.'

'We're about to enter the atmosphere, and should be with you in seven minutes.'

'Copy and good luck. We're putting the champagne on ice.'

Hattie held her breath and shut her eyes.

'Breath, Hattie,' said Yu. 'You can't do that for seven minutes.'

Hattie let the air flow into her mask and gave him a rueful grin.

'I can hold my breath for three minutes, you know,' she said.

'Seriously?' said Bret. 'I don't believe you.'

'Honestly,' said Hattie. 'I practiced for years. My sister and I used to have competitions. We were so stubborn, my mother used to find us turning blue.'

'You're still stubborn,' said Yu. 'I had a mule who stalled less than you do.'

'I don't believe you,' said Hattie. 'Anyway, I like to call it perseverance.'

'That's enough guys,' said Bret. 'Let's just relax. They'll be here in a minute.'

Behind their rover, a couple of robot-driven ones had pulled up and were waiting. Bret, Hattie and Yu gazed upwards through the glass dome of the rover and suddenly, the enormous bulk of the Starship appeared, engines on full thrust as it righted itself and sank towards the ground. Even on Mars, the roar of the engines almost deafened them. Massive clouds of dust rose up and enveloped the craft as it neared its landing place. Some of the dust reached their rover and clouded the window screen which automatically cleaned itself with a brush. As the dust settled, the shape of the Starship became clear in the gloom.

'The eagle has landed,' said Bret.

'Starship to mission crew,' said Chad. 'Are you receiving me?'

'We copy you, Chad. Is everyone okay?'

'Absolutely. Give us an hour to run through the protocols and we'll come down on the lift.'

'Do you want us to wait?'

'No, don't bother. The robots will bring us to the habitats. They sound fantastic.'

'They are. We'll go home and cook some dinner. I'm afraid its space rations only, until we can locate the food.'

'We'll bring more with us. See you guys soon.'

Chapter 25

When the remaining crew members arrived at the central hub, Hattie, Yu and Bret had already removed their space suits and were waiting there for them. Ellie emerged first from the airlock, squealing in delight as she took off her helmet. She rushed towards Hattie with her arms out. Bret put up his arm to stop her.

'Take off your spacesuit first,' he said. 'You'll contaminate her and the habs.'

Ellie stopped short of Hattie and winked at her. Then she stepped into the console which removed her gloves, suit and boots.

'Now?' she said.

Bret rolled his eyes. Ellie squealed again and wrapped an embarrassed Hattie in a warm hug.

'We're really here,' she said. 'Isn't it amazing? I can't believe we got here in one piece.'

Chad, Scotty and Mo entered to less effusive displays of affection. Bret shook their hands with gusto, pumping them up and down as if he wanted to extract water from a well. Hattie gave them al a quick hug, lingering just an extra second in Scotty's embrace. Did he notice? He beamed at her, but then he beamed at everyone. She had never seen him lose his cool. He behaved as if travelling to Mars was something he did all the time, never appearing flustered or defeated. No wonder I've got a crush on him.

Yu on the other hand, seemed bemused. He cracked a shy smile as he welcomed the crew and then hung back, uncertain while everyone talked about the landing and the red dust and the robots. After a while, when everyone had taken off their suits and calmed down a little, Bret held up his hands for silence.

'Right,' he said. 'Now we're all here. We need to assign people to their habitats. There are two complete residential habs ready. At present we are all living in Homer—'

'Homer?' said Chad. 'Like the Simpsons?'

'Yes. The NASA scientists who named the kilopower farm Krusty, have continued the theme. Anyway, as I was saying, we have been living in Homer for convenience but now we are all here...'

He pulled out his all-in-one and tapped the screen.

'Hmm, yes, since the clinic is in Marge, it makes sense for Yu to be there. Hattie, Mo and Scotty, can you move over there too? Chad and Ellie, you're with me in Homer.'

Ellie's hand shot up.

'I'd like to be in Marge too. I'll be working with Hattie most of the time so it makes sense for us to be in the same building.'

Brad sighed.

'Okay. Scotty, can you come with me and Chad? It seems we'll have a bachelors' pad.'

'Party on,' said Chad, trying to high five Scotty who pretended not to notice.

Crestfallen, Hattie tried to think of a burning reason why Mo should swap instead of Scotty. She waited for him to suggest it, since he always went on and on about being one of the boys, but he just nodded.

'Okay then, let's get settled in. Can the people without suits on evacuate the hub so Chad can empty the rovers more efficiently?'

Once the supplies were placed in the central hub, Bret pressurised it again and all the astronauts could circulate

160

without their suits. Hattie and Scotty got into the lift to travel to the top floor of Homer. He grimaced at her.

'That didn't go the way I'd planned,' he said. 'I'd much prefer to be in Marge with the girls.'

'Why didn't Mo offer to share with Bret and Chad? He's a perfect companion for the frat twins.'

'Search me. Maybe he fancies one of you.'

Scotty winked at her. Does he know? Hattie wanted to melt into his arms but the doors opened to reveal Chad emptying Hattie's belongings into a box.

'Hey, couldn't you have waited two minutes?' said Hattie.

'I wanted to be sure to get the pod nearest the restrooms because my stomach's still giving me trouble. Anyway, we'll be living together for five months so we'll have no secrets.'

He dangled a piece of Hattie's underwear in front of her face.

'Honestly, Chad, did you time travel from the Stone age?' said Scotty.

Hattie grabbed her underwear and dropped it into the box.

'And what's this?' said Chad, waving the model of Buzz Lightyear in the air.

'Put that down,' said Hattie. 'You've no right to touch my things.'

Her voice caught in her throat and she tried to snatch the figure. Chad held it just above her head, laughing at her attempts.

'Dammit,' said Bret, stepping out of the lift. 'Put that down and let Hattie finish moving her stuff.'

Hattie entered her sleeping pod and checked all the shelves and drawers, taking her remaining items out and putting them in the box.

'Thanks, Bret,' she said, as he held the lift door for her.

'Why does she have a stupid doll anyway?' said Chad. 'How old is she?'

161

Hattie clutched the box closer. Scotty jumped into the lift with her. Their shoulders rubbed together in the confined space.

'He doesn't mean anything by it. He was abandoned as a baby and brought up by Neanderthals,' said Scotty. 'I won't let him bully you.'

'And what makes you think I will?' said Hattie. 'I'm just keeping my head down until we get settled in. There's no point fighting over dumb stuff.'

'Why did you bring Buzz Lightyear to Mars with you?' said Scotty.

'He's a present from my sister, and my reminder someone loves me.'

'Everyone will love you when they get to know you better. I already do.'

The lift doors opened and they stepped out into the wet lab where the new supplies from the Starship had been stockpiled.

'I'm going to take these to the kitchen,' said Scotty. 'See you later.'

Hattie floated to the Marge habitat with his words ringing in her ears. *I already do.* She was still smiling when she arrived at the sleeping quarters carrying her box. Ellie came bounding up to her and grabbed Buzz Lightyear from the top of it.

'Wow, where did you get this?' she said. 'It's a genuine antique.'

She held it in the air and swooped Buzz around the room making engine noises. Hattie put down the box and held out her hand.

'Please, give it back to me.'

'Lighten up. I won't break it. Hey, what's this?'

The compartment in the base had opened up and a note floated to the ground. Ellie bent over and picked it up. Seeing the panic in Hattie's eyes, she waved it in front of her face.

'What's this then?' she said.

'Nothing. Give it back.'

162

But Ellie unfolded the note and read it, her lips moving.

'Who's Grace?' she said. 'Is she your girlfriend?'

'No and I'd rather you didn't touch my stuff without asking me first.'

Ellie handed back the figure and the note.

'Sorry, I didn't mean to upset you. To infinity and beyond? That sounds like a girlfriend to me.'

'Not that it's any of your business, but Grace is my sister.'

'Your sister? They didn't tell me you had a sister.'

'Well, I do. And you shouldn't read people's private notes.'

'I'm sorry. I can't help being nosey. I love Buzz too. The compartment just sprung open. Forgive me?'

Hattie sighed.

'I guess so.'

'You're so lucky to have a sister. I only have brothers and they're the worst. How come Grace is a secret?'

'She's not. But she works for someone who is against space travel so she hasn't told them about me or our Dad. They'll definitely fire her.'

Ellie frowned.

'Oh, and who does she work for?'

'I can't tell you.'

'Come on. We're on Mars. Who am I gonna tell? The man on the moon?'

Hattie put the note back into the compartment and placed Buzz on top of the box. She sighed.

'The CNP. She works as a PA for some guy in there. They're fanatically against this whole trip. My Dad says they tried to sabotage it using the media.'

Ellie's eyes widened.

'No wonder you're shielding her. That could go horribly wrong if they found out.'

'Don't tell anyone, please. I shouldn't be telling you.'

'My lips are sealed. We are going to be even closer friends, now I know your secret.'

163

'Tell me one of yours,' said Hattie.

Ellie giggled and looked away.

'I've got a crush on Bret,' she said.

'You haven't.'

'I have. I like his All-American-Hero vibe. He's like Captain America.'

'You mean he's plastic?'

'So speaks the girl who cuddles up to Buzz Lightyear. Get unpacked and let's curl up and watch a movie. This whole Mars thing is weirding me out. I need to pretend I'm back at home on a Saturday night.'

'You stay in on a Saturday? No wonder you like Bret. All you need is a pinafore and some curlers.'

'That's what you think.'

Chapter 26

Despite Hattie's longing to collect the samples from Hephaestus Rupes, where the Perseverance rover had left them for collection, the need for fresh food to supplement their diet took priority over EVAs. Wayne's death, and the consequent lack of manpower, forced her to spend her first weeks on Mars inside the greenhouse with Ellie.

The greenhouse was another Marsha structure, shaped like a fat shark fin containing both conventional and aquaponic growing systems, in addition to space devoted to crop research studies. Climate controlled through a propane heater and swamp cooler; it had been designed with broad spectrum grow lights for additional light during the winter months.

Hattie had swallowed her disappointment and dedicated her time to helping Ellie to plant the seeds inside small rock-fibre cubes made from a combination of Mars regolith and coconut husk transported to the planet in sacks by one of the Starships. Mo and Yu helped to wire the habitat for the LED lighting and to set the timers for a nine-hour night and fifteen-hour day cycle.

'Why don't we just leave the lights on twenty-four-seven?' said Hattie. 'Surely the lettuces would grow faster?'

'Too much light isn't good for them. Their leaves will toughen and turn bitter, and the sap will become milky. They'll send up a seed stem too,' said Ellie. 'They'll be full sized in a month and we can harvest a few lettuces before then.'

'I never thought I'd be so desperate for lettuce. I know how rabbits feel.'

'I'm planting cherry tomatoes, red and chilli peppers, radishes and basil as well. They take a little longer but they'll be worth it. And the yields will be great as there are no insects to eat them, or rabbits.'

'Maybe there are some advantages to living in the death zone,' said Hattie.

'Don't call it that,' said Ellie, frowning.

'Hey, I was kidding,' said Hattie.

'Now for the disgusting part. We need nutrients to grow the vegetables so we'll use our own sewage.'

'Gross,' said Hattie.

'It's not that bad. The water has already been siphoned off from the septic tanks and cleaned with UV light. It will be kept inside the tanks under the hydroponic towers and it will circulate inside without coming out again.'

'Where are the towers?'

'Bret said the robots will bring them over today. We can set them up, and now the seedlings have emerged, we can plant them in the growth cavities of the tower. Then, we just sit back and wait.'

'You can wait. I'm going to take a rover and collect the Perseverance samples.'

'Can I come with you?'

'I think Bret wanted to come, but he may be too busy. Let's ask him when we're set up here. These seeds aren't going to plant themselves.'

The women worked steadily until lunchtime and then returned to Homer through the tunnels. The whole crew had assembled for an update by Scotty on the progress of propellant production and other matters.

166

Hattie helped herself to a serving of reconstituted curry and rice, and sat beside Ellie on the couch.

Scotty wiped his mouth and put his plate down on the table. His tight jaw muscles spoke volumes.

'We've got problems,' he said. 'The Moxie that landed from the launch during the last Hohmann window, hasn't been functioning correctly, and the supply of oxygen and methane to the tanks has been minimal.'

'Are we going to suffocate?' said Mo.

'No, but if we don't find a solution, we will be stuck here for years because we won't have enough fuel to leave the planet in the Starship.'

'I thought we had three Moxies in total,' said Bret.

'We do, or should I say did. One of the Moxies was on the Starship that disappeared. The other came with us. I am in the process of setting it up but we can't make fuel fast enough to leave the planet in five hundred days.'

'Can't they send a Starship to collect us?' said Hattie.

'Duh. It won't have fuel to take off either,' said Chad.

'But it could send a module to take us off the surface,' said Hattie, rolling her eyes. 'We could make enough propellant for that.'

'Now, that sounds good,' said Scotty. 'But it would have to make two trips, so I need to calculate how many litres of oxygen and methane we would need to refill it twice.'

'Alternatively, they could send a bigger module like a Dragon capsule and we could all cram in,' said Hattie. 'It takes seven passengers for short trips.'

'You're right. There are ways out of our dilemma,' said Scotty. 'But I thought it best to alert you so we can start working on several right now. I'll alert NASA so the boffins there can concentrate on it.'

'How about the Rassors? Are they managing to dig the ice out from under the regolith?' said Bret.

'The whats?' said Ellie.

'The Rassors. They have buckets at both ends to anchor them to the Earth when they dig. If they only had one bucket, they couldn't get traction in this gravity.'

167

'Duh,' said Chad. 'You should know that.'

'I do know. I just forgot their name.'

'Honestly, Chad. You need to stop pointing out everyone's failings and start working for the team. You've been behaving like a child since Serena died. Please get with the programme,' said Bret.

Chad swallowed and shrugged.

'Sorry, Ellie,' he said. 'Bret's right. I have been a jerk to everyone. I promise to do better.'

'We're all in this together, said Ellie.

'Good. Let's go out to the quarry and check on the diggings, Scotty,' said Bret.

'Can I come too?' said Ellie. 'We're finished for the time being in the greenhouse. Mother Nature has to get working on the seeds now.'

'What about me?' said Hattie.

'You can help Chad to finish setting up the wet lab. Yu is working on the clinic but he's self-sufficient over there.'

Chad sighed.

'Great,' said Hattie, hiding her dismay. *Do you think you're the only one who's unhappy? I'd rather eat broken glass.*

After lunch had been cleared away, Scotty, Bret and Ellie suited up and disappeared into the airlock, Yu went back to his clinic in Marge, and Mo used the dry lab upstairs in Homer to work on solutions to the Moxie dilemma. Hattie and Chad stood looking at the chaos in the wet lab on the ground floor, both fighting their dislike of each other.

'It's like a scene from The Defiant Ones,' said Hattie.

'The what?' said Chad

'An old movie from the nineteen-fifties.'

Chad laughed.

'You look twelve but you've seen movies that are nearly a century old.'

He shuffled his feet and stared at the ground, his jaw muscle working. She waited, and, to her surprise, he raised his head and looked her in the eye.

'Hey, do you want to call a truce? I've been taking out my grief about Serena on you too, and I apologise.'

Hattie grinned.

'What a relief. Truce agreed. But you have to show me how to service the Rassors, and the Moxies.'

'That's some price. I'm not sure I can do that.'

Hattie held out her hand.

'Do we have a deal or not,' she said.

Chad grabbed it and squeezed hard.

'Sure, why not? Less work for me.'

He grimaced.

'Have you changed your mind?' said Hattie.

'No, it's my stomach again. Dammit.'

'Has Yu examined you?'

Chad avoided her inquiring glance.

'I haven't told him, but I will. It's getting worse.'

'So that's why you wanted the sleeping cabin beside the toilets? You should have said.'

'I was embarrassed.'

Hattie punched his arm.

'We'll be living together for five months, so we'll have no secrets,' she said.

'Very funny. I already apologised. Let's get on with it.'

They worked steadily for a couple of hours, and then Chad bent double groaning.

'Are you all right?' said Hattie.

'I have terrible cramps. I've got to go up to the bathroom. Can you go and find Yu?'

'Can't you make it to the clinic? It will be easier if you have to stay there after he examines you.'

'I can try.'

Chad groaned again.

'Put your arm around my shoulder,' said Hattie.

Almost fainting from pain, Chad leant on Hattie as she helped him down the tunnel into the central hub and on into the one leading to Marge. They were halfway along to the habitat when Chad let out a gasp and fell to the floor. Hattie tried to rouse him but Chad did not move. His skin had turned yellow, and his breathing sounded raspy. She rolled him on his side and put her jacket under his head. Then she checked his airways. They were clear but his breaths were shallow and laboured.

What on Earth could be wrong with him?

Hattie jumped up and ran to the habitat, sprinting up the stairs to the clinic.

'Yu, come quick. It's Chad. He's really ill.'

'Where is he?'

'In the tunnel. I tried to bring him here, but he collapsed and he's too awkward for me to carry in that small space.'

'I'll bring the stretcher. We can lie him on that and take him to the clinic in the lift.'

They ran back down the tunnel. Chad lay on the floor, his head still on Hattie's jacket. His eyes were wide open, as if in shock.

'Chad? Oh my God,' said Hattie. 'Is he dead?'

'Let me check,' said Yu.

Yu check Chad's pulse, and shook his head. Then he examined Chad's eyelids and his tongue. Hattie slid to the floor.

'No,' she whispered.

Yu sat down beside her.

'I'm afraid he's gone,' he said.

'But he can't be,' said Hattie. 'He's so young and strong. What happened?'

'I don't know,' said Yu, rubbing his chin. 'How long has this been going on?'

'He had an attack of diarrhoea when we took off in the module. Surely that didn't kill him.'

'It's the origin of the cramps that worries me. He may have been poisoned.'

'But how?'

'I don't know, but I think it's deliberate. It can't be a coincidence after Serena and Wayne. I examined Serena, you know, after she died. I wasn't supposed to but I managed to sneak into her room. She had doubled over in bed like she had stomach cramps, and her tongue had gone the same yellow colour as Chad's.'

'But didn't she die of a heart attack?'

'Maybe not.'

Hattie grasped his arm.

'You mean someone's trying to kill us all?'

'Yes. And worse than that, you and I are being framed.'

Chapter 27

H attie and Yu cleaned Chad's body and dressed him in a new uniform.

'He looks even more like Ken, now he's dead,' said Yu.

'I think Barbie dumped him thirty years ago,' said Hattie. 'What are we going to do when the others return? They'll never believe us.'

'They might if we had the results of Serena's autopsy,' said Yu.

'But how do we get that?'

'Ask your father. He must suspect something's wrong by now. And with Chad dying, he'll be certain.'

'My sister sent me a note when we took off from the Starship in the module. I've been so busy I never reread it. Maybe she knows something. We could ask her.'

Hattie took out her all -in-one and scrolled back to the message. She gasped.

'What?' said Yu.

'Oh my God. I didn't notice before. We were taking off and the module got stuck and I received the message but I didn't get a chance to read it properly and then we crash-landed and—'

'What does it say?' said Yu, grabbing her arm.

'It says *I'm sure everyone is doing their utmost to keep you all safe up there. Remember the astronaut deaths were both accidents. Love you. Gracefool...*'

'And?'

'She signed it Gracefool, but I didn't notice at the time.'

'So?'

'It means she's lying. The opposite is true. It's a game we played as children. She knows the deaths were murder. That means my father does too. Why haven't they told us?'

'Perhaps they were afraid of who might see the message? Write to her.'

'And if whoever is killing us intercepts it? We don't know it's anyone in the crew. All the deaths were caused on Earth. What if they go after Grace?'

'I never thought of that, but we have to do something or Bret and the others will think we killed Chad, and Wayne.'

'I can send Grace a message and sign it with Harriet. She'll know it's a lie.'

'Do it now. Before they get back.'

Hattie made a picture with the message to Grace. *It read Everything's fine here. No problems with Mars crew. Chad's stomach ache was not fatal and he's livelier now. It was lucky Serena's autopsy didn't show problems or we would still be on Earth. Tell Dad. Lots of love Harriet.* She pressed send.

'Will that do the trick?'

'I hope so. My father will guess something's wrong. And when they hear from Bret that Chad is dead, he'll be sure. Until then we've got to persuade the others not to harm us.'

'Why would they do that?

'I know what I'd do, if I discovered someone planned to kill us.'

'But why are they doing this? And who are 'they'?'

'I don't know yet. Maybe Grace can find out. She's super smart.'

'Like you then. I can't believe this is happening to us,' said Yu. 'It's a nightmare beyond my imagination. My parents were so proud of me and now I may never go home.'

173

They covered Chad in a sheet and walked back to the central hub where they sat on the shower bench. The clunking sound of the airlock alerted them to the arrival of the others. Hattie bit her lip.

'Here they come,' she said.

'Wait for them to get into the suit consoles. They'll be trapped there while we explain. And let me do the talking.'

Bret, Scotty and Ellie entered the hub, jostling each other and giggling. They removed their helmets and backed into the suit consoles. Bret spotted Yu and Hattie and he frowned.

'What are you two doing here?' he said. 'Have you had another fight with Chad?'

'I'm afraid he's dead,' said Yu. 'I think he was poisoned.'

Bret's face reddened as he struggled to free himself from the console but could not.

'He can't be. This is a nightmare. How can you know?'

'He's been having stomach cramps since the launch party but he hadn't told anyone because he feared he'd be left behind on Earth.'

'He would've told me,' Bret said, shaking his head.

'I think he died of the same poison as Serena,' said Yu. 'Maybe he ate a piece of her sushi.'

'She died of a heart attack,' said Bret. 'No one ever mentioned poison to me.'

'It can't be a coincidence,' said Scotty, scratching his head. 'That you and Hattie were involved again. Like when Wayne died.'

'Are you crazy?' said Hattie. 'What about Mo? He's here too. What possible motive could we have? Yu only joined the crew a few months ago from China, and as for me—'

'You only joined because Serena died,' said Ellie.

'Are you saying I killed her too? I wasn't even living in staff quarters then.'

Scotty shook his head.

'It looks bad, Hats.'

174

Bret jumped out of the console.

'I'm going to alert NASA right away. Meanwhile, Yu and Hattie are confined to quarters in Marge. Ellie, I want you to move into Homer with us. Where's the body?'

'It's in the clinic,' said Yu.

'We need to put it into storage with Wayne's. Scotty, can you organise that?'

'But someone poisoned Serena,' said Hattie.

'Who did?' said Bret.

'I don't know,' said Hattie. 'But I asked my father to get her autopsied.'

'Didn't she die of heart failure,' said Ellie. 'They must have cremated her by now.'

'My sister doesn't think so,' said Hattie. 'She sent me a warning message.'

'When was that?' said Bret. 'You didn't say anything to me.'

'It was in code. I didn't notice at the time. I—'

'Is that the same sister who works for the Christian National Party,' said Ellie. 'I'd say you've got a pretty good motive for sabotaging the trip.'

Hattie turned to stare at Ellie, her mouth open in shock.

'How could you?' she said. 'I thought we were friends.'

'I'm sorry,' said Ellie. 'My priority is to keep us alive. And it seems yours is the opposite.'

Bret took Hattie and Yu back into the Marge habitat and locked them in despite their protests. Then he turned to Scotty.

'It seems we were wrong after all,' he said.

'What are we going to do with them?' said Scotty.

'I'll ask NASA.'

Chapter 28

D espite the hour, Chuck, who had been asleep when he received the emergency call, had thrown on his clothes and driven straight over to NASA. The stars still twinkled in the sky as he tried, unsuccessfully, to persuade his car to break the speed limit. He swore and flicked through the updates on his all-in-one, snorting as he scrolled past conspiracy theories about the Mars Mission and other scientific truths. He subscribed to these sites in order to keep tabs on them, but sometimes he wished he could turn off the constant bombardment. There was no mention of any update from Mars.

He stopped outside the administration building and the security guard ushered him in, looking up and down the street before opening the door. *It seems conspiracy theories are catching.* Once upstairs, Fredericks appeared in the passageway and let Chuck into his office, his jaw tight and purple bags under his eyes. He shut the door after checking that nobody loitered in the passage outside.

'Where's the fire?' said Chuck.

'We've lost another astronaut.'

'When you say lost—'

'Dead. Chad Farrant. He's dropped dead with stomach cramps.'

'Stomach cramps?'

'Dr Chen Yu thinks he's been poisoned.'

'Like Serena?'

'Quite possibly at the same time. He may have eaten a piece of her sushi.'

'But why the delay in his reaction to the poison?'

'The pathologist tells me that the small amount and his enforced coma will have slowed down the action of the poison. From the minute he woke up, he was living on borrowed time.'

'What about the rest of the crew?'

'That's the problem. They've put Chen Yu and Hattie under house arrest because they were with Chad when he died.'

'But why?'

'Chen Yu and Hattie were the ones who discovered that Wayne had suffocated, and now Bret thinks they are responsible for both deaths.'

'But that's ridiculous,' said Chuck.

'We know that. I've only met Yu a couple of times but my Hattie had no reason to kill anyone. She can't even kill wasps, and she hates them.'

'How can I help?'

'Grace received a cryptic message from Hattie about Serena's autopsy report. Unfortunately, Serena's body was cremated months ago, but from what you told me, the report contained information about the cause.'

'Can't you ask for a copy?'

'I'm afraid it will disappear if we ask for it,' said Fredericks. 'Anyone who can reach out and kill people on a craft in outer space has penetrated NASA's whole system. I wondered if your contact could still lay his hands on a copy? We need to convince the remaining crew members of Hattie and Yu's innocence before it's too late.'

'What are you proposing?'

Fredericks sighed.

'I can't believe I'm saying this, but can you ask your source to get a copy of the report?'

Chuck raised his eyebrows.

'You want us to steal it?'

'Not exactly, just clone it. Look, I know it's a lot to ask. But at least one of my daughters is in danger, and the other one is working incognito in an organisation linked to the murderer. How would you feel?'

'I don't know but I'm worried about them too. Should Grace resign?'

'I tried to make her leave but she thinks she may be able to pick up more information if she stays.'

Chuck sighed.

'I'll try but it will cost me.'

'How much? I don't mind paying.'

'My source takes payment in kind. I'll deal with it.'

'We need to act before the news of Chad's death leaks out.'

'You mean tonight? Wow, okay, let me call her.'

'It's a woman? I don't want to put her in danger.'

'Danger's her middle name. That and commitment.'

Chuck flicked through his all-in-one and tapped on Gina's photo, stopping to admire her red curls and cheeky smile. He couldn't be sure if he hoped she had taken a sleeping pill or not. The call went through and after two or three tones, her furious face appeared on the screen.

'This better be good,' she said. 'Or I'm going to take out a contract on you.'

'Hey, sweetness. Sorry to wake you from your beauty sleep, but we have a mission of the utmost importance to perform.'

'Are you talking about sex again. Because if you are, it will be the last thing you do, you no-good-ratfink.'

'I'm serious. It's a matter of life or death. Please. Don't cut off the call. People may die.'

Gina narrowed her eyes.

'Is this about Serena Hampton again?'

'Yes, but it's not us that's in danger this time, it's the astronauts. Another one has died.'

'Hold the phone.'

Gina's face disappeared from the screen and Chuck could hear her scrabbling about in her bedroom. She reappeared after several minutes with her hair tied back, dressed in a tracksuit.

'Okay, I'm awake now,' she said. 'I'm guessing it's an emergency?'

'You're the best,' said Chuck. 'I'll pick you up in twenty minutes.'

'Are you sure about this?' said Fredericks, after Chuck cut off the call.

'As long as our deal about exclusives holds, I'm in for the long haul,' said Chuck.

'My daughters' lives may be at stake. If you can copy the report, I'll make you the official chronicler of the Mars Mission. You can have an exclusive with the grieving parents too, but you may have to hold off on Chad's mother for a few weeks.'

'It's a deal. My contact can get us into the system and after that it's child's play.'

Chuck's bravado evaporated on the journey to Gina's house, but reinflated as she swept into his car in a cloud of perfume and hair.

'You smell fantastic,' he said.

'In case I get arrested,' said Gina. 'I need to be able to seduce the cop.'

'We won't get arrested. It's just a quick search through the files in the coroner's office and we'll be out of there.'

'Let's hope you're right. I don't know why I agreed to this.'

'We'll be saving people's lives. And I promise to give you exclusive access for at least six months.'

Gina laughed and poked his stomach.

'All this, just for me? What a privilege.'

Chuck blushed.

'I've been working out, you know.'

'Hmm. Not much.'

179

Chuck pretended to sulk but in fact enjoyed being squashed up next to his favourite fireball. They soon arrived at police headquarters and pulled up to the door.

'Okay, we're here. Are you sure you can get in?'

'No, problem. We're just going to waltz through the main entrance. There are no set hours for investigations. We can take the lift to the coroner's floor in the basement.'

Despite Chuck's reluctance, Gina's perfume did the trick, that, and the wink she gave to the security guard. He opened the door for them with a flourish.

'Good evening, Ms Gina.'

'Good evening, George. All well I hope?'

'All's quite around here tonight. Did you forget something?'

'Yes, I just need to clone a couple of files for a press conference. This is Chuck Gomez, who writes crime articles. Is it okay if he comes in with me for a minute.'

'I don't know about that, I... Hey, wait! I recognise you, Mr Gomez. I love your articles about the astronauts.'

'Thanks, Fred. I do my best.'

'Don't touch anything in there.'

'I wouldn't dream of it.'

Gina pulled Chuck's arm.

'Let's go then,' she said, 'Time's a wasting.'

They got into the lift and travelled down a floor.

'Let's hope Fred isn't watching us on his panel,' said Gina.

'I think he had a telenovela on his security screen,' said Chuck. 'There's not a lot of action this time of night.'

The lift shuddered as it descended to the coroner's floor. Chuck wondered how they would explain themselves if it got stuck between floors. His meeting with Saul Taggart, and then his later visit to Saul's widow, had marked Chuck out as a person in interest in Saul's murder. A particularly zealous junior detective sergeant had interrogated him for hours without getting anywhere. Gina had roared with laughter when he related the details to her.

'Well, you are kind of shady looking,' she said, making him cross, as he was going for the look of a mysterious dark stranger.

The eerie glow of background LED lighting illuminated the corridor to the coroner's door, which opened without a fight.

'Shouldn't it be locked,' hissed Chuck. 'I thought this would be trickier.'

Gina shrugged.

'Maybe he forgot. He is getting on in years.'

They crept into the office of his assistant and then Gina spotted the light under the door. She put her hand over Chuck's mouth and pointed. His eyes widened and he opened his palms in question. Gina crept behind the assistant's desk and started the screen. She keyed in a password and entered the system.

'Don't ask,' she whispered. 'It's so we can see what they 're doing in there.'

The screen came on and Chuck gasped.

'It's Serena's autopsy report. Someone is altering it. What do we do?'

'The old one will still be stored on this computer until the new one is saved. I hope I'm in time.'

Gina's fingers flew over the screen opening and closing folders at a speed even Chuck couldn't follow.

'Okay, get ready to clone,' she said.

Chuck tried to establish a connection to the screen, but the battery of his all-in-one had conked out. He shook it.

'Damn. Not now.'

Gina rolled her eyes at him. He looked around in desperation and spotted a cable hanging from the back of the screen and stuck it into the all-in-one. *Thank goodness for universal connections – now that qualified as civilization.*

'Now,' said Gina, who had not appreciated Chuck's manoeuvres. 'It's now or never. Clone it.'

'Done,' said Chuck.

Gina sighed with relief and shut down the screen. She examined Chuck, who hyperventilated with anxiety. She opened her mouth to comment when the sound of someone moving around inside emanated from the office. The legs of a chair scraped across the floor.

'Hide,' hissed Gina, and they both dove under the desk. Chuck had Gina's rear-end in his face, a situation he would normally have enjoyed, but his blood ran cold as the door opened and the silhouette of a skinny man stood out in the light for a second before he walked swiftly to the door, locking it on his exit.

'Shit. We're locked in now,' said Chuck.

'No, we're not. Since the chief got locked in his office over the weekend during a power cut, all doors open from the inside. But we can't lock it.'

'They'll know someone came in.'

Gina gave Chuck a pitying glance.

'They'll know anyway. I used my passcode on the police computer. You'd better be right about this, or I'll be toast.'

'You're the one who told me Serena didn't die of a heart attack.'

'I didn't say that. I said someone told me to back off investigating it, if I knew what was good for me.'

Chuck shrugged.

'We'd better both be right then. A toaster has two slots.'

Chapter 29

T he door to Marge opened with a clunk and Bret stepped inside to find Hattie and Yu hard at work unloading the last pallet of medical supplies. Hattie looked up to see who it was but Yu kept his head down, muttering to himself.

'I received a message from NASA this morning,' said Bret. 'About Serena's autopsy report.'

Yu stood up with a box in his arms.

'And?' he said.

Bret swallowed.

'They say someone poisoned her, and that it's likely Chad died of a smaller dose of the same poison.'

Hattie and Yu waited.

'Look, I'm sorry, okay?' said Bret. 'I need to keep everyone safe. It's my duty. And you've got to admit, you two were in the wrong place at the wrong time.'

'Have you told the others?' said Yu.

'Yes, we'd like you to come to Homer and have coffee with us. We need a reset if we're to work together. Please.'

'I told you,' Hattie said. 'You didn't trust me. How can we work with you?'

'I don't see we have any choice,' said Yu. 'Let's have coffee with the others and see how it goes. We're all adults here and it did look bad.'

Hattie rolled her eyes. She and Yu followed Bret back into Homer and up into the kitchen. A smell of cookies wafted down the lift shaft and Hattie's mouth filled with saliva at the long-mourned treat. She tried not to look around for them as she entered the room. Ellie ran to Hattie and hugged her but she remained rigid.

'I'm so sorry,' she whispered. 'I baked cookies for you with my secret stash of cookie mix. You have Buzz but I have Betty.'

Hattie stepped back.

'You should never have mentioned Grace. I can't believe you did that.'

Ellie sighed and dropped her arms.

'I thought I was protecting the crew from a murderer. What would you have done?'

Hattie relented.

'The same I guess.'

'I'll get the cookies.'

Hattie glanced across at Yu and watched his features crease into a giant beam and Scotty shook his hand. *We've got this.* And then Scotty shuffled up to her, and she fought back tears which he wiped gently from her cheeks.

'Can you ever forgive me?' he said. 'I must have been mad to believe such a thing.'

'We would have been the dumbest killers in the history of murder,' said Yu. 'Both times making sure no one else could have done it.'

'Hmm. I hadn't thought of that,' said Mo. 'It could have been me last time though.'

He grinned and slapped Yu on the back.

'Ow,' said Yu. 'Why do you have to be such a jock? If you injure the doctor, who will cure you?'

'You haven't had much success yet,' said Mo.

'Okay, that's enough,' said Bret. 'I know it scarcely seems credible that we are down to six astronauts, so early in our stay on Mars, but NASA tells me they have good reason to believe that those responsible are on Earth and not among us. They are running a joint operation with the police to hunt down the killers of our fellow crew mates and have a prime suspect in their sights.'

'Do we know why they died?' said Yu. 'Why would anyone kill astronauts?'

'Not yet. But the police have several lines of inquiry.'

'But what about—'

'Look, we've still got serious problems here with making fuel and oxygen, never mind the looming shortage of food if we don't start growing some staples like sweet potatoes and yams. For the time being, I'd like you to finish transferring the seedlings into the towers and monitoring the light and carbon dioxide levels. It's vital that we understand how to maximise production.'

'Will I need an oxygen mask?' said Yu.

'I'm not sure, but wear one to be on the safe side,' said Ellie. 'I've increased the percentage of CO_2 quite a lot recently as plants are happy with much higher levels than we are.'

'Next,' said Bret. 'I'd like to get the Perseverance samples on site. After all, that is our main objective. Hattie and Ellie should go as soon as possible so we need to make a plan for the trip. Mo, can you work with them to establish the protocols and logistics?'

Hattie wanted to refuse but she had no good reason now that Ellie had apologised. And they were running out of crew. Anyway, her lifetime's ambition had edged closer and she couldn't wait to get a sample of Jezero delta sediment under her microscope.

'Have you had any success with that algorithm for the stromatolites?' she asked Mo.

'It's almost ready,' he said. 'I've been busy. But I'll get right on it when you and Ellie leave to collect the samples.'

'It should only be a day trip,' said Bret. 'Hephaestus Rupes is only 30 kilometres away.'

185

'We'll have to leave at first light,' said Hattie. 'I hope the heating works in the rover.'

'I can guarantee you a steady fifteen degrees,' said Scotty.

'That better be centigrade,' said Ellie.

Despite their rapprochement, Ellie did not move back into her room at Marge, so Hattie found herself sharing with Mo and Yu. Mo liked to cook and took over the kitchen. Yu raised an eyebrow at this anachronism.

'Mr Macho likes to wear an apron? Now that's weird.'

'Leave him alone,' said Hattie. 'I'd prefer you didn't cook. We don't want anyone else getting poisoned.'

Besides cooking, Mo spent most of his time holed up in his room 'working'. If anyone knocked on his door, he closed his personal laptop before opening it.

'What does he do in there?' said Hattie.

'Probably watches porn,' said Yu.

'Eu, I wish I hadn't asked.'

Despite their doubts, Mo emerged from his room the next day with a smug look on his face.

'I've done it,' he said. 'When you get back with Ellie, we'll try it out.'

'And what about our trip?'

'All set up. Scotty and Bret will load the large rover with enough oxygen for three days and attach the trailer for carrying the samples back to base. They'll leave it ready at the airlock.'

'Won't the samples be too heavy for us to lift onto the trailer?'

'There's a lift at the back so just put them on that and press the button.'

The temperature outside the habitats was minus fifty-five degrees centigrade as Hattie and Ellie passed through the air lock into the rover. Despite having initiated the heating circuits before they left the hub, the bitter chill had not entirely worn off inside the vehicle. Ellie read the monitor.

'It's still ten below zero,' she said. 'I'm keeping my suit on.'

'Probably the best thing to do anyway, if you've remembered your nappies.'

'I never leave the house without them.'

Hattie grinned.

'At least the boys can't just pee against a tree out here. We may have reached peak equality.'

'Have you noticed any discrimination?'

'I don't think so. Mo and Bret are a bit alpha male, but they seem to respect us. Except...'

'Yu's not a woman.'

'I know. I just felt a bit, them and us. Like I was a foreigner too.'

'It's not what you think. They're from money. They look down on everyone.'

'I know. I'm just being dumb. Let's try to have fun. After all, we are about to create history.'

The rover descended through the lowlands of the Elysium Mons and west towards the Hephaestus Rupes beacon. The Kevlar tires absorbed some of the vibration but the rough terrain kept their speed to ten kilometres per hour. By the time they arrived at the site, they were both rattled to the core.

'My kidneys feel like pate,' said Ellie.

'Can you see the samples?' said Hattie. 'There's no signal on the monitor.'

'That's odd. The coordinates are correct.'

'Let's get out and have a look. Maybe they got covered in dust.'

The two astronauts put their helmets back on and depressurised the rover. They stepped out onto the surface and looked around. The bare landscape spread out before them, scarred by mini faults and crevices all covered in a layer of red dust that puffed into the sir as they placed their feet on it. Behind them Elysium Mons dominated the skyline, its volcanic cone dark and foreboding.

'I don't think I'll ever get over how enormous that mountain is. The eruption must have killed half of the planet.'

'Not that there was anything to kill.'

Hattie turned to stare at Ellie.

'You don't believe life existed on Mars? Why are you here then?'

'It's my job,' said Ellie.

Taken aback by Ellie's cool reaction, Hattie did not comment further but her mind filled with questions. She took out her all-in-one and checked their coordinates.

'The beacon should be about fifty metres north of here,' she said. 'I'm going to look for it.'

When Ellie didn't answer, Hattie followed the trace until she almost fell into a crevice in the rocks. She teetered on the edge and took a cautious glance downwards. The box containing the Perseverance samples sat on a narrow ledge just over half a metre down from the surface. The crevice continued below it, apparently bottomless. Hattie felt a wave of relief flood over her.

'Over here, and bring the ropes with the carabiner clips. We'll need to pull the box out of this crevice.'

Hattie lay on her stomach and attached the clips to the sample box. She passed the ropes to Ellie and stood up again, painting with effort.

'Okay, pull slowly,' she said.

The box slid up with no trouble and they pushed it clear of the gap. Hattie spotted something glinting on the edge of it and bent over to inspect it. She heard a grunt and Ellie fell over her into the crevice.

'Ellie? What the hell?'

Hattie lay down again and peered into the hole. Ellie had her forearms on the ledge where the box had been and her legs dangled into the void. Her eyes were wide with terror.

'Help me,' she whimpered. 'Please.'

Hattie took hold of the straps on Ellie's oxygen unit and pulled with all her might but Ellie had become wedged in the gap. Hattie lay still for a few seconds running scenarios through her mind.

'Okay,' she said. 'You've got to unclip your air tanks and I'll pull the unit out first. Then I'll lift you out.'

'But I won't be able to breath.'

'It will only take a minute at most. You've got to trust me.'

Ellie looked away, biting her lip.

'I don't know if I can,' she said.

'You're going to die, either way, in that case.'

'I'm sorry it's just__'

'Just what? Serena died of poisoning and Wayne by sabotage. What's it got to do with me? Do you think I'm stupid enough to go back to Bret and say I couldn't save you? They'll never believe me.'

Ellie wriggled again but she could not free herself. Then she took a couple of deep breaths.

'Let's do this,' she said.

Hattie reached down and unclipped the unit.

'Ready?'

'Yes.'

'One, two three,' she said and heaved it upwards.

The unit slid out and Ellie scrabbled to hold onto the ledge as her body swung free. Hattie swung the unit onto the ground and reached down again.

'Take my hand,' she said.

Ellie grabbed it and pushed herself up with her other one, trying to get her knee on the ledge. The effort of holding her breath had turned her face puce. Hattie could feel her shoulder muscles stretching and she grimaced with effort. Ellie made a desperate shove and managed to get her knee on the ledge. She stood up and levered herself onto the surface, seizing the emergency mouthpiece from the side of Hattie's oxygen unit and attaching it to her helmet. She took several deep breaths and her face returned to a normal colour.

189

'I'm sorry I doubted you,' she said. 'I'm an idiot. I panicked. Please can you help me replace the unit on my back?'

She held her breath again as Hattie bent down to pick it up and a sharp pain ran down her arm. She squeaked as she lifted it and slid it back into its frame where it automatically linked back to Ellie's helmet.

'Are you all right?' said Ellie.

'Something's damaged,' said Hattie. 'It hurts like hell.'

'Let's get home then.'

'Aren't you forgetting something?'

'Oh, the samples!'

'Can you go and get the rover? I'll wait here.'

Ellie crossed the dusty metres to the rover and got inside. Hattie waited for her to drive it over, holding her throbbing shoulder. Out of habit, she examined the rocks on the ground and saw a piece that caught her eye. It was volcanic, but it had vesicles in it; the prefect sample to test Mo's app. The vesicles might look like stromatolitic texture in a thin section on a slide. Smiling, she put the sample in her outside pocket to examine later. When she raised her head, she noticed Ellie sitting inside the rover staring at her with cold eyes, her face blank. *She's going to leave me here.* But then the rover jolted forward over the short distance to Hattie and the box of samples and Ellie parked the trailer right beside it. She initiated the lift at the back and placed the box of samples on the lift bed.

'Get in then,' she said. 'We haven't got all day.'

Shaken and trying to ignore the searing pain in her shoulder, Hattie got into the rover. Ellie pressurised the cabin and they took off their helmets.

'Phew. That was close,' she said. 'You saved my life back there. I hope your shoulder is okay.'

'No problem,' said Hattie. 'You would have done the same for me.'

But would she? As they drove home, Hattie's doubts only grew.

Chapter 30

C huck parked his car on the corner of the street where Grace Fredericks lived. Gina, his usual partner in crime, had been suspended from work for her role in their escapade at the coroner's office, and she had since blocked his calls. This struck him as unfair, since he had used his influence with Fredericks to get her reinstated almost immediately. He doubted she could bear to be out of the loop for long. It would cost him dinner, but he could afford it after his article on the deaths of the astronauts got national syndication.

To his surprise, he had been invited to a meeting between the police, now investigating Serena Hampton and Chad Farrant's murders, and a NASA team including Fredericks, who were still chasing the origin of the corrupted file which had caused Wayne's hibernation pod to shut down. Chuck had given a presentation on his leads in the investigation, but had neglected to include Grace. He could not explain to himself why he shielded her. She had not exactly been polite to him so far. But her confusion and vulnerability at finding herself so close to the epicentre of the murders had touched him in places he normally keep hidden. Besides, she was his in with Van Horn.

'In summary,' said the Chief of Police. 'We cannot be sure if the killings were the result of a grudge, or whether they will stop now. Our efforts will be concentrated on finding this Harlan Grimes character. We ran his fingerprints through the database but came up with someone who is known to be deceased. It is likely he had them forged to put us off his trail, so we are back to square one.'

'But can we be sure no more murders will occur among the crew?' said Fredericks. 'My astronauts have enormous daily task loads and perils to deal with, without having to worry if one of them is a murderer.'

'Edgar, we know you are worried about Hattie. It's doubly difficult for you. But as far as we know, the threat of danger comes from Earth. Nevertheless, we need your side to monitor all calls, videos and graphics sent from Mars and send them to us through the agreed encrypted channel.'

'And me?' said Chuck.

'You can stand down. I really appreciate your input but we need trained investigators from now on. You might muddy the waters if you interfere.'

After the meeting, Chuck had felt a tap on his shoulder. Edgar Fredericks beckoned him outside into the oven-like parking bay. They stood in the sweltering heat; the air thick with the harsh chirping of insects. A rivulet of sweat ran down Chuck's back.

'Firstly,' said Fredericks. 'I don't know how to thank you for retrieving the autopsy report. Because of you and Gina risking your lives, my daughter is safe on Mars.' He shrugged. 'Well, as safe as it's possible to be on a planet that's trying to kill you.'

'No need to thank me,' said Chuck. 'I'm just glad we got there before they managed to change it. The police are looking into it but Harlan Grimes is still at large.'

'We'd have had no proof without it. Are you sure I can't do anything for you?'

Chuck rubbed his chin.

'There is one thing...'

'Anything. Within reason.'

'I'd like to do interviews with the grieving parents now that enough time has passed. We may also pick up clues to the reasons behind the murders.'

'Okay, but remember what the police chief said about interfering; and be respectful of their grief.'

'Of course. I'm hardly going to do a hatchet job on global heroes.'

'It's a deal then. I'll message you the contact details,' said Fredericks.

'How's Grace, by the way?'

'Holding up, I think. She found Chad's death very shocking.'

'It's not surprising.'

'I'm still nervous about her working at the NCP. We don't know if they were involved in all this. I wouldn't put it past them. They deny the existence of life off this planet.'

'Enough to sabotage the mission?'

'I don't know.'

After the meeting, Chuck had contacted both Serena and Wayne's parents. He had conducted careful, probing interviews, and published them to wide acclaim. The next interview would be with Chad Farrant's mother. Chuck worried that the death might still be traumatic for her, a single woman with no other children. He decided a female presence might be comforting for her and since Gina had cut him off, he rang Grace.

'I'll do anything which brings us closer to catching the killers,' she said.

So, he found himself drumming his fingers on the dashboard and scanning the streets for her neat figure. He dropped his stylus on the floor and suddenly she appeared, knocking on the window. She got into the car, dressed in a light blue shift dress with her afro hair held back by a hairband of the same colour. Effortless style.

'Are you ready for this?' said Chuck. 'We need to be careful not to upset Mrs Farrant more than is necessary.'

'I don't see how we can avoid it,' said Grace. 'But I'll do my best.'

May Farrant lived in a cul-de-sac in Glenwood to the west of Boca Raton. Her shabby house sat between two much smarter versions of the same building. A swinging chair hung in the porch, occupied by a large malevolent-looking black cat who hissed at them as they walked to the door. Chuck rang the doorbell and soon May Farrant appeared, her grey hair unkempt and hanging in hanks from her head, her face destroyed by grief. She coughed, and a cloud of bourbon breath mixed with toothpaste wafted across them, almost obliterating the odour of her unwashed body.

'Mr Gomez?' she said. 'And who's this?'

'I'm Grace Fredericks. My sister Hattie is an astronaut on the mission to Mars.'

May Farrant reached out a scaley hand and touched Grace's cheek.

'Oh, my dear,' she said. 'You must be so worried.'

Grace nodded, speechless. Chuck put a hand on her shoulder.

'We hoped we might talk about Chad and give the world an idea of his character and bravery, if that's okay with you, Mrs Farrant?'

'Call me May. I'm Ms Farrant but it's an alias. I divorced my husband many years ago.'

'Sure, and my name's Chuck, by the way.'

'My son belongs to the world now, don't he? I don't know what I can tell you that hasn't already been said, but I'll do my best. Please sit down.'

They sat on the chintz couches covered in black cat hair and sipped homemade lemonade with far too much sugar in it. Grace's nose wrinkled in disgust at the cat hairs as she furtively tried to brush them off before sitting down. May Farrant didn't seem to notice. She balanced unsteadily on the edge of her chair as if she would flee, or dash out for another gulp of bourbon.

'Where do you want to start?' she said.

194

'Did Chad always want to be an astronaut?' said Chuck.

'Always. But he kept it secret at first.'

'Secret? Why?'

She wagged her finger at them.

'My husband Grant was a member of the NCP.'

She slumped in her chair, shaking her head. Grace tried not to react but Chuck saw the look in her eyes. May Farrant continued.

'Grant didn't believe in space travel. He forbade Chad to watch or read anything about it. But when I left him, I didn't see the point of crushing the boy's interest in space. I saw it as child cruelty and Jesus wouldn't like it. But don't put anything about the CNP in the article. I ran away. I don't want them to find me.'

'

'Of course not. Tell us more about Chad.'

May Farrant had a lot to say about her son's childhood. Chuck could hardly keep up with the stream of stories, all of which could be used in the article, but none enlightening as to the cause of his murder. After half an hour, Grace excused herself to go to the toilet. She didn't really need to go but her stomach had reacted badly to the lemonade and she needed an antacid, pronto. She found the restroom at the end of the upstairs corridor and stepped into a germ's paradise of stained bathroom fittings and a mouldy shower curtain. The empty towel rail made her realise she had entered the wrong room but she spotted a filthy medicine cabinet on the wall. She opened it with caution fearing a cockroach could leap out of it. She scanned the shelves for an antacid, and an old bottle of Tums caught her eye.

As she reached for it, she dislodged a photograph wrapped in a plastic bag which had been hidden behind it. She took out the photo and peered at it. A much younger May Farrant stood beside a smug man, who appeared be her husband, flanked by two small boys in their Sunday best. The noise of someone at the bottom of the stairs made her jump. She cloned the photograph and placed it back in the cabinet without looking closely at it. The Tums tablets had liquified in the bottle so she replaced it with a sigh. Nobody came upstairs so she searched the other restroom and grabbed a Tums from there before returning below.

Chuck had finished his interview with May Farrant, and stood up as Grace entered the lounge.

'Are you ready?' he said. 'We have to be going. Thank you so much for telling us about Chad. He is a loss to NASA, and I hope you will accept my condolences.'

May Farrant waved them off and then Chuck slapped his forehead.

'Damn. I forgot to ask for a photograph. We'll have to run the stock ones.'

'We could go back,' said Grace. 'Or...'

'Or what?'

'I found a photograph upstairs, but I don't suppose we can use it.'

'You did? Why didn't you say anything?'

'I didn't want May to know. It seemed to be hidden for some reason. Perhaps it belonged to Chad'

'Show me.'

Grace flashed the image up on her screen and Chuck took the all-in-one and magnified the faces. His eyes opened wide.

'I don't believe it,' he said. 'Have you had a look at this?'

'I didn't really have time,' said Grace.

'Look now,' said Chuck, and passed her back the telephone.

Grace looked at the image again and focussed on the face of the taller boy. She dropped the all-in-one on the floor of the car.

'I can't believe it.'

'It is him, isn't it? About two hundred pounds lighter though.'

Yes, it's my boss. It's Noah van Horn.'

Chapter 31

H attie winced as Yu injected her shoulder with painkiller.

'Don't move,' he said. 'I'm not an expert with muscle injury. How on earth did you do it?'

'I wrenched it pulling the sample box out of the crevice.'

'Didn't Ellie help you? I thought you two had mended your fences.'

'We have. I just don't like her much. All this close proximity shows people for who they really are.'

Yu grunted.

'Beggars can't be choosers around here. There's not a lot of choice.'

Bret stepped out of the lift with Ellie, and Yu rolled his eyes at Hattie.

'Here come the cops,' he whispered.

'How's she doing?' said Bret, avoiding looking at Hattie with her top off.

'She'll live,' said Yu. 'It's just a sprain.'

Bret grinned at her.

'I hear you tried to hurl yourself into a crevasse,' he said.

'Not quite.'

'You saved Ellie's life,' said Bret.

'Not on purpose,' said Hattie. 'I needed help with the samples.'

197

Bret laughed.

'That was pretty heroic anyway.'

'I followed my instincts. You would have done the same.'

Yu laughed.

'What a dark horse you are, Hattie Fredericks. According to her, she saved a box of samples.'

'She did that too,' said Ellie. 'But without her, I'd be dead.'

'No wonder she damaged her shoulder,' said Yu. 'You're a trooper.'

'Thanks. I had no choice. We need someone to wash the dishes.'

'Well, you certainly won't,' said Bret. 'I can't believe I ever doubted you.'

'All part of the service, Commander,' said Hattie, saluting.

'Are you still in pain, or would you like to coordinate with Mo to get the stromatolite algorithm working?'

'I'm fine. Yu's filled me full of painkiller so I'm floating on air.'

'Hm. I'm not sure if that's a good thing, but we're short-staffed on this gig and we have to make progress. The world is waiting with bated breath for the results of your studies, and you're the only one who can perform the tests.'

'If Mo sorts out the algorithm, anyone will be able to do that,' said Hattie.

'Don't be so modest. You're the expert. Go find him and let's get on with this. It's the main objective of our trip, and time is passing quicker than I'd like.'

Bret left again, and Yu strapped up Hattie's shoulder while Ellie waited.

'There you go,' he said. 'Like new again. Sort of.'

Hattie raised her arm and squeaked.

'Ouch. It doesn't feel like new to me.'

She pulled her top on with caution, wincing in pain.

'What are you smirking at?' she said to Ellie.

'Nothing. Your social skills are still appalling, so you can't be too sick. Let's go and find Mo. He's made a lot of progress and wants you to try out the programme.'

Yu put Hattie's arm in a sling high on her chest.

'Keep your arm raised to give your shoulder a chance to heal,' he said.

Hattie stood up, wobbling for a second before finding her balance.

'How do you feel?' said Ellie.

'Yu's magic potions seem to have done the job. And it's fantastic to have the samples safely on site.'

'Talking of samples, do you want me to prep them for you?' said Yu. 'All that practice on the Starship has made me feel like an expert.'

'That would be great,' said Hattie. 'Ellie's got her hands full with the greenhouse.'

The two women headed for Mo's cabin but found the door shut. Ellie reached out to press the entry button but Hattie stopped her.

'Don't you think we should knock first?' she said.

But Ellie shook her arm free and tapped the button. The door slid open but Mo wasn't inside. Ellie went inside and looked around.

'Honestly,' she said. 'It's the same as any other cabin. I don't know what the big secret is. Oh—'

Her hand flew to her mouth.

'Quick, let's get out of here,' she said.

'Why? What's so shocking?' said Hattie.

She pushed past Ellie and then she saw it; an image of a handsome young naked man with an erection filled the screen.

'Oh goodness,' she said. 'I wasn't expecting that.'

'So much for macho man,' said Ellie.

They both giggled. Mo emerged from the toilets and saw the open door of his cabin. He blanched when he noticed their smirks.

'You went into my cabin?' he said. 'Without my permission?'

Hattie shrugged, avoiding his accusing glance.

'It's not our fault the door was open,' said Ellie.

'You're lying,' said Mo. 'I'd never...'

His voice sounded thick in his throat.

'It's okay,' said Hattie. 'We were just surprised. You never told us you were gay.'

'Is that your boyfriend?' said Ellie. 'He looks good enough to eat.'

Mo blinked rapidly.

'Look,' he said. 'I'm sorry I didn't tell anyone, but I have my reasons.'

'But your actions made you suspect. All that sneaking around,' said Hattie. 'I wondered if you had something to do with the deaths.'

'Me? No, of course not.'

'You were at Homer when Chad died,' said Ellie. 'And you've got the skills to sabotage the hibernation pods. I'm not sure why we should believe you.'

'I'd never—'

'How did you receive that image?' said Hattie. 'I can't imagine NASA letting it through.'

'Encrypted software,' said Mo.

'What?' said Ellie.

'I made an app to bypass the NASA messaging servers so no-one would see my mails.'

Ellie raised an eyebrow.'

'You've got an app? Why do you need it if you're only talking to your boyfriend?'

You don't understand.'

'You're dead right, we don't,' said Hattie.

'I'm from a strict Muslim family. My parents would never forgive me if they found out,' said Mo. 'I'm their only son. I'm supposed to get married and produce heirs.'

'Seriously?' said Hattie. 'In this day and age?'

'Some people still believe that homosexuals are going against God's laws,' said Ellie.

200

'And others think Earth was made in six days. But that doesn't make them right. I'm sorry, Mo. We didn't mean to snoop on you. I promise not to tell anyone.'

'But we want a copy of the app. If you can have private conversations, we want them too,' said Ellie, looking to Hattie for confirmation.

Hattie wanted to disagree, but the thought of uncensored chats with Grace made her long for it too.

'If it's okay with you,' she said.

Mo nodded.

'Sure. Bring your all-in-ones along and I'll set them up later. On one condition; don't tell anyone about any of this.'

'Cross my heart,' said Ellie.

'Can Yu and Scotty have it too?' said Hattie.

Mo sighed.

'What about Bret?'

'Not Bret. He'd probably blab to NASA,' said Ellie. 'And we wouldn't want that.'

When Hattie returned to Mo's cabin with her phone, he took it from her and put it in the drawer.

'Do you want me to send anything for you?' said Mo.

'I've put some images and short videos in a file marked 'home' if you would forward them to Grace. Just tell her not to share them under any circumstances.'

'Are you sending naked photos too?'

Hattie snorted.

'To my sister?'

'Oh. Alright. I'll do that when I get back.'

'Why don't we go and give this app a try? I don't suppose you have anything from Mars with stromatolites in it ready for testing?'

'Not yet, it will take Yu a couple of days to prepare the thin sections for examination. It's very fiddly work. Haven't you got the ones I gave you from Earth?'

'Those are the ones I used to calibrate it.'

'I have a Martian sample I picked up at Hephaestus Rupes. It might have stromatolites in it but I doubt it. I

201

think the stream it came from was too fast flowing. We can cut that now and have a look. I'll set it up in the diamond saw.'

'Okay, and while it cuts, I'll show you how this thing works.'

Chapter 32

G race wavered at the door of Noah van Horn's office, afraid to speak in case it released a torrent of emotions churning inside her. She had withdrawn from him after Harlan Grimes had been revealed as a serial murderer. His bemusement had not hidden his hurt at her rejection of him. He smiled sadly when he spotted her at the door.

'What is it, Ms Dos Reis?'

'Mr Gomez is in reception. He wants to talk to you.'

Van Horn's face reddened.

'Tell him I'm too busy to see him.'

'He insists on seeing you now.'

'Who does he think he is?'

Van Horn levered himself out of his chair. 'I'll send him packing.'

'I don't think—'

Chuck entered the room and strode over to Van Horn's desk.

'Get out before I call the cops,' said Van Horn, puce with rage.

'You'd better sit down,' said Grace. 'This is important.'

Her voice caught in her throat and Van Horn stared at her reaction, mystified.

'Gracie, sweetheart, what's wrong? Has this bastard upset you?'

'Please sit down, Mr van Horn. I've got some unsettling news for you,' said Chuck.

'Do as he says,' said Grace. 'Please.'

Van Horn fell back into his chair which groaned in protest. He crossed his arms over his chest and narrowed his eyes.

'This better be good,' he said.

'Yesterday, Grace and I visited a woman called May Farrant—'

'The astronaut's mother? What on earth were you doing there, Grace?'

Chuck ignored him.

'I went there to research an article about Chad Farrant; a human-interest story.'

'He'd still be alive, if he had stayed on Earth where he belonged,' said Van Horn.

'I'm not sure about that. Mr Farrant was murdered; poisoned by the same person who killed Serena Hampton.'

'That's garbage. Everybody knows she died of a heart attack. And Chad is on Mars. He hasn't had an autopsy yet, so how can you come here spouting this bull at me?'

'I'm afraid it's true. We have the original autopsy report for Serena Hampton.'

The colour drained from Van Horn's face.

'And what's that got to do with me?' he said.

Chuck frowned.

'May I show you a photograph?' he said.

'If you must. Send it to my screen.'

Chuck fumbled with his all-in-one and recalled the family snapshot from May Farrant's house. He transferred the image to Noah van Horn's screen. All his bluster evaporated in an instant.

'But where did you get this? Are you running some sort of scam?'

'No, Mr van Horn. I found it in the bathroom of Chad's mother's house,' said Grace.

'But that's my mother and father. And—'

Van Horn went pale and grabbed the arms of his chair.

'How did she get this photograph?' he said.

'She's in it. May Farrant is your mother. And I'm afraid Chad was your brother,' said Chuck. 'I'm so sorry for your loss.'

'My brother? But they told me he had died in a car crash with my mother. My father said...'

Van Horn rubbed his face in his hands.

'I thought they were dead. You have to believe me. Oh my god.'

He slipped off the chair onto his knees on the floor. 'No, no, no,' he said. 'I can't believe it.'

His body racked with sobs as he laid his forehead on the desk and then began to pound it on the veneer.

Grace ran to stop him and Chuck helped her guide Van Horn back into his seat. They waited while he regained his composure. Finally, he looked up again, his face puffy and tearstained.

'I didn't know,' he said. 'I swear I would never...'

'Commit fratricide?' said Chuck. 'What about Harlan Grimes? I saw him, you know. In the kitchen on the night of the launch dinner. It took me a while to piece together the clues.'

Van Horn straightened up.

'I had nothing to do with the murders,' he said. 'That man exceeded his brief. He had instructions to delay the launch.'

'But how did you know him?' said Grace. 'I could never figure out why you had dealings with a man like that.'

'I had no choice,' said Van Horn. 'I can't question the will of the Lord. The leaders of the NCP are afraid the discovery of life on Mars could destroy the basis for our religion.'

'Is your religion so fragile?' said Chuck. 'Surely that would prove the reach of God into the heavens.'

'I don't know anymore,' said Van Horn. 'I can't believe my brother got to be an astronaut after all. My father never let us do any science or watch any television.

My mother took the brunt of his anger if we disobeyed him. When she disappeared one day with Jerry, I mean Chad, he told me they had died in a car crash. I never questioned it. I'm so glad he got to Mars. He must have died happy.'

'Would you like your mother's details?' said Chuck. 'I'm sure she'd be happy to see you again.'

'Of course. I'm sorry. I'm so confused and sad and happy.'

Chuck took out his trusty notebook and copied the number which he pushed across the desk. Van Horn gazed at it for a while and stroked the scrap of paper before putting it into a drawer. His brow furrowed as he looked up again.

'What's Grace got to do with all of this?' he said.

Grace hung her head and sighed.

'Don't hate me,' she said. 'Hattie Fredericks is my sister.'

Van Horn roared with laughter.

'Now that explains a lot. And Edgar Fredericks is your father? No wonder you used an assumed name to work here.'

'It's my mother's maiden name.'

A shadow crossed Van Horn's face.

'I can't guarantee Hattie's safety,' he said. 'There are forces of evil in the NCP who will stop at nothing to sabotage the mission.'

'How do we expose them?' said Grace.

'I don't know. I wish I did,' said Van Horn. 'I don't have access to the inner circle and there's nothing in writing.'

'We need to find Harlan Grimes,' said Chuck. 'He's the key, but the police can't find him. Are you still in contact?'

'Not exactly. I told him to take a hike after he turned up at my office once. I doubt he would trust me now that he knows the police are looking for him.'

'Are you sure he knows?'

206

'Trust me. If the police have opened an investigation, the NCP are aware of it and they will have warned him.'

'He likes me,' said Grace.

'What did you say?' said Chuck.

'He always makes suggestive comments, doesn't he, Mr van Horn?'

'I don't know what that's got to do with anything. The man is disgusting outside and in.'

'You could use me as bait,' said Grace. 'He might come to a meeting with me if I invented some pretext. He'd never suspect me of trying to trap him.'

'Forget it,' said Van Horn. 'I'd never allow it.'

'There must be a better way,' said Chuck. 'Let me think about it.'

Chapter 33

Hattie let out a long sigh as she finished scanning the tenth sample from the Isidis Planitia basin under her microscope. Her eyes ached from the effort of staring down the lenses at the thin sections of Martian rock. Mo's famous app bleeped at her and flashed red. Still no sign of stromatolites. Perhaps she hadn't reached the deltaic samples yet. There would be no stromatolites in water deeper than ten metres due to the internal microbes relying on light to photosynthesise. She stood up and stretched out her back.

'Damn app doesn't work,' she said, to no-one in particular.

'Don't let Mo hear you say that,' said Scotty, who had appeared at the door of the wet lab. 'He worked for weeks on that programme.'

Hattie spun around, her cheeks pink.

'It's not his fault there are no stromatolites in the samples, but I do blame technology. You should never send a robot to do a man's job.'

'No luck then?'

'All barren so far. There's something not quite right here, but I can't put my finger on it.'

'How about a break? I'm off to check on the Rassors and the progress at the Moxie plant. Do you want to tag along?'

'Does a bear defecate in the woods?' said Hattie. 'That would be excellent. Maybe I'll take some samples out there.'

'Let's grab a bite and then suit up.'

Hattie ate her noodles at speed, burning her tongue in the process. Scotty grinned at her when a loud burp erupted from her throat.

'When I said quick bite, I didn't mean you to wolf down your food without chewing.'

Hattie bit her lip.

'Sorry,' she said. 'I'm just so stoked to get out for an EVA. I spend so much time cooped up in the hab, sometimes it feels like I'm still on Earth.'

'Except for the food,' said Scotty.

'Now that we've got vegetables, I hardly notice.'

'I miss meat. That lab-grown stuff is revolting.'

'Come on then. Let's get ready.'

Scotty shook his head and rejected the rest of his food.

'Lead on Macbeth.'

As their rover crawled up the hill to the ice field in the shadow of Elysium Mons, Hattie gazed out of the window at the extraordinary sight.

'Isn't it amazing?' she said. 'I'd really like to take a hike on the Elysium Planitia sometime before we go home.'

'It is immense. I can't quite take it in, no matter how many times I see it.'

The Rassor fleet came into view, rumbling in the distance as they dug up the frozen ground with rotary drums and dropped the material into dump trucks. The deep sounds were muffled in the thin atmosphere like a host of heavy canvas sails flapping in a dockyard.

'This kind of robot is my favourite,' said Hattie. 'Doing the grunt work without the need for supervision. They never stop work for a cigarette or a pee.'

'How do you know what they do when we're not around?' said Scotty.

'I'm not sure it would be very interesting,' said Hattie.

'Probably not. Okay, next stop the Moxie plant.'

They turned to follow the well-worn road to the Starship base and rolled into the main industrial park where the Starships had been landed and adapted by the robots. Scotty drew up alongside the rocket chosen as their craft for leaving Mars after five hundred days. It had been connected by an insulated pipe to a 3-D printed building with an airlock on the outside. He manoeuvred the rover so that they could enter the airlock and soon they were standing inside with the two Moxie plants. Their breath came out in clouds through the outlets in their helmets. Scotty took out his tablet and took note of the measured quantities of liquified gases that had been transferred to the tanks in the Starship. He rubbed his hands together.

'I'm glad these suits are heated,' said Hattie.

'Those are ice crystals in the air,' said Scotty.

'This set up is pretty impressive. Are we on course to fill up the tanks in time?'

'Despite my initial doubts, it's looking possible. By my reckoning, we could have enough fuel to take off and set off for Earth at the very end of the Hohmann window. If they send a tanker from Earth to meet us in space, we can refuel again, and should land on Earth without any dramas.'

'That's great news.'

'It's going to be close though. The atmospheric conditions will have a big effect on the amount of propellant needed for us to take off from here. I could do with some more fuel to add a safety margin for the delta-v.'

'What about the other Starships?' said Hattie. 'Is there any fuel left in their tanks or did they use it all?'

Scotty turned to her with a look of amazement on his face.

'Why didn't I think of that? You're a genius, Hattie. Their insulation circuits have been switched on to keep the cargoes fresh so if any fuel remains, we can salvage it by decanting it at night into the robot bowser. I'll have to programme that in but it should be possible.'

He grabbed her in an awkward hug and she felt her temperature rise despite the freezing conditions.

'These suits were not made with hugging in mind,' she said, reluctantly freeing herself.

'Oh, don't you worry. One of these days I'll get you without your suit on,' said Scotty.

Hattie laughed.

'Promises, promises,' she said.

She found it hard to concentrate on the journey back to the central hub. Scotty had an effect on her like no-one she had ever come across. His combination of brains, brawn and quiet, country confidence made her hormones somersault. She had a suspicion he felt the same, but he covered his feelings with humour, leaving her guessing.

As they neared the hub, still fantasising about possible outcomes with Scotty, Hattie spotted a shape lying on the ground in the gloom of the approaching night.

'What's that?' she said, pointing.

'I don't know. It wasn't there before we left. Let's go and investigate.'

Hattie screamed first.

'Oh my God. It's Mo. Depressurise the rover quickly.'

'His visor is open. There's no hurry,' said Scotty, in a calm voice.

'But he could be...'

Alive? No, he couldn't. Two minutes was all it took if you went out without a pressurised suit on. Hattie put her head in her hands.

'What is he doing out here with his visor open? It doesn't make any sense.'

The control panel of the rover beeped to indicate that the atmospheric pressure had equalised with the outside. They got out of the rover and Hattie ran to where Mo lay on the ground. Her first look at his white face with red froth frozen around his nose told her he could not be saved. His eyes had sunk back into his head and his mouth had opened in a scream.

'Are you receiving me, Yu,' said Scotty. 'I need a stretcher out here.'

'A stretcher? Is it Hattie? That woman's an accident waiting to happen. We should call her sick note.'

'Hattie's fine. It's Mo. Bring the stretcher to the central hub. We'll bring him inside.'

'Roger that.'

Hattie and Scotty picked Mo up and carried him to the rover. His body was light in the low gravity as if his spirit had left only a shell behind. Hattie stifled her instinct to weep. They put him into the rover and drove to the airlock on the central hub. They dragged Mo inside and waited for the airlock to pressurise.

'What on earth was he doing out there?' said Scotty.

A feeling of dread crept up Hattie's back, making the hairs on the back of her neck prickle in alarm.

'I think I might know,' she said. 'Someone will have to check in Mo's room to see if he left a note.'

'A note?'

'It could be suicide.'

The airlock door opened, and Yu, Bret and Ellie waited in the hub with the stretcher. Their faces fell as they saw Mo's limp body.

'Will he be all right?' said Bret, his face tight.

'He's dead,' said Scotty. 'He went outside and lifted his visor.'

'On purpose?' said Yu.

'I don't know.'

'Can you check his room,' said Hattie. 'There might be a note.'

'A note?' said Bret. 'Are you suggesting—'

'Just do it,' said Scotty.

Yu went to Mo's room and noticed Hattie's all-in-one on Mo's pillow. The message light flashed as he picked it up. A new message had arrived into Hattie's inbox with the heading 'I'm so sorry'. Yu ran back downstairs and into the hub where the crew were removing Mo's space suit.

'He sent you a message, Hattie.'

Hattie removed her gloves and took the unit from Yu. She opened the message and read it out. 'A few days ago, I experienced the greatest shame of my life. I cannot live with it, or you all, after what happened. I hope you will forgive me for deserting you but I can't go on lying to you, or to my family. I'm going outside, I may be some time. Mo.

Hattie's heart froze. *Could he have written this after his conversation with her and Ellie? He had seemed relieved, unburdened, but not ashamed. It didn't make any sense.* She took off her helmet and entered the console to remove her spacesuit. The process seemed to take even longer than usual. She could hear the other's discussing Mo's message. Ellie stood apart from them, as if shocked. As the pressure on her suit released, Hattie couldn't help wondering why Mo would bother putting on his spacesuit if he planned on committing suicide. *Why didn't he just enter the airlock in his uniform and walk outside if he wanted to die? It didn't make any sense.*

'Does anyone know what the hell Mo's talking about?' said Bret.

'I do,' said Hattie.

Chapter 34

M o's death had cast a gloom over the whole crew and people went about their business without talking to each other, each wrapped in their own thoughts. Hattie discovered Mo had installed his app on her all-in-one before dying; another conundrum. *Why would he do that if he was about to commit suicide? It made no sense.* It gave her a lifeline, in those sad days after Mo's death, to be able to send private messages to Grace who tried to cheer Hattie up. She told Hattie that the danger of any more murders on Mars had receded as they had a suspect on Earth, but she did not mention their plan for Harlan Grimes. And Hattie did not voice her fears about Mo. There seemed no point agitating people so far away with unfounded suspicions.

Hattie tried to talk to Ellie about Mo, but Ellie had refused.

'He's dead. He killed himself. What's the point of discussing it? We'll never know why he did it,' said Ellie.

'But the message—'

'I don't want to discuss it.'

Bret had debriefed Hattie about Mo, but he too seemed unable to square the circle on Mo's suicide.

'If what you say is correct, Mo's death just doesn't make sense,' he said.

'But what if he killed himself because of us?' said Hattie.

'You shouldn't feel guilty. Mo was the one keeping secrets. Nobody can stop someone who is determined to kill themselves.'

Her talk with Bret did not prevent Hattie from brooding on Mo's death, but despite her anguish, she forced herself to continue work on the samples. *This is why I'm here, and I'm going to do my job no matter what.* She doubled down on her efforts to find a sign of life in the Perseverance samples. But Mo's app, and her own eyes, told her no sign of life existed, fossilised or otherwise, in these red lumps of rock. No matter how many hours she spent scanning the samples, she couldn't spot any stromatolites in them. Scotty tried to cheer her up by bringing her treats from the greenhouse, but a feeling of hopelessness settled over her. As it looked inevitable that the search for life on Mars would come up empty, at least on this occasion, even Ellie sympathised.

'Some things aren't meant to be. At least you have survived to tell the tale,' she said.

But Hattie kept going. She reviewed her data, and double checked everything. She even made a thin section of the sample she brought back from Hephaestus Rupes to test Mo's app, to make sure it worked correctly. The sample did not look promising either; bland grains of sand in a silty matrix. She had just taken the sample off the microscope when the penny dropped. Her eyes widened and she squeaked in surprise. *It can't be.* She put it back and upped the magnification. Instead of looking for stromatolites, she examined the grains of quartz. They had the aphanitic texture of extrusive rocks. No surprise there.

But then she substituted the slide with one containing the delta sediments from Isidis Planitia. She peered down the microscope and examined the sample. Her head shot up and she gasped. *Calm down woman. This is important.* She rubbed her eyes and looked again. The individual grains in the sample had sharp edges as if they

215

had been crushed, or split apart by the harsh climate. Some of the edges were razor sharp. None of these grains had ever seen a river or been in a delta. *Oh my god. Either the Perseverance rover took the wrong samples, or someone has substituted them since they were taken.*

Yu. She couldn't escape the conclusion, seeing as he had the samples under his care since they arrived in the habitat, and he had made the thin sections. With her record, she couldn't accuse him without proof. She had to be sure. Since Yu rarely left the habitat, and then only to follow the tunnel to the greenhouse, Hattie made her way there. She looked around for a source of samples. The only rocks available in the greenhouse were those brought inside and cleaned of perchlorate for use as soil. She selected a couple of representative pieces from the pile, and brought them to the wet lab. It took her a couple of hours to make some slides with them. She stuck small pieces of rock to several glass slides with epoxy resin. Then she ground the sample down to eighty microns in the vacuum before setting them on the slide ready for observation.

She took a deep breath and inserted one of them under the microscope and focussed the lens on the rock sample. The rock has grains of volcanic rock in a fine matrix. The sharp edges and geological origin of the grains matched those in the samples she had already examined and confirmed her suspicions. Yu had replaced the Perseverance samples with rock from the greenhouse. *But why?* Yu was the last person on Mars, she would have suspected. *Was this linked to the murders? What on earth was going on?*

Whatever the reason, Yu needed to explain himself to Bret rather than her. She had no authority over Yu's actions and as commander of the mission, he would know what to do. If he believed her. To her surprise, not only did he listen to her findings but he agreed with her conclusions. Shortly afterwards, Bret called Yu into a private meeting with Hattie and himself. He pushed the slides across the table towards Yu who turned pale.

'Would you care to explain this?' Bret said.

''Explain what,' said Yu, pushing them back. 'I'm not a geologist.'

'You swapped them,' said Hattie. 'They're not from Isidis Planitia. You took them from the greenhouse.'

Yu looked as if he would faint.

'How did you know?' he said.

'Science,' said Hattie.

'Why did you do it?' said Bret. 'I don't understand. Are you the one who murdered the crew? And Mo?'

'I haven't killed anyone. I swear. Tell him Hattie.'

'You had the chance and the knowledge. Mo trusted you. How did you persuade him to come outside with you? Did you drug him?'

Yu put his head in his hands.

'No, you've got this all wrong. It wasn't me.'

'And the samples?' said Hattie.

Yu shrugged.

'Yes, I did that, but I was coerced.'

'By whom?' said Bret. 'Someone on Mars?'

'No. By the Chinese government.'

'But I haven't seen any emails from them,' said Bret. 'I don't believe you.'

'It's a long story,' said Yu.

'We've got time,' said Hattie.

Yu rubbed his temples.

'Remember when I told you about my parents calling me Yu on purpose?' he said.

'It means universe, planets etc,' said Hattie.

'Well, what I didn't tell you is that my mother is a Uigher and my father is from Taiwan. The perfect storm as far as the authorities are concerned.'

'Didn't China annex Taiwan a few years ago?' said Bret.

'Taiwan has always been part of China, according to them. My father didn't agree. He was a dissident, and marrying a Uigher made him an outcast.'

217

'So how did you get on the space programme?'

'A childless couple who were friends of my parents took me in, and pretended I was theirs. I grew up with them and went to school in Beijing. I fought for my place on the space programme, and I got it. The government treated me like a prince. I am their golden boy.'

'What happened?'

'As soon as Mo gave me his app, I texted my real father to tell him I loved him, forgetting that the Chinese government would now be able to read my messages too. They questioned my guardians and arrested them and both of my parents.'

'Oh my God,' said Hattie. 'That's terrible.'

'What's that got to do with the samples?' said Bret.

'The Chinese Government were furious when you planted the flag of the United States instead of the United Nations, and they were looking for a way to sabotage the voyage. When they found out about my parents, they used their all-in-ones to message me an ultimatum. Either I find a way to sabotage the results or they will shoot my parents and my guardian and send me a bill for the bullets.'

'So, if we find life on Mars, your parents will die?' said Hattie.

'Yes. I'm sorry for ruining the experiment, but you must understand.'

'Mo's app has a lot to answer for,' said Bret. 'This is why we wanted to control the communications. How long have you had the app?'

'A few weeks. Mo gave it to me when I told him I had to know how my parents were. They're old, and frail and...'

He tailed off. Bret sighed.

'Jesus. What a mess. I don't know what to tell you. The main aim of our mission is to find out if there is, or was, life on Mars. We have a plenty of time left and I intend to keep searching.'

'Why don't we get NASA to blackmail the Chinese?' said Hattie.

218

Bret guffawed.

'Seriously? We have three murders, a suicide and an attempted sabotage and you think that blackmail is a good idea?'

'Hear me out. NASA, or our government, can let the Chinese know through secret channels that Yu has been caught in the act trying to sabotage the Mars Mission. They can demand that Yu's parents and guardians and the rest of the family are freed and allowed to travel to any other country they wish, including the United States of America. Failing that, the U.S. will release the news that China has sabotaged the first manned mission to space.'

Yu nodded.

'I agree with Hattie. The loss of face would be too great for them to continue with this scheme. It is the only hope of saving my family. I am happy for you to try.'

'It may not work,' said Bret.

'It might,' said Yu. 'The Chinese Government is ruthless but they are not stupid.'

'Let me deal with it,' said Bret. 'Meanwhile, we have a problem. Where are the original samples?'

'I threw them outside behind the hab. They're all mixed up with the local soil.'

'They're destroyed? What now?'

'I can get new samples,' said Hattie.

'At Isidis Planitia?'

'Yes, we have the original co-ordinates and a much better drill attachment for the rover than the Perseverance had.'

'It's quite a drive. You'd have to stay the night.'

'I can take the large rover and a trailer,' said Hattie. 'It will be easy enough.'

'But what if you break down?' said Bret. 'You'd better take Scotty.'

Hattie blushed.

'Can you spare him?' she said.

'I'll have to. I need Ellie to help me with a project I'm advancing.'

'What about me?' said Yu.

Bret shook his head.

'Normally, I'd throw you in the brig for this sort of offence but we can't afford to go down another man. I need you to run the greenhouses while Ellie maintains the Moxie and Rassor fleets with me.'

'You'll also have to make the thin sections again when I get back,' said Hattie.

Yu smiled.

'It will be a pleasure.'

'Okay,' said Bret. 'Get lost you two, before I change my mind. I have a rather delicate call to make to NASA.'

Chapter 35

Despite all the efforts of Chuck and Van Horn, Grace could not be dissuaded from calling Grimes to set up a sting. Chuck organised them a meeting with Gina so she could brief Grace on the likely scenarios. They met upstairs in the Foxhole at the exact table where Chuck had last seen Saul. He decided not to jinx the occasion by remarking on the coincidence but the déjà vu made him uncomfortable.

Gina turned up looking like Boudica with her bright red hair enhanced by some alchemy in the hairdressers and an artfully tattered dress that showed her fabulous figure. Chuck tried not to stare but her magnetic personality drew his eyes to her. *All she's missing is a breastplate and a spear.*

'You look amazing,' he said, again wondering why he couldn't commit to such a Valkyrie.

'Thanks,' she said, and kissed him on the top of the head.

Before he could protest, Grace came up the stairs, also looking ready for war in some combat trousers and a lacy t-shirt. Her Grace Kelly sunglasses gave her an air of old-world glamour.

'This is Grace,' said Chuck.

Gina raised an eyebrow and gave him a hard stare before giving Grace a warm hug.

'I'm Gina,' she said. 'You must be so worried about your sister.'

Grace hugged her back.

'I was, but now I'm not. We're going to save her.'

'Not so fast,' said Chuck. 'We need to discuss this first.'

Grace rolled her eyes.

'I've spent ten years living like the Virgin Mary,' she said. 'I'd like a little excitement for once, and what's more important than saving my sister?'

Grace and Gina sat side by side on the small couch and Chuck gazed at them. It's like something from the Avengers, he thought.

'It's not like in the movies,' said Gina, swishing her mane of red hair. 'Grimes has already murdered four people. His crush on you won't stop him killing you if he thinks it's a trap.'

'I've been the worst sister in the world and now I've got a chance to redeem myself before he kills Hattie too. You've got to help me do this.'

'We'd like him too. The police need to take this guy down before he kills anyone else.'

'So how will this work?' said Chuck.

'We set up a meeting in a café with only one entrance. Grace lures him to a corner table furthest from the door, and once he's seated, we'll come in from the kitchen, and block the front entrance simultaneously.'

'What if something goes wrong?' said Chuck. 'Do we have a plan B?'

'You'd better carry a panic button in your purse,' said Gina. 'One press and we're on it.'

'When shall we do this?' said Chuck. 'Do we need time to set it up?'

'First we need him to take the bait,' said Gina.

'I'll call him now,' said Grace.

Before they could stop her, she had picked up her all-in-one and dialled Grimes's number. He did not pick up the call, even after three tries, so Grace sent him a text.

222

'Hello Mr Grimes, it's Grace, from the NCP office. I'm worried about Mr Van Horn, and I know you two are friends. Can you meet me to discuss?'

The answer came almost immediately. The ping made all of them jump.

'Just the girl I wanted to see. You saved me the effort of finding you. How about Café Rambert at four o'clock tomorrow afternoon. We can have coffee and a nice chat.'

Grace showed the message to Gina.

'Can we get organised by then?'

'I should think so. I'll talk to the chief. Text him back and say you'll be there.'

'Are you sure about this?' said Chuck.

***

She had been. But now Grace's nerves unsettled her stomach and almost made her throw up. She had arrived outside the café fifteen minutes early and stared through the shiny plate-glass window. Eager shoppers sat around neat tables choosing their favourite from the exquisite cakes on offer. Grace took a deep breath and entered the café. She walked to the corner table with as much nonchalance as she could muster, holding tight to a purse with a shoulder strap which was crossed over her chest for safety. She held in her tummy and glided past a long table containing an office party for someone's birthday. The man at the head of the table did not look as if he enjoyed tea parties. A plump woman with too much blusher on her cheeks was making a speech, and Grace saw him looking at his watch. *He would rather be anywhere else; a bit like me.*

She sat with her back to the wall, staring at the entrance to the café, where people paid their bills and queued for their tables with the same reluctance. A loose thread on the hem of her dress caught her eye and she tugged at it until she unravelled some of the stitching. She tutted and broke it off, balling the thread between her thumb and finger and dropping it onto the floor. The excessive air-conditioning made her shiver and wish she had worn a cardigan. In her purse, she could feel the comforting weight of the panic button pressed into her hands by Gina Flores, Chuck's friend, or was she a girlfriend? Gina had given her a pep talk about keeping the table between herself and Grimes and being subtle in her interaction with him. *Subtle? With that monster?*

A chill ran up her back as she spotted Harlan Grimes peering through the window of the café, his ratty face screwed up with concentration. Grimes vanished and then reappeared in the café near the doorway. She raised a sweaty hand from her purse and gave him a shy wave. Grimes glanced towards her and spotted the gesture. He beckoned her to the door. Uncertain how to react, Grace hesitated. Gina had not given her instructions about this scenario. She shook her head and patted the empty chair beside her. But he did not move, jerking his head towards the exit.

Grace pushed out her chair and, clutching her purse tightly to her side, she made her way through the tables to where he stood. An evil smile creased his thin lips as he watched her approach. He composed his features and the familiar air of menace settled over him as his eyes lost their twinkle and became opaque and dead like a shark. Grace felt a shiver run up his back as she witnessed the transformation. No wonder Grimes was so successful. His chameleon-like ability to change from flippant to ferocious in the blink of an eye unnerved her.

'Here she is,' he said. 'Like a lamb to the slaughter.'

'Good morning to you too,' said Grace. 'I thought we were going to have a coffee. I'm dying for a piece of pecan pie.'

'That's not the only dying you'll be doing if you don't come with me right now,' he said. 'I got a message from

224

Mars last night, and I know who your sister is. You're a stoolie, and you're gonna pay for it.'

Grace froze and tried to slip her hand into her purse. He gripped her arm so tight she almost screamed.

'Give me your purse,' he said.

'Let go of my arm then,' said Grace.

He released it and she lifted the strap over her head pretending to get the buckle stuck in her hair.

'Now look what you made me do,' she said.

He leaned towards her to grab the strap. Grace reached for a latte from a passing waitress's tray and hit him smack in the temple with it. Grimes staggered about, knocking the rest of the drinks off the tray, before careening into the table hosting the office party. He landed square on the plates of cakes and sandwiches, splattering the elegant attendees with icing and lit candles, which were hastily extinguished. The birthday boy did not seem at all put out, rubbing his hands together in glee, shouting 'Awesome'.

Grace stuck her hand into her purse and grasped the panic button, pressing it with all her might.

'He's here,' she screamed, before launching herself after Grimes. She landed on top of him and grabbed a heavy glass plate which she broke over his head. He groaned and fell back into the soggy mess that had been the birthday tea. Blood trickled from his temple and stained the paper table cloth. The birthday boy beamed at Grace as she sat astride Grimes, pieces of cupcake in her hair and a look of shock on her face.

'Are you the stripper?' he said.

Chapter 36

B ret came into the staff meeting with a big smile on his face. He sat down between Scotty and Yu and patted them on the knees.

'I know we've had a rough time,' he said. 'More than rough. But I thought this might cheer you up. I just heard from NASA and they've caught the guy who murdered our colleagues. We're safe now.'

'Except that Mars is still trying to kill us,' said Scotty, but he grinned too.

'Fantastic,' said Hattie. 'Do they know why he did it?'

'Not yet. He's probably a nutcase loner. Anyway, we can relax now and get on with our jobs.'

'As I already discussed with you,' said Hattie. 'I'd like to go back to Isidis Planitia and resample the delta. It's the most likely place to find life near here, and my trained eye might be better at choosing the locations for drilling rather than a robot guided from earth.'

'Agreed,' said Bret. 'You can go as soon as I calculate the logistics for the trip. I'll do that today.'

'A girls' road trip?' said Ellie. 'I can't wait.'

'I'm sorry, but I want Hattie to go with Scotty in case she needs some heavy lifting,' said Bret.

'And he's the man for the job,' said Yu, winking at Hattie who blushed.

'Won't the rovers do that?' said Ellie. 'I'm the geochemist.'

'I want Scotty there in case of breakdowns and computer glitches. You can go on the next EVA. There's plenty of time.'

Ellie crossed her arms and a sulky expression settled over her features. Hattie smirked and tried not to catch Scotty's eye afraid she would blush again.

'Okay then. The greenhouses are flourishing under Dr Yu's management so we'll stick with him there. I'd like you to carry out the experiments on light saturation and water control there.'

'Great,' said Yu. 'I never knew I had green fingers but I'm really enjoying it.'

'I want you with me on maintenance and Moxie watch, Ellie.'

Ellie nodded, sullen.

'At least we still have plenty of skills between us, and more than enough food. We'll be okay if we stick together,' said Scotty.

'And Bret doesn't cook,' said Hattie.

'What about my rehydrated Spaghetti Bolognese?' said Bret.

'I thought you were the murderer,' said Yu.

Hattie looked around the laughing faces of her companions and noticed Ellie still sulking. She elbowed her.

'Next time?' she said. 'It's a big planet.'

Ellie sniffed.

'You don't kid me. I know you prefer Scotty.'

It took two days to get ready for the trip to Isidis Planitia. Bret and Scotty found the drill attachment in Starship 3 after a long search and rigged it up in the centre of the large trailer. They also loaded an array of solar panels, as well as extra oxygen and fuel in insulated tanks.

'That should keep you going indefinitely,' said Bret.

'I reckon it will take us a day to get to the furthest point from here and then we'll work our way back along the delta. I imagine it will take us a couple of days to drill out the samples with the rig. It's about ten times as powerful as the one Perseverance had.'

'It's risky to embark on such a long EVA, but what are we here for otherwise?' said Bret.

'Don't worry about us. Just keep the Moxies running and the rest will look after itself.'

'I guess so. I'm a little jealous of your trip.'

'Why don't we organise an EVA to Mons Elysium when we get back. I'm sure we can think of some scientific research to do up there to make it worthwhile.'

'Isn't the Insight rover up there somewhere? Maybe we can download the information that didn't get transmitted after the comms unit failed.

'Now you're talking. And the girls can take samples of the rocks and do some ground truthing of Mars geology on the ground.'

'What about Yu? We can't leave him behind. He'll never forgive us.'

'Maybe we'll take two rovers and stay the night.'

'Anyway, let's park that for now, and go over our checklists.'

'Don't forget the portable toilet.'

'I'll put that on the trailer and you can drag it into the pressurised pop out tent attached to the rover.'

The next morning, Hattie and Scotty suited up for the trip. Bret and Yu came to wave them off, but there was no sign of Ellie.

'Still sulking then?' said Yu.

'She'll get over it,' said Bret. 'Have a good time and be careful out there.'

Hattie had butterflies in her stomach from excitement and she gave Bret a nervous wave as they entered the airlock.

'Do you want to drive first?' said Scotty. 'I didn't get much sleep last night. I don't want to drive us off a cliff.'

'Great,' said Hattie. 'Get strapped in. I'll put the coordinates of the Jezero Crater into the dashboard.'

'A road trip,' said Scotty. 'I haven't done one of these since I went to a rock concert as a teenager.'

'We don't really need the coordinates for most of the trip,' said Hattie. If we head past Hephaestus Rupes and then swing down south west into the Isidis Planitia, we're nearly there already.'

'And remember what happened last time you went to Hephaestus Rupes? Keep your eye on the road.'

'It wasn't me who fell down a crevice.'

But Scotty had taken off his helmet and shut his eyes in a good imitation of a man who doesn't want to talk. Hattie grinned and with one last glance at the habs, she set course for Jezero Crater. Her internal monologue kept her entertained as she avoided rocks and potholes and hummed to herself. *Mars is a bit boring really. Just red dust and red rocks and not much else. The only excitement came from avoiding the cracks and crevices in the surface and the occasional raised plateau with what looked like caves in its walls. They were probably lava tubes and unlikely to contain any sign of ancient life but they might be worth exploring sometime.*

She waited until Scotty stirred before proposing a driver swap. They put on their helmets and depressurised the car so they could step out and stretch their legs.

'It's not the most comfortable way to travel,' said Hattie.

'I'm still not used to having a nappy instead of pissing up against a bush,' said Scotty.

'You'd be hard pressed to find a bush around here.'

'That's true. I can't wait to stop for the night and get cleaned up.'

'I have a large packet of compostable wet wipes.'

'Oh, the glamour of space travel. I bet no one on Earth realises what goes on in a space suit.'

'We mustn't forget to film our exploits at Jezero,' said Hattie. 'It will make great viewing back at home.'

'Not all of them, I hope,' said Scotty, grinning.

Hattie didn't dare catch his eye.

By the time they arrived at Jezero Crater, the temperature had plummeted to minus sixty Fahrenheit.

'Lucky these suits are thermoregulated,' said Scotty, dragging the portable toilet into the pop-up tent. 'I'm not sure how warm the tent will be.'

'I vote we change and clean-up in the tent, and then seal ourselves into the large rover for the night. There's plenty of room in here if we fold down all the seats.'

'Sound's great. You go first and then I'll cook in there after I brush up.'

'Excellent. What's for dinner?'

'Mac and Cheese and tinned pears with condensed milk.'

'A feast. How did you persuade Bret to give you the condensed milk?'

'I didn't.'

Hattie laughed.

'Okay, see you shortly.'

After dinner, they lay on the large mattress made by the seats and looked at the sky through the picture window. The blue sunset stunned them into an awed silence. Despite their proximity, Scotty did not show any inclination to carry out his threat to hug her or to touch her. After a while, the expectation made Hattie nervous, and she tried to introduce humour to break the ice.

'Blue sky at night, Shepherd's fright,' she said.

'Do you always joke when you're nervous?' said Scotty. 'We don't have to do anything just because we are alone at last. Although I'd really like to if—'

Hattie leaned over and pulled him in for a kiss. He smelled like sweaty liners from the inside of spacesuit but it didn't put her off; she did too. The dry Martian atmosphere had dried and cracked his lips, but they felt soft and warm under hers. Passion permeated through her body like hot tea on a cold day, and her moan escaped into the night, ending their long kiss. Hattie opened her eyes to find him gazing at her, his pupils huge and black with desire. It made her shiver in his arms.

'Are you cold?' he said. 'We could crank up the heating. Or I could find something to cover us.'

'Stop talking and get undressed,' said Hattie.

Scotty laughed.

'Did you turn the coms off? Otherwise, hot mic is going to get a whole new meaning.'

They took off their clothes and then lay facing each other on the cushions. Scotty reached out and stroked Hattie's stomach, sending a thrill through her entire body which made her jump.

'Are you enjoying this?' he said. 'You're not the only one who's nervous you know. I haven't done this for a while.'

'I hadn't realised how much I missed being touched,' she said. 'I'm so sensitive.'

'Why don't we just fool around for a while and see where it takes us?'

Hattie nodded and moved into his arms. A warm glow suffused her whole being as they leaned in for another long, passionate kiss. Finally, they pulled apart. Hattie's cheeks shone pink with desire.

'I want to see what comes next,' she said.

Chapter 37

T he next morning, Hattie woke to find Scotty had already gone to the pop-up tent to wash up. She sat up blinking and hugged herself with glee. The fact she had only slept for a few hours did not diminish her enjoyment at remembering the night before. Their mutual passion had melted any boundaries between them, and while she slept their friendship had expanded into the hidden corners of her heart. She had never been in love before, but this felt different to her. Maybe she had finally found someone to share life with, at least for a while.

'Hey, sleepyhead. Rise and shine, and throw on your liner,' said Scotty. 'I've brought you some coffee and porridge.'

'Shouldn't I get suited up first?'

'And get porridge inside it?'

'True.'

They ate in silence, giving each other shy glances as the tendrils of the last night's passion circled around them, almost visible in the early morning sunshine. They put down their bowls and had a last warm embrace. Then Hattie carried out her ablutions in the tent, and put her spacesuit back on, knowing they wouldn't be able to touch again all day, but also that they still had another night together.

Soon they were both ready for action. Scotty kissed her tenderly before they put on their helmets. Their awkward embrace made them both giggle.

'Comms on?' he said.

Hattie nodded.

'We don't want them to worry about us.'

'True. After all we've been through.'

'That's over now. Anyway, we might be about to change history. This is one of the most momentous days of my life and I intend to enjoy every second of it.'

Scotty leant over to the controls panel and switched on the communications.

'Good morning guys. We've arrived safe and well, and survived the night. Now we're off to drill the delta,' said Scotty.

'Bret here. Excellent news. All good here too. Keep us posted. Over and out.'

They had parked their rover and trailer at the south-western edge of the delta in the Jezero Crater, almost under the wall of the crater to get easy access to the sediments. After packing away the pop-up tent and refilling their air tanks, they located the drone in the trailer and removed it from its box. Scotty unfolded the blades and placed it on the ground, offering the controls to Hattie.

'Can you fly the drone, please?' she said. 'I'd like to make notes on the tablet and select areas for us to drill.'

'Sure, where do you want it?'

'The original samples were taken in a grid over the delta so maybe we should overfly it first. I've put the coordinates in so you can over fly that area.'

Scotty lifted the drone off the ground with great care and sent it to the arm of the delta nearest to them. Hattie monitored the screen as Scotty manoeuvred the drone and criss-crossed the fan deposit. She knitted her eyebrows together and tutted as she zoomed the camera in and out, and studied close-ups of the sediments.

'What's up,' said Scotty.

233

'The cyanobacteria which form the stromatolite reefs need clear, shallow water to photosynthesize and build up them up, a bit like coral polyps.'

'But they're plants?'

'Essentially just mats of algae. But they wouldn't have grown in this delta environment. The size and sharp edges of the rock fragments in these sediments show a violent or turbulent current carried them here. Any stromatolites would have been overwhelmed by the debris flow. We need to look for well stratified rocks with fine layers rather than massive agglomerates of broken rock and sand. Why don't you fly the drone to the edge of the crater just to the east of the mouth of the delta and see if that looks more promising?'

Scotty sent the drone to the base of the cliff and flew it over the sand. Soon Hattie started nodding and grinning at the image on her tablet.

'This looks a lot more like it. Why don't you set the drone down near the bluff and we can drive over in the rover and take a look.'

They jumped back into the rover and drove to the cliff.

'So, these algae don't eat anything?' said Scotty.

'No, but that doesn't mean there wasn't anything to eat. We don't have any idea of the type of lifeforms which may have thrived before the atmosphere boiled off, if any.'

'You mean there could be other animals here?'

Hattie laughed.

'Or plants. In theory, yes, but these stromatolites are the most primitive colonies. They were present on earth three and a half billion years ago, way before any multi-celled creatures. They pumped out oxygen into the sea for two billion years and when it became saturated, into the atmosphere.'

'Stromatolites started life on earth? Why don't I know that? I thought they were just boring microbes like the ones in my smoothies.'

'They can't sing or dance,' said Hattie. 'They haven't evolved for billions of years as far as we know, but finding them would be the first step to establishing the reality of life on Mars.'

'Because they leave trace fossils behind.'

'Yup, stone cauliflowers my tutor called them.'

'And if we find them?'

'All hell will break loose on Earth. We'd certainly never have to beg for budget anymore.'

The rover stopped beside the drone and Scotty turned to Hattie.

'Would you come back here, if they asked you to?'

'Let's get home safely, before I answer that question. Space travel has its compensations...' She winked at him. 'But the doctors will have to decide if it's viable to do another trip or not.'

'If our genes are not cooked, you mean?'

'Exactly,' she said, marking another sampling point on her tablet. 'The engineers might come here next. The geology is amazing and the rocks contain a hidden wealth of minerals that may be worth exploiting. It will take me thirty years to study the samples we bring back, if we ever take any.'

'Point taken,' said Scotty. 'Where shall we drill the first hole?'

They adjusted the boring machine to drill out whole samples of fifty centimetres length in sealed tubes and chose areas which had finer sediments which had turned to dust at the surface. Hattie gave her tablet to Scotty so he could monitor and make notes on the sampling. Then, she took her hammer and all-in-one, and headed for a place where the floor of the crater had been uplifted like a slice of layer cake, showing the laminations from the floor of the crater. She took scale photographs with her all-in-one and made notes on the grain size and roundness and the quantity of matrix around the grains. Some laminations were mud or silt consistency and their grains were not visible.

235

On Earth, I'd have licked that to see which it was.

She took samples of the different layers, storing them in special sealed Kevlar bags, and taking meticulous notes so she could reference them to the log she had drawn on her geology app. The work demanded total concentration. Her modern gloves made it less awkward to do this detailed work but her hands still ached from the pressure inflicted on her fingers. She worked her way methodically down the column until she got to a mudstone overlaying a fine-grained sandstone indicating a transition to a deeper water environment. She introduced the point of her hammer into the rock and managed to break off a portion of the rock containing the boundary between the rock types. The sample had a crack along the boundary of the lamination. Hattie knew that if she could get the rock to split open parallel to the lamination boundary, she'd be able to see the surface of the lake as it appeared millions of years ago.

She put down her hammer and took out her Leatherman multitool and pushed the blade into the crack. She put gentle pressure on the blade and prised the rocks apart. The two sides parted and fell to the ground. Hattie swore and bent down with difficulty to pick them up. She balanced one of them on her hand and took a photograph of it. Then she turned it over. Her heart seemed to stop for an instant as she narrowed her eyes trying to focus on the surface through the dusty visor of her helmet. What the hell? Worm burrows? But how? The hairs on her arms couldn't stand up in her tight suit, but a wave of elation swamped her senses and her heart thundered in her chest. Life on Mars. It's true. Oh my God.

She stood swaying with the sample still in her hand. It should have been the best moment of her life, of anyone's life, so why did a little voice nag in her head? *Stay calm and think. Don't say anything.* Hattie had faith in her intuition but this seemed crazy. *Surely, I should shout this from the rooftops, and yet...*

'Is everything okay there, Hats?' said a voice in her ear. 'Your heart monitor is racing.'

Yu. Trust him to be supervising them so closely. He reminded her of how close they were to being deceived already on this voyage. Discretion was not her strong point, but she decided to keep the discovery a secret until they were safely back in the habitats.

'Hi Yu. I just got out of breath walking too fast. Nothing to worry about. All good here.'

'How's the geology looking?'

'Excellent. You have no idea. I can't wait to get back to the wet lab and examine the samples.'

'I'll be ready to help with the prep for you. Oh, by the way, my parents are back home.'

'That's fantastic. Tell me all about it when I get back.'

She put the two halves of the sample together again with all the care she could muster, and wrapped them carefully in a Kevlar bag, unable to explain to herself why she didn't want to tell anyone about the greatest discovery in the history of space travel. But until she knew who had killed the others and why, she felt as if showing anyone the sample could be signing their death warrant. The fossil represented a deadly danger to all of them, rather than a scientific discovery. She put the sample into her front pocket and zipped it in. Somehow, she refocussed on the job in hand although she patted her pocket a few times to check if she had dreamed it or not. Finishing her log, she radioed Scotty.

'Hey, buddy. I'm wrapping up here now. How's the drilling going?'

'Good timing. I've got ten samples, for you, and I wanted to move the rover to another spot a little further away. Bret needs deeper drill core samples from the centre of the crater. I thought if we drilled those out this afternoon, we could set up camp there and drive back to the settlement tomorrow.'

237

'Great. Let's go then,' said Hattie. 'Come and pick me up.'

'Are you okay? You sound funny.'

'It's the lack of atmosphere.'

'I'm sure we can fix that,' he said.

They set up the drill at the part of the crater where the sediments which filled it were at their thickest and set it going. Scotty picked up the full tubes and laid them out in boxes which he stacked in the trailer. Hattie watched him and took notes.

'Why does Bret want these particular samples,' said Hattie, as she watched the coring machine bore into the ground.

'I think they're part of the survey for metal deposits.'

'But what if we find signs of life in the crater. They can't destroy it. That would be unthinkable.'

'I'm not sure fossil which might be stromatolites are high in Bret's list of priorities, or would stop him organising a mining operation here.'

'Might be? You're dissing my whole career here.'

'You know what I mean.'

'Actually, I don't. Mo died for this.'

'Mo committed suicide.'

'Do you believe that?'

Scotty raised an eyebrow.

'Don't you?'

Hattie swallowed her answer. All her romantic assumptions about Scotty vanished in any instant. I don't know him at all. What if Bret had killed Mo on the orders of some shadowy corporation? What if Scotty had only cosied up to her to keep an eye on her? And Ellie was alone with Yu and Bret. What if they chose her to die next? She didn't suspect any of this. A wave of remorse hit Hattie for doubting her friend. They should have stuck together like Ellie had first proposed. Hattie's hand flew to her chest where the reassuring shape of the rock sample calmed her panic. She had intended to whisper her secret into Scotty's ear after their dinner but the idea now seemed preposterous. And as for having sex again?

She let out a pantomime groan and grabbed her helmet with both hands.

'What's up?' said Scotty.

'Fizzy vision, I'm afraid. I'd better get camp set up and take an early night. I'm in for a massive migraine.'

Chapter 38

Noah van Horn gazed out of the window in his office, mulling over the events of the past few days. In his hand he held the scrap of paper from Chuck's notebook, with his mother's telephone number on it. He longed to hear her voice, but feared she would despise him for being a member of the organisation which had orchestrated her other son's death. His own feelings about the NCP had also mutated into hate, and he contemplated abandoning his whole life and starting again. His natural cowardice stopped him doing both, so he found himself stuck in limbo, in a job he hated which separated him from his family.

Grace knocked softly and came in with his coffee. She had a radiant smile on her face which reflected the total change in her behaviour with him since he had given them Harlan Grime's private phone number. He returned her smile and sat down in his chair.

'Good morning, Mr Van Horn.'

'Good morning, Ms Dos Reis. Is that my coffee?'

He always said this. He knew there was no other explanation for Grace's tray, but he liked routine and his whole world had collapsed. This was one thing he could rely on.

'Milk and two sugars,' she said. 'And some of those sweet cookies you like.'

He beamed.

'Thank you.'

Grace did not leave. She looked at her feet and twirled a bracelet on her wrist.

'Was there something else?' said Van Horn.

'I thought you'd like to know,' said Grace. 'The police arrested Harlan Grimes. They charged him with murder and he's in jail awaiting trial.'

'The astronauts are safe? I'm so glad.'

'Me too. Thank you for saving Hattie.'

Van Horn swallowed.

'I did nothing I shouldn't have done earlier. I'm sorry I ever let them convince me to help him.'

'And your mother? Have you talked to her yet?'

'I'm will soon, but I'm not sure how to tell her about my role in Chad's death.'

'She's your mother. You can't abandon her now. She lost her son, but now she's got another. Tell her. She'll understand.'

After Grace had left, Van Horn sank into his chair and pumped his fist, his delayed reaction to the capture of Harlan Grimes.

'Yes. Yes. Yes!'

The screen in front of him flickered to life. Richard Taylor-Brooks, raised a bushy eyebrow at his triumphant expression.

'Am I disturbing you from the Lord's work?' he said.

'No, sir. Not at all.'

'I have some terrible news. Harlan Grimes has been taken into custody.'

Van Horn rearranged his features into something more suitable.

'I can't believe it. That's awful.'

'Yes, but that's not all. The science officer on Mars has been to the Jezero delta to drill for new samples. I'm told they look very promising. We can't risk news about this getting out to the general public.' He pursed his lips. 'As you know, we have an asset out there who is willing to sacrifice themselves in order to implement a final solution to this problem.'

'An asset?' stuttered Van Horn. 'What solution?'

'The settlement must be destroyed,' said Taylor-Brooks

'Destroyed but what about the astronauts?'

'They will die.'

'But can't we do something else?'

'It's too late. We can't let news of life on Mars become common knowledge.'

Van Horn swallowed.

'But that doesn't mean it's not true,' he said.

'I beg your pardon?'

'Just because you destroy their camp and murder them, doesn't change the facts. Maybe God created more worlds. Maybe—'

'Have you lost your mind? This is blasphemy. You need to clean yourself of these thoughts before the devil takes over. Or is it too late?'

Van Horn bit his lip.

'I thought. I mean. Of course, you're right. But what should I do?'

'Ask the Lord for forgiveness and keep quiet for now. You must do God's work without question or doubt.'

'When will this happen?'

'If there are signs of life in the samples, the asset will obliterate the settlement. It will be over in a matter of days.'

'And if the samples are barren?'

'The astronauts will be heroes when they get home. And we will carry on with our great crusade. Don't tell anyone about this. I've already given the orders.'

'I understand.'

The screen went blank.

Van Horn slumped in his chair. He couldn't escape the doubts any longer. They were real. *He had bought time for the astronauts in vain. How can I let Hattie die now?* He desperately needed to talk to someone, and who better than his mother? She would know what to do, she always had done. Perhaps running away from their fanatically religious father had been a stroke of genius? But why had she left him behind? He needed to find out. He carefully flattened the scrap on paper out onto the desk and connected to her number. A frail voice answered, one that made his heart soar.

'Yes, who is it?'

'It's me, mom. Noah.'

'Noah? Noah who?'

'Your son,' croaked Van Horn.

'Noah? Is it really you?' Her voice caught in her throat. 'But how did you find me?'

'Do you remember the journalist who interviewed you about Chad?'

'Mr Gomez? Yes, of course.'

'His companion that day, Grace, works for me as a personal assistant. She noticed a photograph of us all hidden in the cupboard in a back bathroom. She recognised me in the photo.'

'I'd no idea there was a photo in there. Chad must have hidden it.' She sniffed and Van Horn could hear her blowing her nose. 'I just can't believe it. I thought I'd never see you again. Your father—'

'He's dead, you know.'

'Oh, I didn't. I'm sorry for your loss.'

'He lost me years ago with his violent fanaticism. He told me that you and Jerry had died in a car crash, the day you left. I never questioned it. I'm so glad you're alive but...'

'But what? Can you come and see me?'

'I work for the NCP, mom. I'm pretty sure they murdered Jerry, and I helped them.'

'And how did you do that? Wasn't he on Mars?'

'It's a long story. Not one that paints me in a great light. Do you still want to see me?'

'More than anything in the world.'

'The NCP aren't finished yet. They plan to destroy the base on Mars, but I may be able to prevent them in time. What should I do?'

'Why are you asking me? Didn't I bring you up right? You know what to do.'

'I guess so.'

'Make the call, get the truth out there. Mr Gomez will help you if you let him. And then, come and see me. I'll be waiting for you.'

'Do you still like cinnamon slices?'

Afterwards, Van Horn wept bitter tears, for his brother, for his bad choices, until he had no more to shed. He looked around his opulent office and sighed.

'I never liked this place anyway,' he said out loud, and pressed the intercom. 'Grace, get yourself a box and pack your belongings. I'm just going to make a call and then we're leaving and we're not coming back.'

'Where are we going?' said Grace.

'We're picking up Chuck, and then we're need to visit your father.'

Van Horn drew himself upright in his chair and sucked in his stomach, flexing his shoulders. *I was a physically imposing young man, why did I collapse in a heap? I'm not taking any more shit, and I don't care what the consequences are.* He called Richard Taylor-Brooks, who popped up on his screen still pulling up his fly, his cheeks pink.

'Jesus Christ, Van Horn. Could you have chosen a worse time to call me?'

'There's no need for blasphemy,' said Van Horn, smirking. 'I'm calling to tell you that I quit, and I'm going to spill the beans to the police.'

Taylor-Brooks blinked a couple of times and then he sneered.

'Don't be ridiculous. You're the one who's up to his neck here. You can't tie anything to me. Anyway, you're too chickenshit to carry out your threat.'

Van Horn shook his head.

'You don't know me,' he said. 'Who do you think ratted on Grimes?'

Taylor-Brooks' eyes widened.

'You're fired,' he said. 'Get out, and never come back.'

'Oh, I'll be back,' said Van Horn. 'With the cops.'

He cut off the call and grabbed his external hard drive. Everything had already been backed up to the cloud but head office held the key to the files. Grace had already called a cab and soon they were outside Chuck's house waiting for him to come out. A disappointed Chuck trailed over to their car looking back at Gina, who stood in a negligee in the doorway, rolling her eyes to heaven.

'Did we disturb you?' said Van Horn.

'I'll never get past second base,' said Chuck. 'What's the rush?'

'You'll see,' said Van Horn. 'The shit's about to hit the fan.

***

Edgar Fredericks beckoned them into his office and shut the door.

'I don't believe we've been introduced,' he said, sticking his hand out to Van Horn.

'I'm Noah van Horn, your daughter's boss.'

'Are you indeed? This is a pretty odd mixture of folk. What on Earth's going on?'

'The NCP are behind the murders on Mars,' said Grace. 'Just because Harlan Grimes is behind bars doesn't mean the astronauts are safe yet.'

'But what can they do from here?' said Fredericks

'They told me they have an asset on Mars,' said Van Horn.

'An asset. You mean one of the astronauts?' said Fredericks.

'I guess so.'

Chuck scratched his head.

'Noah told me on the way here that the asset has been sent orders to destroy the settlement, if Hattie finds proof of life in the samples,' said Chuck.

'Then, if we want to avoid a tragedy, we need to get a message through to Hattie,' said Fredericks. 'She must pretend there is nothing in the samples, whether she finds proof or not. We can announce the mistake when they get home safely. We've waited centuries to find out if there is life on Mars. Another few months won't make any difference.'

'But how do we know she's not the asset?' said Chuck.

'I'm her father,' said Fredericks. 'I know.'

'Hattie would never help the NCP. She doesn't even believe in God much,' said Grace.

'It can't be Hattie. She wasn't on the original crew,' said Van Horn.

'And what if they killed Serena so Hattie would go instead?' said Chuck, playing devil's advocate.

They all looked at each other.

'Because she could have hidden Yu's sabotage of the samples, but she went back out to Jezero Crater to get more,' said Grace. 'Does that sound like someone with something to hide?'

'They've all got a motive. Yu tried to replace the samples. Bret is in the pay of massive mining corporations who want to tear the place up. And Scotty, it could be him,' said Chuck.

'Why Scotty?' said Noah.

'I just remembered Scotty didn't come to the launch dinner. He could have been poisoning Serena Hampton's sushi,' said Chuck.

'And Ellie... Maybe Ellie doesn't have one. Should we tell her instead?' said Van Horn.

'I still think we should tell Hattie. They killed one science officer, and they tried to kill Hattie and got Wayne instead. Hattie controls the samples too. She'll know what to do,' said Grace.

246

'Okay, it's agreed. Grace, can you send Hattie one of your cryptic messages on Mo's app? Make sure she knows not to tell anyone about the samples, whatever happens.,' said Fredericks.

'And the rest of us?' said Chuck.

'There must be someone in NASA who facilitated the sabotage of the mission. Somebody switched off Wayne's hibernation pod and played with the oxygen controls in the habitats. I have my suspicions that they also put a block on communications with the fifth Starship. We must find them,' said Fredericks.

'Don't look at me,' said Van Horn. 'I was never in that loop, but what about Grimes? Has he talked yet?'

'They've kept him on ice while the detectives gathered the evidence from his house. I think they were planning on interviewing him tomorrow,' said Chuck.

'I doubt they'll get anything out of him,' said Grace. 'He plays hardball.'

'We have to keep trying everything. Who knows what the NCP have planned? And with an asset on Mars, the killing might not be over yet,' said Chuck.

Chapter 39

Since they had returned from Isidis Planitia, Hattie had spent all her waking hours in the laboratory. She preserved the trace fossil on her first morning back by sealing it in a silicon envelope and concealed it in a 3-D printed box the size of a post-it note. She carried it with her everywhere, afraid to put it down for prying eyes to find. A small piece of slate with infinite value.

Grace's cryptic message had doubled her anxiety. She told Hattie that one of her fellow astronauts had orders to kill them all if she found any proof of life on Mars. *Hadn't they arrested the murderer on earth?* It didn't leave her with a lot of choice. Bret seemed to be the one with the most obvious motive but she felt uncertain about everyone except Ellie. Thank goodness she hadn't given in to the temptation to tell Scotty about her find. She looked for clues as to who it might be, but everyone seemed in high spirits since the murderer had been arrested back on earth. No one mentioned the murders any more and between the five of them, they managed a massive workload without any complaints.

'The others would have loved this. What a pity they didn't live to enjoy it,' said Bret, one evening.

'We're pioneers,' said Yu.

'We could be legends,' said Ellie.

'If Hattie would hurry up and find something, we'd be famous,' said Scotty.

248

'Yeah? Well, if Yu would get off his behind and finish the thin sections, I might have a chance,' said Hattie.

Although she joined in the banter, the effort of not divulging her ground shattering secret weighed her down. During the day, she disguised her anguish by burying herself in work, something that did not go unnoticed.

'Honestly, you're no fun anymore,' said Scotty. 'Have I done something wrong. I hoped we might—'

'I'm sorry, but I don't want anyone to know about us. It's hard enough being taken seriously already, and NASA frowns on relationships between astronauts.'

'Well, if you feel like that.'

'Don't get snotty about it. I'd like to give us a try, if you're still interested, once we land back on Earth, but I can't afford to give in to my feelings here. There's too much at stake. Can you understand that?'

Scotty pouted.

'You're probably right. I just want to kiss you all the time and I know that's unprofessional, but it's true.'

'It's mutual. But please be my friend for now. I need one pretty badly with the pressure I'm under.'

'Of course. Always. Is there anything I can do right now?'

'I'd love a cup of coffee.'

When Scotty had left, Hattie continued to write up her report on the Jezero Crater. She meticulously described every aspect of the geology as evidenced by the laminations in the basin sediments, emphasising their different environments and the fauna expected in such biomes on earth. She didn't mention the trace fossil in case anyone could hack her tablet but every time she touched the container, she pictured a primitive worm slogging his way through the sediment. He even had a name, Wilbur. She imagined the sediment raining down on his burrows. *Wilbur's not gonna like that.*

Yu produced the first set of thin sections after a couple of days. He brought them into the wet lab on a tray, smiling from ear to ear.

'These are the ones,' he said. 'I can feel it in my bones.'

'That's what you said last time.'

'Well, this time my bones are right.'

Hattie grinned.

'You never know.'

But she did. She knew whatever turned up in her slides, she couldn't tell anyone about it. The solar storm raging in space had cut off all communications from Earth for the time being, so she didn't have to lie to anyone yet. What she would do once communications returned remained a mystery to her, but she now had two objectives; confirm the presence of stromatolites, and investigate the possibility more complex life forms also existed on Mars. The concept blew her mind. *What would they find preserved in the muds on Mars? How complex did lifeforms become, before they were obliterated?* Just what could be hidden in the sediments of the Jezero Crater? Her mind boggled.

She slid the thin section under the microscope and studied the first sample, noticing the round volcanic grains and lack of matrix which suggested constant winnowing and currents removing the fine-grained sediment. This kind of coarse-grained environment did not preserve the delicate bodies of early life. She needed mudstones if she were to find more proof of complex life. The body forms of worms and cephalopods did not decay in anoxic environments and sometimes they left ethereal traces behind, like those seen in the Burgess Shale.

Over the next few days, she worked her way through the samples drilled out on their sampling trip. She started to relax as the samples, though favourable, turned up negative for stromatolites. *Maybe the worm tubes were just an artifact after all.* She took images and added keys to the components explaining the environment of deposition and the lack of life. And then she saw it. The hairs on her arms stood up as she recognised layering consistent with algal mats in the slide. She rubbed her eyes and looked again. Mo's app flashed green but she did not need an app to tell her what she was looking at. A stromatolite. Without a shadow of a doubt.

'Is there life on Mars?' she said. 'Yes, there is.'

She pumped her fist and did a jig around the lab before sitting down again and taking images of the slide. As she had predicted, the sample of rock came from the sediments deposited in the calm waters at the borders of the Jezero Crater. She tapped out the description on her tablet, only avoiding the use of the words stromatolite or possible signs of life. A noise behind her made her spin around on her chair. Ellie stood in the doorway staring at Mo's app which still blinked green, her face pale.

'Oh my God,' she said.

'You won't tell anyone will you?'

'Why not? Isn't this why we're all here?'

Hattie jumped up and shut the door.

'Shh. Don't say anything. It's dangerous. No one must know.'

'What do you mean?'

'One of the men has orders to kill us all if I find signs of life on Mars.'

Ellie's eyes became like saucers.

'Who told you that?' she said.

'I got a message from my sister before the solar flares cut off communications.'

Ellie's jaw worked but she seemed stunned. She walked over to the microscope and peered down the lens.

'That's it? That's your proof? Couldn't you be wrong?'

Hattie bristled.

'I could be, but Mo's app and my experience tell me I'm right. Anyway, that's not the only proof.'

'It isn't? I don't think I want to know. It might be dangerous.'

Hattie took a deep breath.

'You're right. It would be. But believe me, I'm sure.'

Ellie bit her lip.

'It's a pity you can't tell anyone,' she said. 'We should have a party to celebrate.'

'Maybe we could have a party anyway. It's Bret's birthday tomorrow.'

'You're kidding.'

'My all-in-one told me,' said Hattie.

'What will we do for drink?'

'I think Yu's been experimenting in the greenhouse. He's got a garbage bin full of fermented liquid he made from grain that wouldn't germinate.'

'Beer? Seriously?'

'You better ask him.'

'Have you got any chocolate left? We could pool our resources and make a cake.'

'It will probably be disgusting.'

'So will the beer.'

Chapter 40

Despite their increased workload, nobody objected to the idea of a party to celebrate Bret's birthday. Since the solar flares had blocked communications with their loved ones, the crew had become closer out of necessity. Hattie and Yu still slept in Marge, but all the meals and socialising happened in Homer. Scotty wanted to move to Marge but he couldn't come up with an excuse.

'It's probably for the best,' said Hattie, even though she hungered for another night with him.

'There's a long time remaining before we go home,' said Scotty. 'I may not last.'

Yu produced a Kevlar bin full of a green liquid with scum on the top and announced Chateau Chen ready for drinking. Bret tried a glass, pronouncing it quite disgusting and burping loudly.

'Honestly,' said Ellie. 'Are we having a frat party?'

'It's my party, and I can burp if I want to,' said Bret. 'Anyway, we can't be adults all the time. It gets boring.'

'Hattie burps anyway so we won't notice the difference,' said Yu.

'It's better than farting,' said Scotty.

All the crew contributed some of their precious stores to make a cake for Bret, and a dressing for the salad from the greenhouse. Yu had come up trumps by growing the first tomatoes and peppers on Mars, as well as various types of lettuce and some tiny radishes. A frozen chicken they were saving for Thanksgiving got taken out of storage and readied for the oven.

'Real meat,' said Scotty. 'My mouth's watering.'

Ellie spent the evening before the party watching chick-flicks with Hattie on the couch in Marge. They had become closer again since Hattie got back from Isidis Planitia. Ellie sighed.

'Honestly,' she said. 'I could write the scripts for these movies. I knew what would happen from the moment she met him.'

'That's why they're popular. No surprises and a happy ending,' said Hattie.

'What about you and Scotty? Did anything happen out there?'

'Out where?'

'You don't fool me. You shared a tent for two nights. Didn't you share bodily warmth?'

'Sort of. It's complicated.'

'Why. He likes you and you like him.'

'I'm not sure of his motives. Sometimes I feel like he's the one.'

'But the other day, you said it could be Bret.'

'It could be Yu.'

'Me?' Ellie jumped up, her face thunderous, and her eyes flashing in anger. 'Why are you accusing me?'

Hattie roared with laughter.

'Yu not you, dumb ass.'

Ellie rolled her eyes.

'Only kidding,' she said.

'We're all paranoid these days,' said Hattie. 'I thought the worry was over but now we're back to square one. I knew Mars would try to kill us. I never thought an astronaut would.'

'It'll soon be over,' said Ellie. 'Maybe your sister got the wrong end of the stick. They must feel paranoid too, being too far away to help us.'

'Maybe.'

But Hattie didn't think so. Grace had been quite explicit. On the other hand, Hattie couldn't find out who it was because communications were down. *Surely, they knew by now? Grace said they were close to finding out but gave no clues. And she couldn't tell Grace her secret for fear of it leaking out. It's up to me. If the killer doesn't know I've found life, he won't act.*

Even with the burden she carried, Hattie found herself looking forward to Bret's party. When it came, it brought out the best in everyone. The smell of roast chicken and the availability of alcohol made it seem more real. They only had their NASA uniforms to wear, but Scotty had constructed some alien headbands with antennae attached for everyone to wear. He also rigged up some flashing lights beside the space cleared for dancing.

'You won't catch me wiggling my ass out there,' said Bret.

'If you drink enough of my beer, you'll be out there naked,' said Yu.

Ellie started to Vogue and soon they were all at it, trying to outdo each other with the awkwardness of their poses. Hattie fell over onto the couch and Scotty feigned a similar accident to land on top of her where he sneaked a quick kiss in the chaos.

'Oh, unlucky,' said Yu.

'A coincidence?' said Ellie, wagging her finger. 'I don't think so.'

Hattie dragged herself away from Scotty's embrace, blushing and denying it.

'I'd need my gloves on to touch another astronaut,' said Bret.

'I'd need more than beer to touch you,' said Ellie.

'Me, why?' said Yu.

'Not Yu, you,' said Ellie. 'I'm getting déjà vu here.'

Hattie giggled.

They all sat down to eat and demolished the chicken in double quick time.

'That was out of this world,' said Bret.

'Hardly surprising seeing as we're on Mars,' said Yu.

'Yum,' said Hattie, licking her fingers. 'What luxury. I'm never going to diss chicken again. Not that I did before.'

'I'm too full to dance now,' said Yu.

Hattie noticed Ellie heading for the lift. She followed her and tapped her on the shoulder.

'Hey, girlfriend, are you wimping out on me. I can't dance with three men by myself.'

Ellie jumped.

'Oh, I'll be back with a bang,' she said. 'I'm preparing a surprise for us. You're going to love it.'

'Do you need help?'

'No, I've got this.'

Ellie gave Hattie a hug and whispered 'I'm sorry,' in her ear, before getting into the lift. Hattie stood there for several seconds. *What was she sorry for? Ellie was such a dark horse.* She approached Bret who had challenged Scotty to an arm wrestle. The two men were bright red in the face with exertion. Bret held up his free hand to stop Hattie from talking. She waited until Scotty knocked over his beer and they lifted their arms out of the pool of green liquid advancing over the table.

'Ellie's gone to organise a surprise. Do you know anything about it?' she said.

'I think she said something about fireworks. She is a chemist after all,' said Bret.

'Fireworks? Is that wise?' said Hattie.

'It should be safe enough. We're miles from the fuel stores,' said Scotty. 'Anyway, you owe me a dance. Come on, Fredericks. Let's see you move that booty.'

As they hit the floor, Yu changed the music to something slow and moody. Hattie couldn't resist the chance to snuggle up to Scotty and sniff in his manly odour. *Could he really be a murderer?* The notion seemed faintly ridiculous. She wrapped her arms around his neck and winked at him. He glanced around to see if anyone was looking and gave her a passionate kiss.

Yu noticed but he distracted Bret by going through the contents of the salad with him. Hattie thought she might faint with passion.

Suddenly, the habitat shook on its foundations and a muffled roar came from outside.

Bret stood up and looked around.

'What the fuck was that?' he said, swaying. 'An earthquake?'

'There was only one shockwave. It felt like an explosion,' said Scotty. 'It must have been a big one if we could hear it.'

'Where's Ellie?' said Yu.

'She didn't come back,' said Hattie.

'Holy shit,' said Bret, staring out of the window. 'Look at that.'

They pressed themselves against the quadruple glazing and looked out towards the Starships. A massive fire leapt to the heavens.

'What the hell?' said Scotty.

'Yu, get the clinic ready. Ellie may be injured. Scotty and Hattie, come and get suited up with me.'

Despite all their efforts, it took them twenty minutes to exit the hub and get into the rover. Bret drove towards a fire that had almost burned out by the time they arrived. The building containing the Moxies had been obliterated and the Starship had opened up like a giant metal tulip. The fuel bowser sat undamaged beside Starship 3 where it had been placed to down load the remaining fuel from the tank. No one spoke. And then Ellie staggered into view.

'Get her into the rover,' said Bret, but seeing the rover, she started to run away.

Hattie jumped out and ran after her. Ellie disappeared behind the wreckage of the spaceship and Hattie followed her. Ellie had collapsed onto the ground. Hattie bent over her.

'What happened?' she said.

'You shouldn't have told me,' said Ellie. 'I never wanted to kill you, but I had my orders.'

'You did this?' said Hattie. 'I hope it was worth it.'

'There can't be life on Mars,' said Ellie. 'It's against God's will.'

She shut her eyes and gave a big sigh.

Hattie tapped her radio.

'She's gone, guys. Come and help me carry her.'

They drove Ellie's body back to the hub and removed their suits before dealing with hers. Then they carried her to the clinic and laid her down on the stretcher. Apart from a slight trickle of blood oozing from her nose, she looked like a porcelain doll. Her fair curls framed her pretty face.

'Be warned,' said Bret. 'Beauty outside can hide the monster within.'

Hattie sniffed.

'She told me she was sorry,' she said. 'I should have guessed.'

'Don't be ridiculous,' said Scotty. 'No one knew.'

'A deadly rose among the blunted thorns. She had us all wrapped around her finger,' said Bret.

'Did you get her phone?' said Hattie.

'It's right here,' said Yu. 'Why?'

'She can't have been working alone,' said Scotty. 'Hattie's right. We need to upload all her communications.'

'Won't they be encrypted?' said Yu.

'Someone will know how read them. Nobody's safe until we find out who's responsible for all this,' said Scotty.

'But won't they get intercepted by the same person who's been sabotaging the mission from NASA?' said Bret.

'Send them to Chuck Gomez,' said Hattie. 'He's the one who figured out who killed Serena. We can trust him.'

'Transmit the data as soon as the communications are back. Let's get to bed,' said Bret. 'Scotty and I will do a damage appraisal in the morning and we'll make a plan.'

No one said anything but Hattie knew they were done for. She lay in bed unable to sleep until dawn. Ellie had just killed them all.

Chapter 41

The grim news arrived on Earth two days later. Edgar Fredericks had just finished eating breakfast with his wife when he got the call from NASA. He listened intently, turning his back on his wife so she could not read his face. He nodded, and made conciliatory noises, and then hung up. He composed himself and then returned to the table and took his wife's hand, patting it in an abstract manner as he searched for a way to tell her the news.

'What is it?' she said. 'What's wrong? Tell me.'

'We finally got through to Mars again. Unknown to us, the NCP had an asset embedded in the crew of the Mars Mission. Astronaut Ellie Barrett sabotaged the Moxie plant two days ago, blowing up the reserves of methane and oxygen stored in the Starship. The explosion killed her.'

Juana's eyes widened in horror as she took in the news.

'And Hattie?'

'She's safe. They all are, but there's a problem.'

'They have plenty of supplies, don't they?' said Juana.

'Well, they have adequate fuel due to the reserves on the other Starships, and apart from a couple of melted cables, the kilopower farm will still produce plenty of power for heating and lighting in the habitats. But I'm afraid oxygen reserves, or the lack of them, are the elephant in the room.'

Juana choked on her coffee.

'What do you mean?'

'I'm afraid that without a large Moxie plant, the oxygen reserves will quickly deplete, and the astronauts will eventually asphyxiate. Ellie has sentenced them all to death, including our girl.'

'But there must be something you can do.'

'We're going to do everything we can, but it may not be enough.'

'But, but she'll die if you can't fix it,' said Juana, choking back a sob.

'I'm so sorry darling. It's heart breaking, but they're so far away. We will try until the last minute, but it looks hopeless.'

'Is there anything I can do?'

'Will you please stay on line for her today? I have to go to NASA and fight for Hattie and the other astronauts. Maybe we can come up with something, but Hattie needs you now. She needs her mother.'

Tears started to leak down Juana's face.

'Can you call Grace, please?' she said. 'And get her to come. I can't face this alone. Hattie will be too brave and pretend she's not afraid. Grace will know how to talk to her.'

'Okay, darling. I may not be home for a couple of days. Can you hold the fort?'

'Yes, sweetheart. I'll do my best. Call me if you need anything.'

Edgar Fredericks entered NASA and went directly to his office to contact the President of the United States, a call which summed up the situation. The man had wept on hearing the news about the disaster, and begged Fredericks to do something.

'Can't we send a rescue mission? Or adapt something to produce oxygen? What about the greenhouse? Plants produce oxygen, don't they?'

'We would need acres of vegetables to keep all four of them alive. We don't have anywhere to grow all the necessary plants, and the water supplies would not last.'

'Are they all going to die? Can't we put them back to sleep until they are rescued?'

'I'm afraid the hibernation pods were destroyed in the explosion. I'm sorry, Mr President. I'm not saying we've stopped trying, but the oxygen will only last them another week or so, and unless we find a solution by then, this voyage will end in tragedy.'

The President sighed.

'Oh my God,' he said. 'Your daughter is out there. I'm sorry. I got so caught up in this dreadful disaster that I forgot how tragic this is for you personally.'

'Thank you, sir. Hattie's having the time of her life out there. I don't think she'd give it up to be safe. They'll find a way to make peace with the world.'

'God bless you. And, thank you for your service to our country.'

'We haven't given up yet. I have the best brains on planet Earth working on a solution.'

I'm praying for you. Anything you need is yours. Just ask.'

'God bless America,' said Fredericks.

Afterwards he wept alone in his office. He couldn't believe Hattie would die. She had been so excited to fulfil her dreams and they were about to be ended by a bunch of religious fanatics. He needed to do something positive while he waited for his scientists to exhaust the possibilities for saving her. Then his all-in-one rang. He had meant to block all calls, but in his distress he had forgotten. He grabbed the unit intending to refuse the call. Then he saw it was from Chuck Gomez and flashed up as urgent. Despite his distress, he answered.

'Chuck, I presume you've heard? I'm not available to talk to you right now. Sorry.'

'Wait, don't go. I just received a large download from Hattie. She says they're the files from Ellie's all-in-one.'

'But why did she send it to you?'

'I guess that the astronauts still believe there's an NCP asset in NASA.'

'Give them to the police then. Their forensic data unit should be able to remove the encryption,' said Fredericks.

'Have the police got anything from Grimes yet?'

'No. They searched his house and didn't find any links to the NCP.'

'What about Taggart?'

Chuck gasped.

'Taggart. I'd forgotten. Oh my God. He's the key. We need to look at the evidence the police took from Grime's place. Listen leave it with me. I'll give Gina a ring and ask her to look through the boxes. I'll get on it straight away. It's not over until it's over.'

'I'm grateful, Chuck. You were the only one who realised the astronauts' deaths were not an accident. At least you tried.'

Chuck cleared his throat.

'Edgar, I wanted to say how sorry I am about Hattie. I feel like part of the family now, and my heart is breaking for you.'

'Thanks, Chuck. I know she would appreciate that. We're going to revenge her. She'll know. She'll be watching us.'

***

Noah van Horn stood at the door of his mother's house, clutching the bag of cinnamon buns in his sweaty hand. He pressed the door bell and waited for her to open it. Adrift for the first time in his life, he had shut the door on his religious past and decided to start anew. Meeting his mother seemed like going backwards and he wasn't at all sure of his own motives. His trepidation increased as

263

May Farrant opened the door. She didn't look anything like the mother he remembered. Her grey hair and saggy neck disturbed him. He hesitated as she looked him up and down.

'Don't you look just like your father?' she said. 'I guess you can't help it.'

And then she smiled and held out her arms.

***

When the doorbell rang after eight o'clock at night, Sybil Reisner prevaricated. Nobody came to see her in the evenings. What if a burglar had decided to use the front door? She certainly couldn't do anything to prevent him ransacking the house. The doorbell rang again and her natural curiosity got the better of her. She went into the hall and noticed the slight silhouette of a woman through the glass panels. Who on earth was doing house calls at this hour?

She opened the door to find Grace Fredericks standing in the gloom, her face a picture of misery.

'Why Grace. I haven't seen you for ever so long. What brings you this way?'

'Hello, Mrs Reisner. I've been thinking about Hattie, and I came to ask you a favour.'

'You poor child. I've been praying for your sister every night. Morty's waiting for her, you know. He told me so. You don't need to worry. He'll take care of her.'

Grace's eyes filled with tears.

'Thank you. I know he will. He loved Hattie too.'

'What can I do for you?'

'I know it sounds stupid, but I'd like to use your telescope for a minute. I want to feel closer to her.'

'Oh my goodness. I can't imagine what you're going through, and your poor parents must be devastated.

Come with me. I had planned to do a little star gazing myself.'

Grace followed Sybil Reisner up the rickety stair case to the attic viewing platform.

'What a fantastic view. The night is so clear I can see a million stars.'

'That's exactly what your sister liked to say. She and Morty used to stay up here for hours. I never knew why until he died. Now I come up here to feel closer to him, just like you want to do with your sister. I've got the telescope pointed at Mars. You need to adjust the focus for your eyesight.'

Grace bent down and looked through the eye piece. She held her breath as the planet came into view, clearer than she imagined.

'Hi Hattie,' she whispered. 'It's me, Grace.'

Chapter 42

B ret cleared his throat. He had massive bags under his eyes, and his slumped shoulders told Hattie all she needed to know.

'Scotty and I have done a thorough review of our remaining assets and I'm afraid it's not good news,' he said.

'We have plenty of food, fuel and water for the time being. If we adopt severe rationing, we might even survive until the next Hohmann transfer window.' said Scotty. 'But our oxygen reserves are critical. Unless we come up with something soon, we are not going to make it. And I'm all out of ideas, I'm afraid.'

'I know this is not what you wanted to hear,' said Bret. 'And as commander of this mission, I feel personally responsible, but facts are facts. Your families will be informed officially by NASA when we are gone, but I suggest we all contact our loved ones and send them loving messages to remember us by.'

'How soon will we run out of oxygen?' said Yu.

'Including the EVA units and storage in the rover, I estimate we have enough for about a week,' said Scotty.

'We can't just sit here waiting to die,' said Yu. 'There must be something we can do.'

'Technically, I'm all out of ideas, but the guys back home are working on it. To be honest, I don't want to give you false hope. We need to get our affairs in order,' said Bret.

'I'm not going to sit here waiting to suffocate,' said Yu. 'I have to do something more positive.'

Hattie put her arm around his shoulders.

'Yu's right. I don't know about you guys, but I've always wanted go up to Elysium Planitia and have a stroll up to the flanks of Elysium Mons,' said Hattie. 'Who's with me?'

'Are you crazy? Who wants a stroll at a time like this?' said Bret, rolling his eyes.

'Me,' said Yu. 'I've been stuck inside the greenhouse for months. If I'm going to die, I'd like to go on an EVA first.'

'I like it,' said Scotty. 'If we have to go, let's leave in style. We can take the last of the oxygen up with us and let it run out watching the sunset.'

'I vote we take our luxuries up there and have a picnic too,' said Hattie.

'A picnic? Are you all mad?' said Bret.

'I've got some great cookies,' said Scotty.

'And I've got some delicious noodles we can rehydrate,' said Yu. 'It looks like you are out voted, Bret. It would be a pleasure to suffocate with my friends after a great day out. I vote yes.'

'Me too,' said Scotty.

'And me,' said Hattie. 'Bret?'

Bret shook his head, but he smiled.

'Okay, you win, but we have to leave this place ready for the next crew before we go. The next few days will be devoted to finishing our reports and transmitting all our data back to NASA. I'd like to be professional to the end.'

'Fair enough,' said Scotty. 'The rover robots are doing a good job categorising and storing the scrap. The spare parts will be useful for anyone arriving here. I'll get the large rover ready for the picnic.'

Despite the ghastly cloud hanging over them, a new enthusiasm gripped the astronauts, and they completed all their tasks in good humour to the sound of music at high volume. They ate the most delicious things still left in the stores with mixed salads from the greenhouse and hung out watching old movies on the television.

'My vegetables are going to outlive me,' said Yu, stuffing a tomato in his mouth.

'They'd probably make better astronauts,' said Scotty.

'Honestly, you two. Are you ever serious?' said Bret.

'Not often,' said Yu.

In the excitement of preparing for the picnic, they almost forgot why they were going, but when Scotty announced that the oxygen levels in the habitats would soon start reducing, their predicament became very real. They sent their last messages to NASA with a promise to transmit their last position so their bodies could be found. Since it took thirty minutes for messages to go back and forth to Earth, there was no way of having a meaningful talk with their families. Hattie transferred all of her personal photographs and files to Grace with the instruction to destroy anything that might cause a problem. She told her parents she loved them more than the universe and sent love to Mrs Reisner. There didn't seem any point dwelling on what she was about to do.

They got into the large rover after sealing the hub for the last time, pulling a trailer with the back-up oxygen units on it, enough to last until evening. Hattie took Buzz Lightyear with her, and a photograph of her family printed out and tucked into the drawer underneath him. She felt light headed but strangely calm. Scotty sat beside her in the rover and took her hand. They had spent a couple of nights together in Marge now that nobody cared what anyone did with their last days alive. His love had taken the edge off their awful situation and she felt grateful for it.

Ahead of them, Elysium loomed red and purple, unfeasibly enormous.

'Would you look at that?' said Bret. 'It's taller than Everest, you know.'

They rose up to the Elysium Planitia and motored for several hours until they got to the ridge where they would watch the sun set. Then they sat in the rover with their helmets off, eating and drinking to their hearts' content, and singing along to Hattie's musical collections.

'Do you think the Beatles are the best pop group ever?' said Yu.

'I like Oasis,' said Scotty.

'What about more recent bands like Grundle?' said Hattie.

'What about them?' said Bret, and helped himself to another square of chocolate.

'Who feels sick?' said Scotty.

'Me,' said Hattie. 'Shall we go for a stroll?'

The four astronauts did not go far from the rover as they were worried about having enough oxygen in their units. Bret took out the helicopter and they all had turns flying it up the mountain slopes until Yu managed to crash it.

'You owe the US Government about a gazillion dollars,' said Hattie.

'Just as well I won't be here to pay it.'

As the afternoon wore on, they all returned and switched units.

'Last call for oxygen,' said Yu.

'Let's get a good seat for the sunset,' said Bret.

They mounted the ridge and watched in awe as the sun turned blue and slid down the sky. The shadows lengthened and the colours deepened around them. Elsyium Mons behind them, turned a dark crimson and purple. Hattie gazed out across the plain below them to the horizon and tried to take it all in. It seemed her that she had never seen anything so beautiful.

'It's not a bad place to die,' said Yu.

'Should we say a prayer?' said Scotty. 'I'm not very religious but—'

'What the hell is that?' said Hattie, jumping to her feet.

'What, Hats?' he said. 'I was getting all spiritual over here and you've wrecked the mood.'

'That. Can't you see it. Over there.'

The suns rays hit something in the distance and the resulting flash illuminated the area again.

'What the hell?' said Bret.

'It's something metallic,' said Hattie. 'Oh my God. Could it be the lost Starship?'

'Don't get over excited. It's more likely to be the Insight rover,' said Scotty. 'But it could be. I can't believe it.'

'How far away is it?' said Bret.

'The sensor on the robot arm on the rover could tell us,' said Hattie.

The four astronauts ran to the vehicle and jumped in. Bret drove up to the crest and measured the distance using the laser sight. He nodded and sealed the rover.

'It's about a two-hour drive from here. I wish we could check before we go over there. It might be a false hope, and the oxygen will last until we get there, but I'm not sure how much longer than that,' said Bret. 'A couple of hours perhaps.'

'Take off your helmets. I'm going to route the oxygen from the units into the rover, one by one until we run out,' said Scotty. 'Let me know if you are feeling sleepy or get a headache and I'll change the unit.'

Yu started crying.

'If I hadn't crashed the helicopter, you could have sent it to find out.'

'Don't be silly. We're dead anyway if we don't go,' said Hattie.

'But we have enough oxygen to return to the habs,' said Bret. 'What if they have sent us a solution.'

'And do what? Suffocate there instead? They can't save us now. It's too late.' said Scotty. 'I vote we risk

270

driving towards it. If we run out of oxygen, we'll fall asleep as the carbon dioxide level gets too high.'

'It's our only chance,' said Hattie.

'Is that the consensus?' said Bret.

All the astronauts put up their hands.

'Put on your seatbelts. I'm going to drive like Sebastian Loeb,' said Bret.

'Who the hell is he?' said Yu.

'Some rally car hero,' said Scotty.

Bret pointed the car directly at the point of light and put in coordinates. He removed the speed restriction and grabbed the steering wheel.

'Hold on,' he said. 'And try not to breathe. We might just make it.'

He drove as fast as he could taking as few risks as possible. The rover almost overturned on a few occasions as he swerved to avoid a collision but he drove doggedly on. After about an hour, they rounded a bend and were greeted with the sight of the lost Starship gleaming in their headlights. A spontaneous cheer broke out in the rover and they all exchanged high-fives.

'We're saved,' said Yu.

'Can you message NASA?' said Scotty. 'If they have found the guy who turned off Wayne's pod, they can reactivate the Starship communication for us.'

'Brilliant idea,' said Bret. 'Sent the text, Yu and ask them to find us some oxygen or we're all going to suffocate.'

'We've got to get there first,' said Scotty. 'There's a crevasse separating us from it. We can't cross that on foot. We'll have to go around.'

'How much air have we got left?' said Bret.

'If I got out it would last longer,' said Yu.

'Don't be ridiculous,' said Hattie. 'What if we need a doctor? It's all of us, or none of us. Right or left, Scotty?'

'Right,' said Scotty, and Bret swung the rover parallel to the ravine.

'I'm not going to stop until I find somewhere to cross,' he said.

He switched up the music.

'And no singing,' he said. 'Driver's choice.'

Chapter 43

C huck tried not to lose his cool with the woman at the reception of the police headquarters. The new receptionist had taken out a nail file and worried a hang nail on her index finger with it. She chewed a piece of gum with her mouth half open.

'Please can you call Gina Flores for me,' he said. 'This is extremely important.'

'I'm sorry,' said the receptionist. 'I don't have the authority.'

'But the astronauts are in danger,' said Chuck.

The woman rolled her eyes at him.

'They're always in danger. There's nothing you or I can do about it.'

'You don't understand—'

'Listen, sir. We're all glad you're such an upstanding citizen but if you don't get lost, I'll have them arrest you for harassment.'

'The chief of police is a friend of mine. Ask him?'

She snorted.

'That corny line won't work with me. I'm friends with the President, you know, but I don't go to the White House and demand to see him when he's busy.'

Chuck tried his all-in-one again. *Gina, pick up, please.* Where was she? After another ten minutes of silent standoff, the inner door opened and Gina came out, panting.

'Sorry, I was practicing self-defence in the gym and I left my all-in-one on silent.'

'Isn't that forbidden?'

'Who's gonna know? What's the big rush. Is there a fire?'

'It's vital that I see the evidence boxes from Harlan Grimes's apartment. We need to trace the mole who's been intercepting and passing on communications in NASA.'

'But Grimes is a dead end. We didn't find anything.'

'I'd still like to look. This might be our last chance to find out who's behind this. Can you get me in?'

'Let me talk to the boss. You're in his good books right now. Stay here.'

Gina strode off leaving him in a cloud of patchouli and lavender. The tips of her hair flicked him in the face as she turned away but he leaned in rather than out of the way. He caught to receptionist glaring at him and tapped the side of his nose. She sat down so that he could only see the top of her resentful head. Minutes later, Gina came back.

'Okay, but you can't take anything away. We have a chain of custody to keep here.'

Chuck resisted the temptation to tell her he already knew that.

'I cross my heart and hope to die,' he said.

Gina made a disbelieving grunt and buzzed him in. He followed her through the glass-walled corridors towards the back of the building, past the rooms full of detectives and forensic teams of all shades. Finally, they arrived at a small windowless room with a metal table and two chairs. Seven or eight boxes sealed with blue and white evidence tape sat on the floor.

'There you go,' said Gina. 'Knock yourself out.'

Chuck heaved the boxes of evidence onto a metal table and wiped his forehead.

'I think I need to get back into the gym,' he said.

Gina snorted.

274

'And when did you ever enter a gym?' she said. 'My investigations have not yielded up any proof.'

Chuck sucked in his stomach.

'I work out,' he said.

'Whatever,' said Gina. 'Why don't you put your biggest muscle to work here and find something useful? I think you're wasting your time though. The detectives interviewing Grimes came up with a big fat zero as regards his NCP connections. The gun they found on him links him directly to the murder of Saul Taggart, but they didn't find anything hinting at an affiliation of any kind with the NCP.'

'But what was he doing in Noah's office? Why did Grace hear him talking about the murdered astronauts before the news was out?'

'I know you're fond of Grace, but has it ever occurred to you that she might be lying?'

'About what?'

'Maybe her boss is the mastermind. Maybe we should be focussing on Noah.'

Chuck blew out through his lips and shook his head.

'It so isn't Noah. He has just been manipulated all his life. There's not a wicked bone in his body. Did your boys get anything out of him during questioning?'

'Nothing. He collapsed in a heap and told us everything before we even asked him. I must admit. I can't believe he's a criminal mastermind. I don't think he even believes in God much anymore.'

'So not him then.'

'Not him.'

Chuck opened one of the boxes.

'There must be something in here that they missed.'

'I doubt it. My guys have been through this evidence with a fine-tooth comb and they didn't come up with anything.'

'Maybe they were looking for something different?'

'What do you mean?'

'Well, they arrested him for murder, which they believed to be linked to the NCP. It stands to reason they concentrated on communications; hard drives, data sticks, cloud storage, Grime's all-in-one and back-ups,' said Chuck.

'They did. And while they could find evidence of several conversations with Noah Van Horn, they didn't unearth any other connections to the NCP.'

'But we're looking for something else.'

'Like what?'

'I don't know, but I will when I see it.'

'Let's take three boxes each,' said Gina. 'Then we can compare notes.'

For the next hour, they took articles out of the boxes one by one, showing them to each other with much shaking of heads and disappointed sighs. When they were finished, Chuck put his head in his hands.

'I don't understand it. I was so sure... Wait. What's that box over there?'

'Oh, it's full of some computer printouts of some sort. It's all gobbledegook. Nothing there for us.'

Chuck froze.

'What did you say?'

'Computer printouts.'

'Oh my God. Quick. Open it up and show me some of them.'

Mystified, Gina lifted out a wedge of paper and dropped it in front of Chuck.

'I know what this is,' he said. 'Saul told me he printed out the data from Wayne's hibernation pod failure to review it at home, but when I went there, it had gone. This is the proof we need.'

'But it's only zeros and ones. How will we ever find out?'

'Let's go through the pages. Maybe Saul made some notes.'

'Okay. But it's a long shot.'

They each took half of the paper and started their way through it. Soon zeros and ones seemed to float across Chuck's vision making him feel disorientated. Suddenly, Gina banged the table.

'It's here. You were right. Oh my God.'

'What? Show me,' said Chuck.

Gina placed a piece of printout in front of him. On it was just one word written in Saul's scrawl. It read 'sabotage?' and he had underlined a long number in the left-hand margin of the print out.'

'What does it mean?' said Gina.

'I'm not sure, but I hope we can identify the saboteur from the code.'

He stood up.

'Come on. We need to go to NASA straight away.'

Gina got permission to use a squad car and they shot across town towards the Space centre. Edgar Fredericks waited for them downstairs and ushered them into his office, his face grey with worry.

'The astronauts have found the fifth Starship,' he said. 'They are on their way there to see if the Moxie has been functioning.'

'Thank God,' said Gina. 'Will they be saved?'

'I don't know. The oxygen in their rover is about to run out and will be at zero by the time they get there. The Starship is not receiving communications from us, so we can't open it. I have the whole building working on it. We must find a way of unblocking the Starship computers, before the astronauts asphyxiate.'

'We might be able to help,' said Chuck.

'What have you got for me?' said Fredericks. 'Quick. Hand it over.'

'We found this,' said Chuck, and pulled a photocopy out of his pocket.

'What is it?' said Fredericks.

'We were hoping you could tell us,' Chuck said.

'It's a data printout,' Gina said.

'Yes, I can see that, but of what? Hang on a minute.'

Fredericks tapped on his screen.

'Elaine, can you send me one of the programmers, please. Preferably, someone who isn't a Christian.'

'And how will I know that?' she said.

'Look, I know it's an odd request, but it's incredibly important. I'll explain, I promise. Tell them to run.'

Five minutes later, Ethan Barzim stood nervously in Edgar Fredericks's office, holding his chest and panting.

'You wanted to see me, sir?'

'Yes, Ethan, we need your help. Can you please look at this piece of paper and tell me what you see?'

Ethan took the paper and flattened out the crease. Then he sat on the spare chair and read it to himself mouthing the words. After a minute, he looked up.

'What does it say?' said Chuck.

'It's a shutdown instruction,' said Ethan. 'For something electronic. An override mechanism.'

Chuck let out a roar and hugged Gina. Fredericks leapt to his feet, his eyes almost bulging out of his sockets. Ethan's mouth dropped onto his chest at the reaction to his simple explanation. He looked around uncertain whether to stay or go.

'Oh my God,' said Fredericks. 'It's him, the saboteur.'

'The what?' said Ethan.

'Someone murdered Wayne Odoyu, and put a communications block on the fifth Starship,' said Chuck.

'But who wrote it, Ethan?' said Gina. 'It's incredibly important.'

'I don't know. But it's easy to find out,' he stammered.

'How?' said Fredericks. 'This is vital information. We can't make a mistake.'

Ethan swallowed and returned his gaze to the paper.

'The number in the column on the left,' he said, pointing. 'It corresponds to the computer on which it was written. You should be able to trace the person who wrote it from the time stamp on the document. We all log on and off our stations and it's impossible to delete that information.'

'And could you trace the person that wrote this instruction?' said Chuck.

Ethan looked at his feet.

'Um, I could. But would they get into trouble because of me?'

'Because of you? No, definitely not,' said Fredericks.

'Okay, it won't take me long.'

Ethan had already started for the door.

'Ethan? Can you use my computer?'

'Yes, sir. They're all linked up to the mainframe.'

'Sit in my chair and please hurry. This is a life-or-death situation. Minutes matter.'

'No pressure,' said Chuck, and forced out a laugh.

Gina had gone green with anxiety, and she sank into a chair while Chuck and Fredericks stood behind Ethan watching with incomprehension as his fingers flashed over the keyboards. Every now and then, he scratched his head, but soon his smile appeared and broadened. He sat back in his seat.

'There you go,' he said. 'Station four. Michael Forrest.'

'Is he in today?' said Chuck.

'Sure, I saw him earlier,' said Ethan. 'He's in the communications centre.'

'What does he look like?' said Gina

'He's the one with the large crucifix hanging from his neck. You can't miss him.'

'He's religious?' said Chuck

'You could say that. He's not supposed to wear it to work, but he takes it out once he's at his desk.'

'He's got a communications block on the missing Starship. If he's logged on, can you unblock it?' said Fredericks.

'Yes, but he has to be logged in.'

'We need to distract him,' said Chuck. 'So we can grab him and stop him logging out. Then Ethan can do his magic.'

'How do we do that?' said Fredericks.

Gina tossed her hair back.

'Honestly,' she said, unbuttoning the top of her blouse and plumping up her breasts. 'He's a computer geek. How hard can it be? I'll do it. Just enter the aisle from the other side to me and jump on him.'

'Now I'm distracted,' said Chuck.

Ethan's eyes nearly popped out of his head. And Gina gave him a playful slap.

'See? It works,' she said.

Chapter 44

After fifteen minutes of hectic driving, the astronauts finally came to a place where the crevasse pinched in and then out again. A large boulder blocked the way across.

'That's us screwed,' said Bret. 'How the hell are we going to move that out of the way?'

'This is the end of the road, folks,' said Yu. 'We're not going to make it.'

'There must be something we can do,' said Hattie.

'We only have one oxygen unit,' said Scotty. 'We can't get enough people out of the vehicle at once to push it.'

'Maybe I can get it to roll,' said Bret. 'I'll give it a try. Put on your helmets and share the oxygen using your emergency connections to the console. I'll depressurise the rover.'

Once they were attached and the rover depressurised, Bret got out and walked up to the rock. He planted his feet on the ground.

'He's crazy,' said Yu. 'He'll never move it.'

'He has to try,' said Scotty.

Bret shoved at the rock from all angles and inserted a crowbar underneath it, straining with all his might, but he could not shift it.

'I'm sorry guys. There's no way we can move that, we can try driving further along to find another crossing but

I think this is our last chance. If we could split it, we might have a chance but—'

Hattie slapped her forehead.

'We can,' she said. 'I forgot that I had brought the Sierra Blaster with me,' said Hattie.

'Say what?' said Bret.

'It's a contraption I use to blast open boulders when I'm doing prospecting. I thought it might be handy on our trip in case we saw something interesting.'

Scotty roared with laughter.

'We're all about to die, and Hattie is still thinking about rocks.'

'How does it work?' said Bret.

'We need to drill a couple of small-bore holes into the rock and then insert a cartridge in each and blast it. With luck the boulder should split down the middle.'

'Should?' said Yu. 'And what if it doesn't'

'Have you got any better ideas?' said Hattie.

'Okay, guys. Don't waste time arguing. Let's get organised. We haven't much time. How many units still have oxygen in them?'

'Two,' said Scotty. 'I can put one on and go out to drill the holes.'

'And then you can give it to me, and I'll go out and blow the charges,' said Hattie.

'And where are we going to get a drill?' said Yu.

'It's part of the kit,' said Hattie.

Minutes later, Scotty stood outside drilling into the rock with all his might. He had to swap out the drill bits to increase the size of the hole. Bret looked at his watch.

'Is everyone feeling all right?' he said.

'The oxygen gauge is still in the green zone,' said Yu. 'But only just.'

Scotty gave a thumbs up and came back to the rover. He gave the oxygen unit to Hattie who headed outside. Moments later, she came back.

'Has anyone got any water?' she said.

'I've got a small amount. Are you thirsty?' said Yu.

282

'No, but you might just have saved us. These things work much better if the borehole is filled with water.'

'Why is that?' said Yu.

'Who cares, just give her the water,' said Bret.

Hattie went back to the boulder and tipped the water into the hole. Then she pushed the blast-head rod into it, and loaded a large rock on top of the blast head, grunting with effort.

'What's she doing?' said Bret.

'You'll see,' said Scotty.

Hattie stepped back and blew the charges. After a momentary lull, there was a popping sound and to her immense relief, the boulder split in two and rocked backwards. One of the halves fell into the crevasse. The other wobbled in the middle of the road. Hattie tried pushing it but she couldn't budge it.

'Hattie, come back. We can push that half out of the way with the vehicle,' said Bret.

Hattie got back into the rover and took off her unit.

'You'll need to hook that up to the rover,' said Scotty. 'I'm getting a headache.'

Yu had fallen asleep, but Hattie shook him awake.

'Don't do that,' she said. 'You might never wake up.'

'What if I don't want to see what happens next?'

'What if you do?'

Chapter 45

The sight of Gina flicking her red hair and sticking her ample chest out as she sashayed down the computer aisle towards him, seemed to mesmerise Michael Forrest. He didn't even notice Chuck behind him before it was too late. Chuck wrapped his arms around Forrest and pulled his chair away from the computer in one movement.

'Now,' he said, and Ethan grabbed another chair from the vacant station beside him and started searching through Forrest's computer for the block sequence.

'Leave me to it,' he said. 'I've got this.'

'It's too late,' said Forrest, laughing. 'They have no oxygen left. They'll all be dead in minutes.'

'Not if I've got anything to do with it,' said Ethan.

He put his head down and swiped through screens at a pace Chuck had never even imagined possible. Then he grunted and started typing.

'There you go,' he said. 'I've removed the block. If they're still alive, they should be able to communicate with the Starship.'

A cheer erupted from the consoles around them as the fifth Starship came online. Fredericks tottered over to them and shoved Forrest in the chest before pumping Ethan by the hand. He looked as if he would faint. He turned even greyer than usual and wavered on his feet.

'You've got him?' he said. 'I can't believe it.'

'Ethan is a genius,' said Chuck. 'I think he needs a raise.'

'He can have my job if he wants it,' said Fredericks. 'What's happening?'

'The Starship communications are unblocked. We will have to wait for feed from the rover to know if they made it on time or not.'

Chapter 46

A fter an agonising half hour, the rover finally arrived at the foot of the Starship. They all stared up at the huge shape looming above the rover, apparently unscathed by its trip to Mars.

'How are we doing for oxygen?' said Bret.

'Not good,' said Scotty. 'We've almost exhausted the last tank and we're now using the small amount in the rover. I estimate we have about fifteen minutes left.'

'Can you communicate with the Starship's computer yet?' said Hattie. 'If you can get it to send the lift down from the cargo bay, we might be able to go and get a unit from the suiting up area. They should be full of oxygen. This Starship is fitted out just like ours.'

'And it has a Moxie unit in the cargo bay,' said Scotty. 'I wonder if it has switched itself on or not. It's too dark to tell if the robots have set up kilopower units for electricity.'

'But first we need to get into the spacecraft. How will we get to the cargo door if there is no oxygen left in the units?' said Yu.

'I can do it,' said Hattie.

'I won't allow that,' said Bret. 'It's my responsibility.'

'You don't understand,' said Hattie. 'I can hold my breath for three minutes. If I don't wear a unit, I can sprint through the ship and find the oxygen quicker than any of you.'

'But what if the lift takes longer than three minutes?' said Yu.

'We can time it,' said Scotty.

'It's our only hope,' said Hattie. 'Please let me try.'

Bret tapped furiously on the console, muttering to himself. 'Come on, damn you. Come on'. He kept tapping. A tense silence fell on the crew. Hattie started to feel sleepy. She shook herself awake. Bret swore softly and starting tapping again. Suddenly the cargo door half way up the Starship opened, showering dust on the ground below, and the lift descended slowly downwards.

'Thank God,' said Bret. 'NASA came up trumps.'

'How long did the lift take to come down?' said Scotty.

'Two minutes,' said Yu.

'I can do this,' said Hattie. 'You have to let me try.'

'Okay. But hyperventilate in here first. As soon as you are inside the Starship, I will shut the cargo door and repressurise the area for you. The tanks should be in the changing section. Good luck.'

Hattie took a couple of quick breaths directly from the last unit and stuck on her helmet.

'See you shortly, guys, and if not, it's been an honour.'

She took one more breath and then jumped outside the rover. The door shut behind her and she ran over to the lift. As she leapt on board, she snagged her suit on a random piece of jagged metal sticking out of the barrier around it. The lift started upwards. Hattie held her breath, trying to slow her heart rate but realised her suit had started to depressurise. She had to breath out slowly or risk her lungs bursting.

'Oh my God,' said Yu, who monitored her life signs on his tablet. 'Her suit's depressurising. She's not going to make it.'

'Don't say that,' said Scotty. 'Come on, Hattie. Nearly there.'

They watched the lift make its painful progress up to the door. Hattie fell to her knees as the door approached. She kept trying to breath out and then she felt the bubbles forming on her tongue. I'm going to die like Mo. She fell into the door hitting the emergency close button as she collapsed.

'Is she alive?' said Scotty.

But Yu had passed out.

'We're goners,' said Bret. 'See you in the next world.'

Hattie came to after a couple of minutes as the cargo bay pressurised and filled with oxygen. She struggled to stand up but only managed to get to all fours. She crawled to the changing unit, but there were no oxygen units on the walls.

'Where are they? They're supposed to be here.'

She tried not to panic.

'Do you receive me, Bret?'

Silence. Hattie could feel her panic mounting. They've suffocated. Please no.

'Scotty, are you there? Don't leave me alone here.'

She slumped to the floor and lay panting. Breath, breath, breath. Suddenly she heard a cough in her ear.

'Who's that?' she said.

'It's us, Hats. We're saved. The Starship detected the low oxygen levels in our vehicle and sent its robot rover to inject oxygen into the cabin. Are you okay?'

Hattie panted, her lungs agony with every breath.

'You mean I didn't have to do this?'

Scotty laughed.

'Are you okay?'

'I will be. My suit tore on the way up. I'll get into the console when I feel better and generate another one.'

'You won't need it now. Just relax. We'll be up there soon.'

Chapter 47

T he police arrived to take Michael Forrest away within minutes as Gina had already alerted them to the real possibility of an arrest. Ethan kept Forrest's phone and had cloned the contents onto the NASA hard drive before handing it over to the police. He patiently reviewed the communications while the room around him settled into a tense wait for signs of life from the astronauts.

The minutes went by with agonising slowness as the whole of NASA downed tools and stared at their screens, praying, hoping, wishing for a miracle. The press had been alerted and correspondents had swarmed into the centre from all over town. A live feed had been set up and excited broadcasters were filling the awful wait with every scientific fact they could garner from the tense scientists. The clock ticked down to twenty minutes and still no answer was received. Then one of the team shouted.

'An automated rover has mobilised from the Starship and pumped oxygen into the astronauts' vehicle. We have three, no, four, life signs.'

A massive cheer went up in the communications room and bedlam ensued with the whole department hugging and kissing and generally going berserk. Fredericks leaned over and checked with the woman before allowing himself a tear. He bit his lip and took out his all-in-one, tapping the screen and swaying with happiness. The pale face of his wife and daughter who were holding each other's hands for comfort, swam into view through his blurred vision. He smiled at them.

'She's alive,' he said. 'Our girl's going to make it.'

Grace screamed so loudly that her cry filled the room. Everyone came to Fredericks and slapped him on the back and waved at Juana and Grace. They hugged and cried and laughed and couldn't speak at all from happiness. Chuck had grabbed Gina and was kissing her like his life depended on it. Ethan, who had never had so much attention in his whole life sat stunned on his chair. Then he tugged Chuck by the sleeve.

'Sir, I know you're busy, but I thought you'd like to know...'

Chuck came up for breath, his lips rosy and swollen, trying not to look impatient.

'Do you know a Richard Taylor-Brooks?' said Ethan. 'He's the guy who ran the operation to sabotage the mission. It's all here. Messages, videos, files.'

'He's the leader of the NCP,' said Chuck. 'Oh my God, we've got him.'

Gina picked up her all-in-one and called the police chief who ordered an immediate arrest. A squad car in the vicinity radioed back to say that Taylor-Brooks was on his way to the airport and they were on his tail.

'Come on then,' said Gina. 'You don't want to miss this.'

Chuck and Gina jumped into their squad car and drove to the airport at top speed, siren blaring. Gina drove straight past the departures hall making Chuck shout and grab her arm.

'He won't be getting a commercial flight,' she said. 'Trust me. That guy thinks he's better than everyone else. He's got a charter ordered. He must have realised the game was up when he saw the feed from NASA.'

Gina roared into the parking lot of the Charter section and radioed her location to the other squad cars. She and Chuck jumped out of the car and headed for the

290

entrance. She flashed her coroner's badge at the door, and crossed the floor with Chuck right behind her. They dashed outside onto the tarmac and looked around. A gleaming Lockheed waited with engines on. Suddenly Taylor-Brooks appeared from an office on the side wall of the hanger. Gina broke into a sprint.

'Stop right there,' she said. 'You're under arrest.'

Taylor-Brooks froze, stunned for a second, then he tried to run for the aircraft steps. But his momentary hesitation was his undoing, Gina caught him as he put his foot on the bottom step and threw him to the ground.

'How dare you,' he said. 'Don't you know who I am?'

'Oh we know exactly who you are,' said Chuck. 'That's why you're about to go down for the rest of your life.

The hangar filled with the sound of sirens and soon Richard Taylor-Brooks had been cuffed and pushed into the back of a squad car.

'We make a good team,' said Chuck, kissing Gina with gusto.

'Not bad,' she said. 'But you still owe me dinner.'

Chapter 48

Hattie tottered into the communal area of the Starship the next morning and headed for the kitchen. Her eyes throbbed and her lungs felt as if they had been trampled by a herd of bison. To her embarrassment, the three men were waiting for her. They applauded and cheered her every step making her blush and shake her head.

'Hattie Fredericks, bad ass,' said Scotty. 'Who'd have believed it?'

'Please stop,' said Hattie. 'I did it to save myself as much as you.'

'That's no excuse for being a hero,' said Bret.

'I don't buy it,' said Scotty. 'She saved us all.'

'She must love us,' said Yu.

Hattie's eyes filled with tears despite herself.

'Of course I do,' she said, biting her lip.

'I'm not sure how I feel about reverse harem,' said Bret. 'But give me a hug anyway.'

All four astronauts joined in a group embrace and wept tears of joy and relief.

'I got a message from the President of the United States this morning,' said Bret. 'Congratulating us on surviving. We're all going to get a medal. Isn't that amazing.'

'A medal?' said Scotty. 'I'd prefer a large pension.'

'And a life-long tax exemption,' said Hattie.

Scotty high fived her.

'I wish I could talk to my family without the delay,' said Yu. 'My mother told me the government is using my background to call for unity and peace. It's so odd to be able to talk openly to them again, and so frustrating to wait so long between messages.'

A wave of nausea hit Hattie who sank into a chair.

'Are you okay?' said Yu. 'You're lucky you didn't suffer from the bends.'

'I'm alive,' said Hattie. 'Luckily I remembered to breath out when I felt my suit begin to depressurise.'

'Lucky the new design takes time to loosen,' said Scotty.

'I didn't realise I had damaged it until I felt it releasing its grip.'

'It was lucky all around,' said Bret. 'I can't imagine how NASA located the communications to the Starship block so quickly.'

'I'm sure we'll hear all about it,' said Yu. 'Here's a bowl of porridge. Scotty is going to update us on progress.'

Hattie plonked her bowl down on the table, still embarrassed by her reception.

'First the good news,' said Scotty. 'Despite being cut off from communications with earth, the automatic programming of the Starship still worked perfectly. Once the spacecraft had landed, the robot rovers came down from the cargo bay and started work. They set up the kilopower units which started to generate electricity for heating and cooling in the spacecraft. One of the two Moxie plants initiated once the power came on, and has produced enough liquid oxygen to get the project going again. Also, there are pallets of food and medicine supplies in the cargo hold.'

'Meaning we won't starve or suffocate in the short term. But we have a problem,' said Bret.

'What a novelty,' muttered Yu.

'Nothing we can't deal with,' said Bret.

'We need to empty the oxygen from this spaceship and transport its contents to the hub,' said Scotty.

'Why don't we bring everything up here?' said Hattie.

'No ice for the Rassors. And the greenhouse is well established now, it would be a pity to tear it up and start again,' said Bret. 'So we need to transfer this spaceship and all its contents to the original hub.'

'It's just a question of priorities,' said Scotty. 'The refrigerated bowser is operational so we only need to send it the coordinates of this Starship and it will transfer the oxygen to the hub. We can divide the oxygen over three journeys, to make sure we don't lose it all in an accident.'

'Once we have oxygen stored back at the hub, and have set up one of the Moxies at the habs, we'll move back ourselves,' said Bret. 'Then we can organise the transfer of the rest of the cargo and eventually the Starship itself.'

'Fantastic,' said Yu. 'Then we can get on with the purpose of the trip.'

'Ah,' said Hattie. 'I should have said something earlier.'

Bret rolled his eyes.

'What now?'

'I found stromatolites. That's why Ellie tried to kill us. The NCP didn't want us to find life on Mars.'

The three men turned to stare at her.

'You found life on Mars?' said Scotty.

'And you haven't told us?' said Bret.

'What a dark horse,' said Yu.

'I've told you now,' said Hattie.

'Don't you think we ought to tell Earth the news?' said Bret.

'Haven't they had enough excitement for one day?' said Scotty, and laughed.

'Send the message,' said Bret.

'Me?' said Hattie.

'Yes, you, Hattie Fredericks.'

294

Other Books by PJ Skinner

Individual books in the Sam Harris Adventure Series

The first book in the Sam Harris Series sets the scene for the career of an unwilling heroine, whose bravery and resourcefulness are needed to navigate a series of adventures set in remote sites in Africa and South America. Based on the real-life adventures of the author, the settings and characters are given an authenticity which will connect with readers who enjoy adventure fiction and mysteries set in remote settings with realistic scenarios.

Set in the late 1980s themes such as women working in formerly male domains, and what constitutes a normal existence, are examined and developed in the context of Sam's constant ability to find herself in the middle of an adventure or mystery. Sam's home life provides a contrast to her adventures and feeds her need to escape. Her attachment to an unsuitable boyfriend is the thread running through her romantic life, and her attempts to break free of it provide another side to her character.

Fool's Gold - Book 1

Sam's dream job awaits in the jungle, but so does a dangerous secret; Will her first adventure be her last?

When geologist Sam Harris finishes university, she is determined to make her mark in a man's world. But exploration roles are hard to come by. Desperate for her first job, Sam accepts a contract with Mike Morton, a dodgy entrepreneur, searching for gold in the remote rainforests of Sierramar. Sam soon questions her decision, as she struggles with a violent colleague, and living conditions in the field. But everything changes when she photographs some Inca steps hidden deep within the jungle, which may lead to an ancient archaeological site.

Mike sends her back to the site to search for artefacts with a drunken historian. But rumours about priceless Inca relics have spread among their team, and Sam is deep in the jungle, far from help. Can she trust her colleagues, or is one of them planning to take the fabled treasure for himself?

Hitler's Finger - Book 2

The second book in the Sam Harris Series sees the return of our heroine Sam Harris to Sierramar to help her friend Gloria track down her boyfriend, the historian, Alfredo Vargas.

A missing historian, a vengeful journalist, some unhinged Nazis and a possible pregnancy. Has Sam gone too far on her return to Sierramar? Historian, Alfredo Vargas, and journalist, Saul Rosen, have disappeared while searching for a group of fugitive Nazi war criminals. Sam and her friend Gloria join forces to find them and are soon caught up in a dangerous mystery. A man is murdered, and a sinister stranger follows their every move. Even the government is involved. Can they find Alfredo before he disappears for good?

The background to the book is the presence of Nazi war criminals in South America which was often ignored by locals who had fascist sympathies during World War II. Themes such as tacit acceptance of fascism, and local collaboration with fugitives from justice are examined and developed in the context of Sam's constant ability to find herself in the middle of an adventure or mystery. Sam's home life provides a contrast to her adventures and feeds her need to escape. Her continuing attachment to an unsuitable boyfriend is about to be tested to the limit.

The Star of Simbako - Book 3

The third book in the Sam Harris Series sees Sam Harris on her first contract to West Africa to Simbako, a land of tribal kingdoms and voodoo.

A fabled diamond, a jealous voodoo priestess, disturbing cultural practices. What could possibly go wrong?

Nursing a broken heart, Sam Harris goes to Simbako to work in the diamond fields of Fona. She is soon involved with a cast of characters who are starring in their own soap opera, a dangerous mix of superstition, cultural practices and ignorance (mostly her own). Add a love triangle and a jealous woman who wants her dead and Sam is in trouble again. Where is the Star of Simbako? Is Sam going to survive the chaos?

This book is based on visits made to the Paramount Chiefdoms of West Africa. Despite being nominally Christian communities, Voodoo practices are still part of daily life out there. This often leads to conflicts of interest. Combine this with the horrific ritual of FGM and it makes for a potent cocktail of conflicting loyalties. Sam is pulled into this life by her friend, Adanna, and soon finds herself involved in goings on that she doesn't understand.

The Pink Elephants – Book 4

The fourth book in the Sam Harris Series presents Sam with her sternest test yet as she goes to Africa to fix a failing project. A failing project, beleaguered pygmies and endangered elephants. Can Sam save them all or will she have to choose?

Sam gets a call in the middle of the night that takes her to the Masaibu project in eastern Lumbono. The project is collapsing under the weight of corruption and chicanery engendered by management, both in country and back on the main company board. Sam has to navigate murky waters to get it back on course, not helped by interference from people who want her to fail. When poachers invade the elephant sanctuary next door, her problems multiply. Can Sam protect the elephants and save the project or will she have to choose? The day to day problems encountered by Sam in her work are typical of any project manager in the Congo which has been rent apart by warring factions, leaving the local population frightened and rootless. Elephants with pink tusks do exist, but not in the area where the project is based. They are being slaughtered by poachers in Gabon for the Chinese market and will soon be extinct, so I have put the guns in the hands of those responsible for the massacre of these defenceless animals. The themes of this novel are impossible choices and brave decisions.

The Bonita Protocol - Book 5

An erratic boss. Suspicious results. Stock market shenanigans. Can Sam Harris expose the scam before they silence her? It's 1996. Geologist Sam Harris has been around the block, but she's prone to nostalgia, so she snatches the chance to work in Sierramar, her old stomping ground. But she never expected to be working for a company that is breaking all the rules.

When the analysis results from drill samples are suspiciously high, Sam makes a decision that puts her life in peril. Can she blow the lid on the conspiracy before they shut her up for good?

The Bonita Protocol is the fifth book in the Sam Harris Adventure series. If you like gutsy heroines, complex twists and turns, and heart pounding action, then you'll love PJ Skinner's thrilling novel.

Digging Deeper - Book 6

A feisty geologist working in the diamond fields of West Africa is kidnapped by rebels. Can she survive the ordeal or will this adventure be her last? It's 1998. Geologist Sam Harris is desperate for money so she takes a job in a tinpot mining company working in war-torn Tamazia. But she never expected to be kidnapped by blood thirsty rebels.

Working in Gemsite was never going to be easy with its culture of misogyny and corruption. Her boss, the notorious Adrian Black is engaged in a game of cat and mouse with the government over taxation. Just when Sam makes a breakthrough, the camp is overrun by rebels and Sam is taken captive.

Will anyone bother to rescue her, and will she still be alive if they do?

Concrete Jungle - Book 7 (series end)

Armed with an MBA, Sam Harris is storming the City - But has she swapped one jungle for another?

Forging a new career was never going to be easy, and Sam discovers she has not escaped from the culture of misogyny and corruption that blighted her field career.

When her past is revealed, she finally achieves the acceptance she has always craved, but being one of the boys is not the panacea she expected. The death of a new friend presents her with the stark choice of compromising her principals to keep her new position, or exposing the truth behind the façade.

Will she finally get what she wants or was it all a mirage?

All of the books are available in paperback. Please go to your favourite online retailer to order them.

Sam Harris Adventure Box Sets

Sam Harris Adventure Box Set Book 1-3
Sam Harris Adventure Box Set Book 2-4
Sam Harris Adventure Box Set Book 5-7

The Green Family Saga
Rebel Green – Book 1

Relationships fracture when two families find themselves caught up in the Irish Troubles.

The Green family move to Kilkenny from England in 1969, at the beginning of the conflict in Northern Ireland. They rent a farmhouse on the outskirts of town, and make friends with the O'Connor family next door. Not every member of the family adapts easily to their new life, and their differing approaches lead to misunderstandings and friction. Despite this, the bonds between the family members deepen with time.

Perturbed by the worsening violence in the North threatening to invade their lives, the children make a pact never to let the troubles come between them. But promises can be broken, with tragic consequences for everyone.

If you like family sagas in an authentic Irish setting, Rebel Green will thrill and move you in equal measure. Buy it now

Africa Green – Book 2

Will a white chimp save its rescuers or get them killed?

Journalist Isabella Green travels to Sierra Leone, a country emerging from civil war, to write an article about a chimp sanctuary. Animals that need saving are her obsession, and she can't resist getting involved with the project, which is on the verge of bankruptcy. She forms a bond with local boy, Ten, and army veteran, Pete, to try and save it.

When they rescue a rare white chimp from a village frequented by a dangerous rebel splinter group, the resulting media interest could save the sanctuary. But the rebel group have not signed the cease fire. They believe the voodoo power of the white chimp protects them from bullets, and they are determined to take it back so they can storm the capital.

When Pete and Ten go missing, only Isabella stands in the rebels' way. Her love for the chimps unlocks the fighting spirit within her. Can she save the sanctuary or will she die trying?

All of the individual books are available in paperback at your favourite online retailer

Connect with the Author

About the Author

The author has spent 30 years working as an exploration geologist managing remote sites and doing due diligence of projects in more than thirty countries. During this time, she has been collecting tall tales and real-life experiences which inspired her to write the Sam Harris Adventure Series chronicling the adventures of a female geologist as a pioneer in a hitherto exclusively male world.

PJ has worked in many countries in South America and Africa in remote, strange and often dangerous places, and loved every minute of it, despite encountering her fair share of misogyny and other perils. She is now writing these fact-based adventure books from the relative safety of London but still travels all over the world collecting data for her writing.

The Sam Harris Adventure Series is for lovers of intelligent adventure thrillers happening just before the time of mobile phones and internet. It has a unique viewpoint provided by Sam, a female interloper in a male world, as she struggles with alien cultures and failed relationships.

PJ's childhood in Ireland inspired her to write Rebel Green, about an English family who move to Ireland during the beginnings of the Troubles. She has written a follow-on in the same Green Family Saga called Africa Green which follows Isabella Green as she goes to Sierra Leone to write an article on a chimpanzee sanctuary. She is now writing a third in the series, Fighting Green, about Liz Green's return to live in Ireland.

She is now mulling a series of Cosy Mysteries, or a book about... You'll have to wait and see. to get informed of her new releases.

If you would like updates on the latest in the Sam Harris Series or to contact the author with your questions please click on the following links:

You can follow the author on or on

Please subscribe to the for updates and offers